John Dene Of Toronto

Toronto

A Comedy Of Whitehall

by

Herbert Jenkins

John Dene Of Toronto
A Comedy Of Whitehall
by Herbert Jenkins

ISBN: 978-93-57278-47-8

Published by

DOUBLE 9 BOOKS

2/13-B, Ansari Road
Daryaganj, New Delhi – 110002
info@double9books.com
www.double9books.com
Tel. 011-40042856

ABOUT THE AUTHOR

The British author Herbert George Jenkins (1876–8 June 1923) also owned the Herbert Jenkins Ltd. publishing business, which made many of P. G. Wodehouse's books available.

Jenkins' parents are from Norfolk, and Greyfriars College is where he received his education, according to his obituary in The Times. Before starting his own publishing business in 1912, he worked as a journalist for a while before spending about 11 years at The Bodley Head. He remained single and passed away on June 8, 1923, in Marylebone, London, at the age of 47 following a six-month illness.

Jenkins' light fiction is what is most well-known, but his first work was a biography of George Borrow. William Blake was admired by him, and he did study into his high treason trial and the location of his missing tomb before producing a book on him in 1925.

Jenkins established Herbert Jenkins Limited, his own publishing house, in 1912. Its offices were in a small, five-story building from the late 19th century on London's Duke of York Street, just off Jermyn Street.

CONTENTS

CHAPTER I.
THE COMING OF JOHN DENE

"Straight along, down the steps, bear to the left and you'll find the Admiralty on the opposite side of the way."

John Dene thanked the policeman, gave the cigar in his mouth a twist with his tongue, and walked along Lower Regent Street towards Waterloo Place.

At the bottom of the Duke of York's steps, he crossed the road, turned to the left and paused. Nowhere could he see an entrance sufficiently impressive to suggest the Admiralty. Just ahead was a dingy and unpretentious doorway with a policeman standing outside; but that he decided could not be the entrance to the Admiralty. As he gazed at it, a fair-haired girl came out of the doorway and walked towards him.

"Excuse me," said John Dene, lifting his hat, "but is that the Admiralty you've just come out of?"

There was an almost imperceptible stiffening in the girl's demeanour; but a glance at the homely figure of John Dene, with its ill-made clothes, reassured her.

"Yes, that is the Admiralty," she replied gravely in a voice that caused John Dene momentarily to forget the Admiralty and all its works.

"Much obliged," he said, again lifting his hat as she walked away; but instead of continuing on his way, John Dene stood watching the girl until she disappeared up the Duke of York's steps. Then once more twirling his cigar in his mouth and hunching his shoulders, he walked towards the doorway she had indicated.

"This the Admiralty?" he enquired of the policeman.

"Yes, sir," was the reply. "Did you want to see any one?"

John Dene looked at the man in surprise.

"Why should I be here if I didn't?" he asked. "I want to see the First Lord."

The man's manner underwent a change. "If you'll step inside, sir, you'll see an attendant."

John Dene stepped inside and repeated his request, this time to a frock-coated attendant.

"Have you an appointment?" enquired the man.

"No," responded John Dene indifferently.

The attendant hesitated. It was not customary for unknown callers to demand to see the First Lord without an appointment. After a momentary pause the man indicated a desk on which lay some printed slips.

"Will you please fill in your name, sir, and state your business."

"State my business," exclaimed John Dene, "not on your life."

"I'm afraid — —" began the man.

"Never mind what you're afraid of," said John Dene, "just you take my name up to the First Lord. Here, I'll write it down." Seizing a pen he wrote his name, "John Dene of Toronto," and then underneath, "I've come three thousand miles to tell you something; perhaps it's worth three minutes of your time to listen."

"There, take that up and I'll wait," he said.

The attendant read the message, then beckoning to another frock-coated servitor, he handed him the paper, at the same time whispering some instructions. John Dene looked about him with interest. He was frankly disappointed. He had conceived the administrative buildings of the greatest navy in the world as something grand and impressive; yet here was the British Admiralty with an entrance that would compare unfavourably with a second-rate hotel in Toronto.

He turned suddenly and almost ran into a shifty-eyed little man in a grey tweed suit, who had entered the Admiralty a moment after him. The man apologised profusely as John Dene eyed him grimly. He had become aware of the man's interest in his colloquy with the attendant, and of the way in which he had endeavoured to catch sight of what was written on the slip of paper.

John Dene proceeded to stride up and down with short, jerky steps, twirling his unlit cigar round in his mouth.

"Excuse me, sir," said the attendant, approaching, "but smoking is not permitted."

"That so?" remarked John Dene without interest, as he continued to roll his cigar in his mouth.

"Your cigar, sir," continued the man.

"It's out." John Dene still continued to look about him.

The attendant retired nonplussed. The rule specifically referred to smoking, not to carrying unlit cigars in the mouth.

At the end of five minutes, the attendant who had taken up John Dene's name returned, and whispered to the doorkeeper.

"If you will follow the attendant, sir, he will take you to see Sir Lyster's secretary, Mr. Blair."

"Mr. — —" began John Dene, then breaking off he followed the man up the stairs, and along a corridor, at the end of which another frock-coated man appeared from a room with a small glass door. He in turn took charge of the visitor, having received his whispered instructions from the second attendant. John Dene was then shown into a large room with a central table, and requested to take a seat. He was still engaged in gazing about him when a door at the further end of the room opened and there entered a fair man, with an obvious stoop, a monocle, a heavy drooping moustache, and the nose of a duke in a novelette.

"Mr. John Dene?" he asked, looking at the slip of paper in his hand.

"Sure," was the response, as John Dene continued to twirl the cigar in his mouth, with him always a sign either of thought or of irritation.

"You wish to see the First Lord?" continued the fair man. "I am his secretary. Will you give me some idea of your business?"

"No, I won't," was the blunt response.

Mr. Blair was momentarily disconcerted by the uncompromising nature of the retort, but quickly recovered himself.

"I am afraid Sir Lyster is very busy this morning," he said, diplomatically. "If you——"

"Look here," interrupted John Dene, "I've come three thousand miles to tell him something; if he hasn't time to listen, then I'll not waste my time; but before you decide to send me about my business, you just ring up the Agent-General for Can'da and ask who John Dene of T'ronto is; maybe you'll learn something."

"But will you not give me some idea——" began the secretary.

"No, I won't," was the obstinate reply. "Here," he cried with sudden inspiration, "give me some paper and a pen, and I'll write a note."

Mr. Blair sighed his relief; he was a man of peace. He quickly supplied the caller's demands. Slowly he indited his letter; then, taking a case from his pocket, he extracted an envelope which he enclosed with the letter in another envelope, and finally addressed it to "The First Lord of the Admiralty."

"Give him this," he said, turning to Mr. Blair, "and say I'm in a hurry."

Nothing but a long line of ancestors prevented Mr. Blair from gasping. Instead he took the note with a diplomatic smile.

"You wouldn't do for T'ronto," muttered John Dene as the First Lord's private secretary left the room. Two minutes later he returned.

"Sir Lyster will see you, Mr. Dene," he said with a smile. "Will you come this way? I'm sorry if——"

"Don't be sorry," said John Dene patiently; "you're just doing your job as best you can."

Whilst John Dene was being led by Mr. Blair to the First Lord's private room, Sir Lyster was re-reading the astonishing note that had been sent in to him, which ran:

"DEAR SIR,—

"I am John Dene of Toronto, I have come three thousand miles to tell you how to stop the German U-boats. If I do not succeed, you can give the enclosed £50,000 to the Red Cross.

"Yours faithfully,
"JOHN DENE."

Sir Lyster Grayne was a man for whom tradition had its uses; but he never allowed it to dictate to him. The letter that had just been brought in was, he decided, written by a man of strong individuality, and the amazing offer it contained, to forfeit fifty thousand pounds, impressed him. These were strange and strenuous days, when every suggestion or invention must be examined and deliberated upon. Sir Lyster Grayne prided himself upon his open-mindedness; incidentally he had a wholesome fear of questions being asked in the House.

As the door opened he rose and held out his hand. Sir Lyster always assumed a democratic air as a matter of political expediency.

"Mr. Dene," he murmured, as he motioned his visitor to a seat.

"Pleased to meet you," said John Dene as he shook hands, and then took the seat indicated. "Sorry to blow in on you like this," he continued, "but my business is important, and I've come three thousand miles about it."

"So I understand," said Sir Lyster quietly.

John Dene looked at him, and in that look summed him up as he had previously summed up his secretary. "You wouldn't do for T'ronto," was his unuttered verdict. John Dene "placed" a man irrevocably by determining whether or no he would do for Toronto.

"First of all," said Sir Lyster, "I think I will return this," handing to John Dene the envelope containing the cheque for fifty thousand pounds.

"I thought it would tickle you some," he remarked grimly as he replaced the cheque in his pocket-book; "but I'll cash in if I don't make good," he added. "You know anything about submarines?" he demanded; directness was John Dene's outstanding characteristic.

"Er——" began the First Lord.

"You don't," announced John Dene with conviction.

"I'm afraid——" began Sir Lyster.

"Then you'd better send for someone who does," was the uncompromising rejoinder.

Sir Lyster looked at his visitor in surprise, hesitated a moment, then pressing a button said, as Mr. Blair appeared:

"Will you ask Admiral Heyworth to come here immediately?" Mr. Blair retired. "Admiral Heyworth," explained Sir Lyster, "is the Admiralty authority on submarines."

John Dene nodded. There was a pause.

"Wouldn't you like to ring up the Agent-General for Can'da and find out who I am?" suggested John Dene.

"I don't think that is necessary, Mr. Dene," was the reply. "We will hear what you have to say first. Ha, Heyworth!" as the Admiral entered, "this is Mr. John Dene of Toronto, who has come to tell us something about a discovery of his."

Admiral Heyworth, a little bald-headed man with beetling brows and a humorous mouth, took the hand held out to him.

"Pleased to meet you," said John Dene, then without a pause he continued: "I want your promise that this is all between us three, that you won't go and breeze it about." He looked from Sir Lyster to Admiral Heyworth. Sir Lyster bowed, Admiral Heyworth said, "Certainly."

"Now," said John Dene, turning to the Admiral, "what's the greatest difficulty you're up against in submarine warfare?"

"Well," began Admiral Heyworth, "there are several. For instance——"

"There's only one that matters," broke in John Dene; "your boats are blind when submerged beyond the depth of their periscopes. That so?"

The Admiral nodded.

"Well," continued John Dene, "I want you to understand I'm not asking a red cent from anybody, and I won't accept one. What I'm going to tell you about has already cost me well over a million dollars, and if you look at me you'll see I'm not the man to put a million dollars into patent fly-catchers, or boots guaranteed to button themselves."

Sir Lyster and the Admiral exchanged puzzled glances, but said nothing.

"Suppose the Germans were able to sink a ship without even showing their periscopes?" John Dene looked directly at the Admiral.

"It would place us in a very precarious position," was the grave reply.

"Oh, shucks!" cried John Dene in disgust. "It would queer the whole outfit. You soldiers and sailors can never see beyond your own particular backyards. It would mighty soon finish the war." He almost shouted the words in the emphasis he gave them. "It would mean that troops couldn't be brought from America; it would mean that supplies couldn't be brought over here. It would mean good-bye to the whole sunflower-patch. Do you get me?" He looked from Sir Lyster to the Admiral.

"I think," said Sir Lyster, "that perhaps you exaggerate a lit——"

"I don't," said John Dene. "I know what I'm talking about. Now, why is the submarine blind? Because," he answered his own question, "no one has ever overcome the difficulty of the density of water. I have."

Admiral Heyworth started visibly, and Sir Lyster bent forward eagerly.

"You have!" cried Admiral Heyworth.

"Sure," was the self-complacent reply. "I've got a boat fitted with an apparatus that'll sink any ship that comes along, and she needn't show her periscope to do it either. What's more, she can see under water. If I don't deliver the goods"—John Dene rummaged in his pocket once more and produced the envelope containing the cheque—"here's fifty thousand pounds you can give to the Red Cross."

Sir Lyster and Admiral Heyworth gazed at each other wordless. John Dene sat back in his chair and chewed the end of his cigar. Sir Lyster fumbled for his eye-glass, and when he had found it, stuck it in his eye and gazed at John Dene as if he had been some marvellous being from another world. The Admiral said nothing and did nothing. He was visualising the possibilities arising out of such a discovery.

It was John Dene who broke in upon their thoughts.

"The Huns have got it coming," he remarked grimly.

"But——" began Admiral Heyworth.

"Listen," said John Dene. "I'm an electrical engineer. I'm worth more millions than you've got toes. I saw that under water the submarine is only a blind fish with a sting in its tail. Give it eyes and it becomes a real factor—*under water*." He paused, revolving his cigar in his mouth. His listeners nodded eagerly.

"Well," he continued, "I set to work to give her eyes. On the St. Lawrence River, just below Quebec, I've got a submarine that can see. Her search-lights——"

"But how have you done it?" broke in the Admiral.

"That," remarked John Dene drily, "is my funeral."

"We must put this before the Inventions Board," said Sir Lyster. "Let me see, this is Friday. Can you be here on Tuesday, Mr. Dene?"

"No!"

Sir Lyster started at the decision in John Dene's tone.

"Would Wednesday——"

"Look here," broke in John Dene, "I come from T'ronto, and in Can'da when we've got a good thing we freeze on to it. You've got to decide this thing within twenty-four hours, yes or no. Unless I cable to my agent in Washin'ton by noon to-morrow, he'll make the same offer I've made you to the States, and they'll be that eager to say 'Yep,' that they'll swallow their gum."

"But, Mr. Dene——" began Sir Lyster.

"I've been in this country fourteen hours," proceeded John Dene calmly, "and I can see that you all want gingering-up. Why the hell can't you decide on a thing at once, when you've got everything before you? If a man offers you a pedigree-pup for nothing, and you want a pedigree-pup, wouldn't you just hold out your hand?"

John Dene looked from one to the other.

"But this is not exactly a matter of a pedigree-pup," suggested Admiral Heyworth diplomatically. "It's a matter of—er——"

"I see you haven't got me," said John Dene with the air of a patient schoolmaster with a stupid pupil. "You," he addressed himself in particular to Sir Lyster, "have said in public that the most difficult spot in connexion with the submarine trouble is between the Shetlands and the Norwegian coast. You can't help the U-boats slipping through submerged. Suppose the *Destroyer*—that's the name of my boat—is sort of hanging around there, *with eyes* and some other little things she's got, what then?"

"Both Sir Lyster and I appreciate all you say," said the Admiral; "but, well, we are a little old fashioned perhaps in our methods here." He smiled deprecatingly.

"Well," said John Dene, rising, "you lose the odd trick, that's all; and," he added significantly as he took a step towards the door, "when it all comes out, you'll lose your jobs too."

"Really, Mr. Dene," protested Sir Lyster, flushing slightly.

John Dene swung round on his heel. "If you'd spent three years of your life and over a million dollars on a boat, and come three thousand miles to offer it to someone for nothing, and were told to wait till God knows which day what week, well, you'd be rattled too. In T'ronto we size up a man before he's had time to say he's pleased to meet us, and we'd buy a mountain quicker than you'd ask your neighbour to pass the marmalade at breakfast."

Whilst John Dene was speaking, Sir Lyster had been revolving the matter swiftly in his mind. He was impressed by his visitor's fearlessness. A self-made man himself, he admired independence and freedom of speech in others. He was not oblivious to the truth of John Dene's hint of what would happen if another nation, even an allied nation, were to acquire a valuable invention that had been declined by Great Britain. He remembered the Fokker scandal. He decided to temporise.

"If," continued John Dene, "I was asking for money, I'd understand; but I won't take a red cent, and more than that I go bail to the tune of a quarter of a million dollars that I deliver the goods."

He strode up and down the room, twirling his cigar, and flinging his short, sharp sentences at the two men, who, to his mind, stood as barriers to an Allied triumph.

"If you will sit down, Mr. Dene," said Sir Lyster suavely, "I'll explain."

John Dene hesitated for a moment, then humped himself into a chair, gazing moodily before him.

"We quite appreciate your—er—patriotism and public-spiritedness in——"

"Here, cut it out," broke in John Dene. "Do you want the *Destroyer* or don't you?"

Sir Lyster recoiled as if he had been struck. He had been First Lord too short a time for the gilt to be worn off his dignity. Seeing his Chief about to reply in a way that he suspected might end the interview, Admiral Heyworth interposed.

"May I suggest that under the circumstances we consult Mr. Llewellyn John?"

"That's bully," broke in John Dene without giving Sir Lyster a chance of replying. "They say he's got pep."

Bowing to the inevitable, Sir Lyster picked up the telephone-receiver.

"Get me through to the Prime Minister," he said.

The three men waited in silence for the response. As the bell rang, Sir Lyster swiftly raised the receiver to his ear.

"Yes, the Prime Minister. Sir Lyster Grayne speaking." There was a pause. "Grayne speaking, yes. Can I come round with Admiral Heyworth and an—er—inventor? It's very important." He listened for a moment, then added, "Yes, we'll come at once."

"Now, Mr. Dene," said Sir Lyster, as he rose and picked up his hat, "I hope we shall be able to—er——" He did not finish the sentence; but led the way to the door.

The three men walked across the Horse Guards Quadrangle towards Downing Street. The only words uttered were when Sir Lyster asked John Dene if he had seen the pelicans.

John Dene looked at him in amazement. He had heard that in British official circles it was considered bad taste to discuss the war except officially, and he decided that he was now discovering what was really the matter with the British Empire.

As the trio crossed the road to mount the steps leading to Downing Street, the girl passed of whom John Dene had asked the way. Her eyes widened slightly as she recognised John Dene's two companions; they widened still more when John Dene lifted his hat, followed a second later by Sir Lyster, whilst Admiral Heyworth saluted. In her surprise she nearly ran into a little shifty-eyed man, in a grey suit, who, with an elaborate flourish of his hat, hastened to apologise for her carelessness.

"That's the girl who showed me the way to your back-door," John Dene announced nonchalantly. Sir Lyster exchanged a rapid glance with the Admiral. "If I was running this show," continued John Dene,

"I'd get that door enlarged a bit and splash some paint about;" and for the first time since they had met John Dene smiled up at Sir Lyster, a smile that entirely changed the sombre cast of his features.

On arriving at no, Downing Street, the three callers were conducted straight into Mr. Llewellyn John's room. As they entered, he rose quickly from his table littered with papers, and with a smile greeted his colleagues. Sir Lyster then introduced John Dene.

Mr. Llewellyn John grasped John Dene's hand, and turned on him that bewilderingly sunny smile which Mr. Chappeldale had once said ought in itself to win the war.

"Sit down, Mr. Dene," said Mr. Llewellyn John, indicating a chair; "it's always a pleasure to meet any one from Canada. What should we have done without you Canadians?" he murmured half to himself.

"Mr. Dene tells us that he has solved the submarine problem," said Sir Lyster, as he and Admiral Heyworth seated themselves.

Instantly Mr. Llewellyn John became alert. The social smile vanished from his features, giving place to the look of a keen-witted Celt, eager to pounce upon something that would further his schemes. He turned to John Dene interrogatingly.

"Perhaps Mr. Dene will explain," suggested Sir Lyster.

"Sure," said John Dene, "your submarine isn't a submarine at all, it's a submersible. Under water it's useless, because it can't see. As well call a seal a fish. A submarine must be able to fight under water, and until it can it won't be any more a submarine than I'm a tunny fish."

Mr. Llewellyn John nodded in eager acquiescence.

"I've spent over a million dollars, and now I've got a boat that can see under water and fight under water and do a lot of other fancy tricks."

Mr. Llewellyn John sprang to his feet.

"You have. Tell me, where is it? This is wonderful, wonderful! It takes us a year forward."

"It's on the St. Lawrence River, just below Quebec," explained John Dene.

"And how long will it take to construct say a hundred?" asked Mr. Llewellyn John eagerly, dropping back into his chair.

"Longer than any of us are going to live," replied John Dene grimly.

Mr. Llewellyn John looked at his visitor in surprise. Sir Lyster and the Admiral exchanged meaning glances. The Prime Minister was experiencing what in Toronto were known as "John's snags."

"But if you've made one— —" began Mr. Llewellyn John.

"There's only going to be one," announced John Dene grimly.

"But— —"

"You can but like a he-goat," announced John Dene, "still there'll be only our *Destroyer*."

Sir Lyster smiled inwardly. His bruised dignity was recovering at the sight of the surprised look on the face of the Prime Minister at John Dene's comparison.

"Perhaps Mr. Dene will explain to us the difficulties," insinuated Sir Lyster.

"Sure," said John Dene; then turning to Admiral Heyworth, "What would happen if Germany got a submarine that could see and do fancy stunts?" he demanded.

"It might embarrass— —" began the Admiral.

"Shucks!" cried John Dene, "it would bust us up. What about the American transports, food-ships, munitions and the rest of it. They'd be attacked all along the three thousand miles route, and would go down like neck-oil on a permit night. You get me?"

Suddenly Mr. Llewellyn John struck the table with his fist.

"You're right, Mr. Dene," he cried; "they might capture one and copy it. You remember the Gothas," he added, turning to Sir Lyster.

"Sure," was John Dene's laconic reply.

"But how can we be sure they will not capture the *Destroyer*?" enquired Sir Lyster.

"Because there'll be John Dene and a hundred-weight of high-explosive on board," said John Dene drily as he chewed at the end of his cigar.

"Then you propose— —" began Admiral Heyworth.

"I'll put you wise. This is my offer. I'm willing to send U-boats to merry hell; but only on my own terms. I won't take a cent for my boat or anything else. It's my funeral. The *Destroyer* is now in Canada, with German spies buzzing around like flies over a dead rat. If you agree, I'll cable to my boys to bring the *Destroyer*, and it won't be done without some fancy shooting, I take it! You," turning to Admiral Heyworth, "will appoint an officer, two if you like, to come aboard and count the bag. I'll supply the crew, and you'll give me a commander's commission in the Navy. Now, is it a deal?"

"But——" began Sir Lyster.

"You make me tired," said John Dene wearily. "Is it or is it not a deal?" he enquired of Mr. Llewellyn John.

With an effort the Prime Minister seemed to gather himself together. He found the pace a little breathless, even for him.

"I think it might be arranged, Grayne," he said tactfully. "Mr. Dene knows his own invention and we might enrol his crew in the Navy; what do you think?" Mr. Llewellyn John abounded in tact.

"I take it that you understand navigation, Mr. Dene?" ventured the Admiral.

"Sure," was the reply. "You come a trip with me, and I'll show you navigation that'll make your hair stand on end. Sorry," he added a moment after, observing that Admiral Heyworth was almost aggressively bald.

"That's all right," laughed the Admiral; "they call me the coot."

"Well, is it a deal?" demanded John Dene, rising.

"It is," said Mr. Llewellyn John, "and a splendid deal for the British Empire, Mr. Dene," he added, holding out his hand. "It's a great privilege to meet a patriot such as you. Sir Lyster and Admiral Heyworth will settle all details to your entire satisfaction."

"If they do for me, I want you to give the command to Blake, then to Quinton, and so on, only to my own boys; is that agreed?"

"Do for you?" queried Mr. Llewellyn John.

"Huns, they're after me every hour of the day. There was a little chap even in your own building."

"We really must intern these Germans——" began Mr. Llewellyn John.

"You're barking up the wrong tree, over here," said John Dene with conviction. "You think a German spy's got a square head and says 'Ach himmel' and 'Ja wohl' on street-cars. It's the neutrals mostly, and sometimes the British," he added under his breath.

"In any case you will, I am sure, find that Sir Lyster will do whatever you want," said Mr. Llewellyn John as they walked towards the door.

For the second time that morning John Dene smiled as he left No. 110, Downing Street, with Sir Lyster and Admiral Heyworth, whilst Mr. Llewellyn John rang up the chief of Department Z.

CHAPTER II.
JOHN DENE'S WAY

As Sir Lyster entered Mr. Blair's room, accompanied by John Dene and Admiral Heyworth, he was informed that Sir Bridgman North, the First Sea Lord, was anxious to see him.

"Ask him if he can step over now, Blair," said Sir Lyster, and the three men passed into the First Lord's room. Two minutes later Sir Bridgman North entered, and Sir Lyster introduced John Dene.

For a moment the two men eyed one another in mutual appraisement; the big, bluff Sea Lord, with his humorous blue eyes and ready laugh, and the keen, heavy-featured Canadian, as suspicious of a gold band as of a pickpocket.

"Pleased to meet you," said John Dene perfunctorily, as they shook hands. "Now you'd better give me a chance to work off my music;" and with that he seated himself.

Sir Bridgman exchanged an amused glance with Admiral Heyworth, as they too found chairs.

In a few words Sir Lyster explained the reason of John Dene's visit. Sir Bridgman listened with the keen interest of one to whom his profession is everything.

"Now, Mr. Dene," said Sir Lyster when he had finished, "perhaps you will continue."

In short, jerky sentences John Dene outlined his scheme of operations, the others listening intently. From time to time Sir Bridgman or Admiral Heyworth would interpolate a question upon some technical point, which was promptly and satisfactorily answered. John Dene seemed to have forgotten nothing.

For two hours the four sat discussing plans for a campaign that was once and for all to put an end to Germany's submarine hopes.

During those two hours the three Englishmen learned something of the man with whom they had to deal. Sir Bridgman's tact, cheery personality and understanding of how to handle men did much to improve the atmosphere, and gradually John Dene's irritation disappeared.

It was nearly three o'clock before all the arrangements were completed. John Dene was to receive a temporary commission as commander as soon as the King's signature could be obtained. The *Destroyer* was entered on the Navy List as H4, thus taking the place of a submarine that was "missing." John Dene had stipulated that she should be rated in some existing class, so that the secret of her existence might be preserved. In short, sharp sentences he had presented his demands, they were nothing less, and the others had acquiesced. By now they were all convinced that he was right, and that the greatest chance of success lay in "giving him his head," as Sir Bridgman North expressed it in a whisper to Sir Lyster.

A base was to be selected on some island in the North of Scotland, and fitted with wireless with aerials a hundred and fifty feet high, "to pick up all that's going," explained John Dene, conscious of the surprise of his hearers at a request for such a long-range plant. Here the *Destroyer* was to be based, and stores and fuel sufficient for six months accumulated. This was to be proceeded with at once.

"I shall want charts of the minefields," he said, "and full particulars as to patrol flotillas and the like."

Admiral Heyworth nodded comprehendingly.

"By the way," he said, "there's one thing I do not quite understand."

"Put a name to it," said John Dene tersely.

"How do you propose to keep at sea for any length of time without recharging your batteries?"

"We shall be lying doggo most of the time," was the reply.

"Then in all probability the U-boats will pass over you."

"We shan't be lying at the bottom of the sea, either," said John Dene.

"What!" exclaimed Admiral Heyworth, "but if your motor's cut off, you'll sink to the bed of the sea—the law of gravity."

"The *Destroyer* is fitted with buoyancy chambers, and she can generate a gas that will hold her suspended at any depth," he explained. "This gas can be liquefied in a few seconds. Her microphone will tell her when the U-boats are about; it's my own invention."

Sir Lyster looked from one to the other, unable to grasp such technicalities; but conscious that Admiral Heyworth seemed surprised at what he heard.

"It's up to you to see that none of your boys start dropping depth-charges around," said John Dene.

He went on to explain that he proposed a certain restricted area for operations, and that the Admiralty should issue instructions that no depth charges were to be dropped on any submarine within that area until further notice.

"There's one thing I must leave you to supply," said John Dene, as he leaned back in his chair smoking a cigar. John Dene chewed the end of a cigar during the period of negotiations, and smoked it when the deal was struck.

"And what is that?" asked Sir Bridgman.

"I shall want a 'mother' — —"

"A mother!" ejaculated Sir Lyster, looking from John Dene to the First Sea Lord, who laughed loudly. Sir Lyster always felt that Sir Bridgman should have left his laugh on the quarter-deck when he relinquished active command.

"A 'mother,'" he explained, "is a kangaroo-ship, a dry-dock ship for salvage and repair of submarines. Yes, we'll fit you out."

Sir Lyster looked chagrined. He had found some difficulty in mastering naval technicalities. When war broke out he was directing a large dock from which vast numbers of troops were shipped to France. He had shown such administrative genius, that Mr. Llewellyn John had selected him for the post of First Lord of the Admiralty, with results that satisfied every one, even the Sea Lords.

John Dene then proceeded to indicate the nature of the alterations he would require made in the vessel, showing a remarkable knowledge of the British type of mother-ship.

"You ought either to be shot as a spy or made First Sea Lord," said Sir Bridgman, looking up from a diagram that John Dene had produced.

"The Hun'll try to do the shooting; and as for my becoming Sea Lord, I should be sorry for some of the plugs here."

John Dene's thoroughness impressed his three hearers. Everything had been foreseen, even the spot where the *Destroyer* was to be based. The small island of Auchinlech possessed a natural harbour of sufficient size for the mother-ship to enter, after which the entrance was to be guarded by a defensive boom as a safeguard against U-boats.

John Dene explained that a month or five weeks must elapse before the *Destroyer* would be ready for action. In about three weeks she could be at Auchinlech, crossing the Atlantic under her own power. Another week or ten days would be required for refitting and taking in stores.

"When you've delivered the goods you can quit, and I shall be pleased to see your boys again in four months."

John Dene regarded his listeners with the air of a man who had just thrown a bombshell and is conscious of the fact.

"Four months!" ejaculated Sir Lyster.

"Yep!" He uttered the monosyllable in a tone that convinced at least one of his listeners that expostulation would be useless.

"But," protested Sir Lyster, "how shall we know what is happening?"

"You won't," was the laconic reply.

"But——" began Sir Lyster again.

"If no one knows what is happening," interrupted John Dene, "no one can tell anyone else."

"Surely, Mr. Dene," said Sir Lyster with some asperity in his voice, "you do not suspect the War Cabinet, for instance, of divulging secrets of national importance."

"I don't suspect the War Cabinet of anything," was the dry retort, "not even of trying to win the war." John Dene looked straight into Sir Lyster's eyes.

There was an awkward pause.

"Who's going to guarantee that the War Cabinet doesn't talk in its sleep?" he continued. "I'm not out to take risks. If this country doesn't want my boat on my terms, then I shan't worry, although you may," he added as an afterthought. "No, sir," he banged his fist on the table vehemently. "This is the biggest thing that's come into the war so far, and I'm not going to have anyone monkeying about with my plans. I'm going to have a written document that I've got a free hand, otherwise I don't deal, that's understood."

"But——" began Sir Lyster once more.

"Excuse me, Grayne," broke in Sir Bridgman, "may I suggest that, as we are all keenly interested parties, Mr. Dene might give us his reasons."

"Sure," said John Dene without waiting for Sir Lyster's reply. "In Can'da a man gets a job because he's the man for that job, leastwise if he's not he's fired. Here I'll auction that half the big jobs are held by mutts whose granddad's had a pleasant way of saying how d'ye do to a prince. If any of them came around you'd have me skippin' like a scalded cat, and when I'm like that I'm liable to say things. I'm my own man and my own boss, and I take a man's size in most things. I'm too old to feel meek at the sight of gold bands. I want to feel kind to everybody, and I find I can do that in this country better when everybody keeps out of my way."

John Dene paused, and the others looked at each other, a little nonplussed how to respond to such directness.

"It's been in my head-fillin' quite a while to tell you this;" and John Dene suddenly smiled, one of those rare smiles that seemed to take the sting out of his words. "I'd be real sorry to hurt anybody's feelings," he added, "but we've got different notions of things in Can'da."

It was Sir Bridgman who eased the situation.

"If ever you want a second in command, I'm your man," he laughed. "Straight talk makes men friends, and if we do wrap things up a bit more here, we aren't so thin-skinned as not to be able to take it from the shoulder. What say you, Grayne?"

"Yes—certainly," said Sir Lyster with unconvincing hesitation.

"You were mentioning spies," said Admiral Heyworth.

"So would you if they'd plagued you as they've plagued me," said John Dene. "They've already stolen three sets of plans."

"Three sets of plans!" cried Sir Lyster, starting up in alarm.

John Dene nodded as he proceeded to relight the stump of his cigar. "One set in T'ronto, one on the steamer and the other from my room at the Ritzton."

"Good Heavens!" exclaimed Sir Lyster in alarm, "what is to be done?"

"Oh! I've got another three sets," said John Dene calmly.

Sir Lyster looked at him as if doubtful of his sanity.

"Don't you worry," said John Dene imperturbably, "one set of plans was of the U1, the first boat the Germans built, the second set was of the U2, and the third of the U9."

Sir Bridgman's laugh rang out as he thumped the table with his fist.

"Splendid!" he cried. Sir Lyster sank back into his chair with a sigh of relief.

"By the way, Dene," said Sir Bridgman casually, "suppose the *Destroyer* was—er—lost and you with her."

"I've arranged for a set of plans to be delivered to the First Lord, whoever he may be at the time," said John Dene.

"Good!" said Sir Bridgman. "You think of everything. We shall have you commanding the Grand Fleet before the war's over."'

Sir Lyster said nothing. He did not quite relish the qualification "whoever he may be at the time."

"About the spies," he said after a pause. "I think it would be advisable to arrange for your protection."

"Not on your life!" cried John Dene with energy. "I don't want any policemen following me around. I've got my own—well," he added, "I've fixed things up all right, and if the worst comes to the worst, well there aren't many men in this country that can beat John Dene with a gun. Now it's up to me to make good on this proposition." He looked from one to the other, as if challenging contradiction. Finding there was none, he continued: "But there are a few things that I want before I can start in, and then you won't see me for dust. You get me?" He looked suddenly at Sir Lyster.

"We'll do everything in our power to help you, Mr. Dene," said Sir Lyster, reaching for a clean sheet of paper from the rack before him.

"Well, I've got it all figured out here," said John Dene, taking a paper from his jacket pocket. "First I want a written undertaking, signed by you," turning to Sir Lyster, "and Mr. Llewellyn John that I'm to have four months to run the *Destroyer* with no one butting in."

Sir Lyster nodded and made a note.

"Next," continued John Dene, "I want a mothership fully equipped with stores and fuel sufficient for four months."

Again Sir Lyster inclined his head and made a note.

"I'll give you a schedule of everything I'm likely to want. Then I want an undertaking that if anything happens to me the command goes to Blake and then to Quinton. If I don't get these things," he announced with decision, "I'll call a halt right here."

"I think you can depend upon Sir Lyster doing all you want, Mr. Dene," said Sir Bridgman; "and when you see the way he does it, perhaps you'll have a better opinion of the Admiralty."

Sir Lyster smiled slightly. He had already determined to show John Dene that nowhere in the world was there an organisation equal to that of the Admiralty Victualling and Stores Departments.

"You help John Dene and he's with you till the cows come to roost," was the response; "and now," he added shrewdly, "you'd better get the cables to work and find out something about me."

"Something about you!" queried Sir Lyster.

"You're not going to trust a man because he talks big, I'll gamble on that. Well, you'll learn a deal about John Dene, and now it's time you got a rustle on."

"In all probability our Intelligence Department knows all about you by now, Mr. Dene," said Sir Bridgman with a laugh. "It's supposed to be fairly up to date in most things."

"Well," said John Dene, as he leaned back in his chair, puffing vigorously at his cigar, "you've treated me better'n I expected, and you won't regret it. Remembering's my long suit. I don't want any honour or glory out of this stunt, I just want to get the job done. If there are any garters, or collars going around, you may have 'em, personally I don't wear 'em,—garters, I mean. A couple of rubber-bands are good enough for me."

Sir Bridgman laughed, Sir Lyster smiled indulgently, and Admiral Heyworth rose to go.

"There's only one thing more; I want a room here and someone to take down letters."

"I will tell my secretary to arrange everything," said Sir Lyster. "You have only to ask for what you require, Mr. Dene."

"Well, that's settled," said John Dene, rising. "Now it's up to me, and if the *Destroyer* doesn't give those Huns merry hell, then I'm green goods;" and with this enigmatical utterance he abruptly left the room, with a nod, and a "See you all in the morning."

As the door closed, the three men gazed at each other for a few seconds.

"An original character," said Sir Lyster indulgently. "Going, Heyworth?" he enquired, as Admiral Heyworth moved towards the door.

"Yes, I've hardly touched the day's work yet," was the reply.

"Never mind," said Sir Bridgman, "you've done the best day's work you're likely to do during this war."

"I think I agree with you," said Admiral Heyworth as he left the room.

"Well, Grayne, what do you think of our friend, John Dene?" inquired Sir Bridgman as he lighted a cigarette.

"He's rather abrupt," said Sir Lyster hesitatingly, "but I think he's a sterling character."

"You're right," said Sir Bridgman heartily. "I wish we had a dozen John Denes in the Service. When the colonies do produce a man they do the thing in style, and Canada has made no mistake about John Dene. He's going nearer to win the war than any other man in the Empire."

"Ah! your incurable enthusiasm," smiled Sir Lyster.

"What I like about him," remarked Sir Bridgman, "is that he never waits to be contradicted."

"He certainly does seem to take everything for granted," said Sir Lyster, with a note of complaint in his voice.

"The man who has all the cards generally does," said Sir Bridgman drily. "Dene will always get there, because he has no axe to grind, and the only thing he respects is brains. That is why he snubs us all so unmercifully," he added with the laugh that always made Sir Lyster wish he wouldn't.

"Now I want to consult you about a rather embarrassing question that's on the paper for Friday," said Sir Lyster.

Unconscious that he was forming the subject of discussion with the heads of the Admiralty, John Dene, on leaving the First Lord's room, turned to the right and walked quickly in the direction of the main staircase. As he reached a point where the corridor was intersected by another running at right angles, the sudden opening of a door on his left caused him to turn his head quickly. A moment later there was a feminine cry and a sound of broken crockery, and John Dene found himself gazing down at a broken teapot.

"Oh!"

He looked up from the steaming ruin of newly brewed tea into the violet eyes of the girl who had directed him to the Admiralty. He noticed the purity of her skin, the redness of her lips and the rebelliousness of her corn-coloured hair, which seeming to refuse all constraint clung about her head in little wanton tendrils.

"That's my fault," said John Dene, removing his hat. "I'm sorry."

"Yes; but our tea," said the girl in genuine consternation; "we're rationed, you know."

"Rationed?" said John Dene.

"Yes; we only get two ounces a week each," she said with a comical look of despair.

"Gee!" cried John Dene, then he asked suddenly: "What are you?"

The girl looked at him in surprise, a little stiffly.

"Can you type? Never mind about the tea."

"But I do mind about the tea." She found John Dene's manner disarming.

"I take it you're a stenographer. Now tell me your name. I'll see about the tea." He had whipped out a note-book and pencil. "Hurry, I've got a cable to send."

Seeing that she was reluctant to give her name, he continued: "Never mind about your name. Be in the First Lord's room to-morrow at eleven o'clock; I'll see you there;" and with that he turned quickly, resumed his hat and retraced his steps.

Without knocking, he pushed open the door of Mr. Blair's room, walked swiftly across and opened the door leading to that of the First Lord.

"Here!" he cried, "where can I buy a pound of tea?"

If John Dene had asked where he could borrow an ichthyosaurus, Sir Lyster and Sir Bridgman could not have gazed at him with more astonishment.

"You can't," said Sir Bridgman, at length, his eyes twinkling as he watched the expression on Sir Lyster's face.

"Can't!" cried John Dene.

"Tea's rationed—two ounces a week," explained Sir Bridgman.

"Anyhow I've got to buy a pound of tea. I've just smashed up the teapot of a girl in the corridor."

"I'm afraid it's impossible," said Sir Lyster with quiet dignity.

"Impossible!" said John Dene irritably. "Here am I giving more'n a million dollars to the country and I can't get a pound of tea. I'll see about that. She'll be here in this room to-morrow at eleven o'clock," and with that the door closed and John Dene disappeared.

"I've told a girl to be here at eleven o'clock to-morrow. She's going to be my secretary," he explained to Mr. Blair as he passed through his office.

Mr. Blair blinked his eyes vigorously. He had seen Sir Lyster and Admiral Heyworth leave the Admiralty with John Dene, he gathered that they had had a long interview with the Prime Minister, then they had returned again and, for two hours, had sat in consultation with the First Sea Lord. Now the amazing John Dene had made an appointment to meet some girl in the First Lord's room at eleven o'clock the next morning.

As John Dene left the Admiralty puffing clouds of blue content from his cigar, the shifty-eyed man, in a grey suit, who had been examining the Royal Marines statue, drew a white handkerchief with a flourish from his pocket and proceeded to blow his nose vigorously. The act seemed to pass unnoticed save by a young girl sitting on a neighbouring seat. She immediately appeared to become greatly interested in the movements of John Dene, whilst the man in the grey suit walked away in the direction of Birdcage Walk.

"Where's the tea?" was the cry with which Dorothy West was greeted as she entered the room she occupied with a number of other girls after her encounter with John Dene.

"It's in the corridor," she replied.

"Oh! go and get it, there's a dear; I'm simply parched," cried Marjorie Rogers, a pretty little brunette at the further corner.

"It's all gone," said Dorothy West; "a Hun just knocked it out of my hand. He smashed the teapot."

"Smashed the teapot!" cried several girls in chorus.

"Oh! Wessie," wailed the little brunette, "I shall die."

"Why did you let him do it?" asked a fair girl with white eyelashes and glasses.

"I didn't," said Dorothy; "he just barged into me and knocked the teapot out of my hand, and then made an assignation for eleven o'clock to-morrow in the First Lord's room."

"An assignation! The First Lord's room!" cried Miss Cunliffe, who by virtue of a flat chest, a pair of round glasses, and an uncompromising manner made an ideal supervisor. She was known as "Old Goggles." "What do you mean, Miss West?"

"Exactly what I say, Miss Cunliffe. He asked me if I was a stenographer, and then said that I was to see him at eleven o'clock to-morrow morning in the First Lord's room. What do you think I had better do?"

"Who is he? What is he? Do tell us, Wessie, dear," cried Marjorie Rogers excitedly.

"Well, I should think he's either a madman or else he's bought the Admiralty," said Dorothy West, her head on one side as if weighing her words before uttering them. "He's the man I saw this morning with Sir Lyster Grayne and Admiral Heyworth, going to call on the Prime Minister—at least, I suppose they were; they went up the steps into Downing Street. But ought I to go at eleven o'clock, Miss Cunliffe?" she queried.

"I'll make enquiries," said Miss Cunliffe. "I'll see Mr. Blair. Perhaps he's mad."

"But what are we going to do about our tea?" wailed Marjorie. "I'd sooner lose my character than my tea."

"Miss Rogers!" said Miss Cunliffe, whose conception of supervisorship was that she should oversee the decorum as well as the work of the other occupants of the room.

"I believe she did it on purpose," said she of the white eyelashes spitefully to a girl in a velvet blouse.

"You had better brew to-morrow's tea to-day, Miss West," said Miss Cunliffe.

"Yes, do, there's a darling," cried Marjorie. "I simply can't wait another five minutes. Why, I couldn't lick a stamp to save my life. Borrow No. 13's pot when they've finished with it, and pinch some of their tea, if you can," she added.

And Dorothy West went out to interview the guardian of No. 13's teapot.

CHAPTER III.
DEPARTMENT Z.

I

"Mr. Sage there? Very well, ask him to step in and see me as soon as he returns."

Colonel Walton replaced the telephone-receiver and continued to draw diagrams upon the blotting-pad before him, an occupation in which he had been engaged for the last quarter of an hour.

Since its creation two years before, he had been Chief of Department Z., the most secret section of the British Secret Service, with Malcolm Sage as his lieutenant.

Department Z. owed its inception to an inspiration on the part of Mr. Llewellyn John. He had conceived the idea of creating a secret service department, the working of which should be secret even from the Secret Service itself. Its primary object was that the Prime Minister and the War Cabinet might have a private means of obtaining such special information as it required. Department Z. was unhampered by rules and regulations, as devoid of conventions as an enterprising flapper.

In explaining his scheme to Mr. Thaw, the Chancellor of the Exchequer, Mr. Llewellyn John had said, "Suppose I want to know what Chappeldale had for lunch yesterday, and don't like to ask him, how am I to find out? I want a Department that can tell me anything I want to know, and will be surprised at nothing."

With Mr. Llewellyn John to conceive a thing was to put it into practice. He did not make the mistake of placing Department Z. under the control of a regular secret service man.

"I'm tired of red-tape and traditions," he had remarked to Mr. Thaw. "If I go to the front, they won't let me speak to a man lower than a brigadier, whereas I want the point-of-view of the drummer-boy."

Mr. Llewellyn John had heard of Colonel Walton's exploits in India as head of the Burmah Police, had seen him, and in five minutes the first Chief of Department Z. was appointed. From the Ministry of Supply, Mr. Llewellyn John had plucked Malcolm Sage, whom he later described as "either a ferret turned dreamer, or a dreamer turned ferret," he was not quite sure which.

In discovering Malcolm Sage, Mr. Llewellyn John had achieved one of his greatest strokes of good fortune. When Minister of Supply his notice had been attracted to Sage, as the man who had been instrumental in bringing to light—that is official light, for the affair was never made public—the greatest contracts-scandal of the war. It was due entirely to his initiative and unobtrusive enquiries that a gigantic fraud, diabolical in its cleverness, had been discovered—a fraud that might have involved the country in the loss of millions.

Mr. Llewellyn John had recognised that this young accountant had done him a great service, perhaps saved him from a serious political set-back. Incidentally he discovered that Sage was a very uneasy person to have in a Government-department. Sage cared nothing for tradition, discipline, or bureaucracy. If they interfered with the proper performance of his duties, overboard they went. He was the most transferred man in Whitehall. No one seemed to want to keep him for longer than the period necessary for the formalities of his transfer.

"Uneasy lies the Head that has a Sage," was a phrase some wag had coined. If a man wanted to condemn another as too zealous, unnecessarily hard-working, or as a breaker of idols, he likened him to Sage.

The chief of the department from which Mr. Llewellyn John took Malcolm Sage when Department Z. was formed is said to have wept tears of joy at the news. For months he had striven to transfer his unconventional subordinate; but there was none who would have him. This unfortunate chief of department had gone through life like a man wanting to sell a dog of dubious pedigree. In the Ministry he was known as Henry II, and Sage came to be referred to as Beckett.

In Department Z. Sage found his proper niche. Under Colonel Walton, a man of few words and great tact, he had found an ideal chief, one who understood how to handle men.

As John Dene had left 110, Downing Street, with Sir Lyster and Admiral Heyworth, Mr. Llewellyn John had rung up Colonel Walton and requested that full enquiries be made at once as to John Dene of Toronto, and a report submitted to him in the morning. That was all. He had given no indication of why he wanted to know, or what was John Dene's business in London.

Hardly a day of his life passed without Mr. Llewellyn John having cause to be thankful for the inspiration that had resulted in the founding of Department Z. Nothing seemed to come amiss, either to the Department or its officials. They never required an elaborate filling-up of forms, they never asked for further particulars as did other departments. They just got to work.

Mr. Llewellyn John had, once and for all, defined Department Z. when he said to Mr. Thaw, "If I were to ask Scotland Yard if Chappeldale had gone over to the Bolshevists, or if Waytensee had become an Orangeman, they would send a man here, his pockets bulging with note-books. Department Z. would tell me all I wanted to know in a few hours."

In his first interview with Mr. Llewellyn John, previous to being appointed to Department Z., Malcolm Sage had bluntly criticised the Government's methods of dealing with the spy peril.

"You're all wrong, sir," he had said. "If you spot a spy, you arrest, imprison or deport him, according to the degree of his guilt. Any fool could do that," he had added quietly.

"And what would you do, Sage?" inquired Mr. Llewellyn John, who never took offence at the expression of any man's honest opinion, no matter how emphatically worded.

"I should watch him," was the laconic reply. "Just as was done before the war. You didn't arrest spies then, you just let them think they were safe."

For a few moments Mr. Llewellyn John had pondered the remark, and then asked for an explanation.

"If you arrest, shoot or intern a spy, another generally springs up in his place, and you have to start afresh to find him; he may do a lot of mischief before that comes about." Sage gazed meditatively at his finger-nails, a habit of his. "On the other hand," he continued, "if you know your man, you can watch him and generally find out what he's after. Better a known than an unknown danger," he had added oracularly.

"I'm afraid they wouldn't endorse that doctrine at Scotland Yard," smiled Mr. Llewellyn John.

"Scotland Yard is a place of promoted policemen," replied Sage, "regulation intellects in regulation boots."

Mr. Llewellyn John smiled. He always appreciated a phrase. "Then you would not arrest a burglar, but watch him," he said, glancing keenly at Sage.

"The cases are entirely different, sir," was the reply; "a burglar invariably works on his own, a spy is more frequently than not a cog of a machine and must be replaced. He seldom works entirely alone."

"Go on," Mr. Llewellyn John had said, seeing that Sage paused and was intently regarding his finger-nails of his right hand.

"Even when burglars work in gangs, there is no superior organisation to replace destroyed units," continued Sage. "With international secret service it is different; its casualties are made good as promptly as with a field army."

"I believe you're right," said Mr. Llewellyn John. "If you can convince Colonel Walton, then Department Z. can be run on those lines."

Malcolm Sage had found no difficulty in convincing his chief, a man of quiet demeanour, but unprejudiced mind. The result had been that Department Z. had not so far caused a single arrest, although it had countered many clever schemes. Its motto was "The Day" when it could make a really historical haul.

The progress of Malcolm Sage had been remarkable. Colonel Walton had quickly seen that his subordinate could work only along his own lines, and in consequence he had given him his head. Sage, on his part, had discovered in his chief a man with a sound knowledge of human nature, generously spiced with the devil.

As Sage entered, Colonel Walton ceased his diagrams and looked up. Sage was as unlike the "sleuth hound" of fiction as it is possible for a man to be. At first glance he looked like the superintendent of a provincial Sunday-school. He was about thirty-five years of age, sandy, wore gold-rimmed glasses and possessed a conical head, prematurely bald. He had a sharp nose, steel-coloured eyes and large ears; but there was the set of his jaw which told of determination.

Seating himself in his customary place, Sage proceeded to pull at the inevitable briar, without which he was seldom seen. For a full minute there was silence. Colonel Walton deliberately lighted a cigar and leaned back to listen. He knew his man and refrained from asking questions.

"They're puzzled, chief"—Sage knocked the ashes from his pipe into the ash-tray on the table—"and they're getting jumpy," he added.

Colonel Walton nodded.

"Twice they've ransacked John Dene's room at the Ritzton and found nothing."

"Does he know?" enquired Colonel Walton.

Sage nodded.

"John Dene's a dark horse," he remarked with respect in his voice, "and the Huns can't make up their minds."

"To what?" enquired the chief.

"To give up the shadow for the substance," he remarked, as he pressed down the tobacco in his pipe. "They want the plans, and they want to prevent the boat from putting to sea."

Colonel Walton nodded comprehendingly.

"They'll probably try to scotch her on the way over; but they won't know her route. They'll be lying in wait, however, in full strength in home waters. He's a bad psychologist," added Sage, as he knocked the ashes out of his pipe.

"Who?" enquired Colonel Walton.

"The Hun," replied Sage, as he sucked away contentedly at his pipe. "He's never content to go for a single issue, or he'd probably have got the Channel ports. He's not content with concentrating on John Dene and his boat, he's after the plans. That's where he'll fail. Smart chap, John Dene."

For some moments the two men smoked in silence, which was finally broken by Sage.

"They'll try to get hold of John Dene, unless he's very careful, and hold him to ransom, the price being the plans."

"Incidentally, Sage, where did you get all this from?" enquired Walton.

Sage gazed at his chief through his gold-rimmed spectacles. "About three hundred yards west of the Temple Station on the Underground."

Colonel Walton glanced across at his subordinate; but refrained from asking further questions. "Have you warned Dene?" he enquired instead.

"No use," replied Sage with conviction. "Might as well warn a fly."

Colonel Walton nodded understandingly. "Still," he remarked, "I think he ought to be told."

"Why not have a try yourself?" Sage looked up swiftly from the inevitable contemplation of his finger-nails.

For fully a minute Colonel Walton sat revolving the proposal in his mind. "I think I will," he said later.

"He'll treat you like a superannuated policeman," was the grim retort.

"The Skipper wants to see us at eleven," said Colonel Walton, looking at his watch and rising. The "Skipper" was the name by which Mr. Llewellyn John was known at Department Z. Names were rarely referred to, and very few documents were ever exchanged. Colonel Walton picked up his hat from a bookcase and, followed by Sage, who extracted a cap from his pocket, left the room and Department Z. and walked across to Downing Street.

As Colonel Walton and Malcolm Sage were shown into Mr. Llewellyn John's room, the Prime Minister gave instructions that he was not to be disturbed for a quarter of an hour.

"Was the John Dene Report what you wanted, sir?" enquired Colonel Walton, as he took the seat Mr. Llewellyn John indicated.

"Excellent," cried Mr. Llewellyn John; then with a smile he added, "I was able to tell Sir Lyster quite a lot of things this morning. The

Admiralty report was not ready until late last night. It was not nearly so instructive."

The main facts of John Dene's career had not been difficult to obtain. His father had emigrated to Canada in the early eighties; but, possessing only the qualifications of a clerk, he had achieved neither fame nor fortune. He had died when John Dene was eight years old, and his wife had followed him within eighteen months. After a varied career John Dene had drifted to the States, where as a youth he had entered a large engineering firm, and was instantly singled out as an inventor in embryo.

Several fortunate speculations had formed the foundation of a small fortune of twenty thousand dollars, with which he returned to Toronto. From that point his career had been one continual progression of successes. Everything he touched seemed to turn to gold, until "John's luck" became a well-known phrase in financial circles.

Unlike most successful business-men, he devoted a large portion of his time to his hobby, electrical engineering, and when the war broke out he sought to turn this to practical and patriotic uses.

"And when may we expect Mr. Dene's new submarine over?" enquired Malcolm Sage casually.

"Mr. Dene's new submarine!" Mr. Llewellyn John's hands dropped to his sides as he gazed at Sage in blank amazement. "His new submarine," he repeated.

"Yes, sir."

"What on earth do you know about it?" demanded Mr. Llewellyn John, looking at Sage with a startled expression.

"John Dene has invented a submarine," proceeded the literal Sage, "with some novel features, including a searchlight that has overcome the opacity of water. The thing is lying on the St. Lawrence River just below Quebec. Yesterday he called to see Sir Lyster Grayne, who brought him here with Admiral Heyworth."

Mr. Llewellyn John gazed in bewilderment at Malcolm Sage, his eyes shifted to Colonel Walton and then back again to Sage.

"But," he began, "you're watching us, not the enemy. Did you know of this?" he turned to the chief of Department Z.

Colonel Walton shook his head. "I haven't seen Sage since you telephoned yesterday until a few minutes ago," he said.

"Where—how——?" Mr. Llewellyn John paused.

"It's our business to know things, sir," was Sage's quiet reply.

"And yet you didn't report this to——" began Mr. Llewellyn John.

"It saves time telling you both at once," responded Sage, looking at his chief with a smile.

"Suppose you tell us how you found out," suggested Mr. Llewellyn John a little irritably.

"Does that matter, sir?" Sage looked up calmly from an earnest examination of the nail of his left forefinger.

For some moments Mr. Llewellyn John gazed across at Malcolm Sage, frowning heavily.

"Sage has his own methods," remarked Colonel Walton tactfully.

"Methods," cried Mr. Llewellyn John, his brow clearing, "it's a good job he didn't live in the Middle Ages, or else he'd have been burned. I'm not so sure that he ought not to be burned now." He turned on Sage that smile that never failed in its magical effect.

"There are one or two links missing," said Sage. "I want to know where and when the *Destroyer* will arrive, and what steps you are taking in regard to John Dene."

"All arrangements will be left in Mr. Dene's hands. He is——" Mr. Lewellyn John paused.

"A little self-willed," suggested Sage.

"Self-willed!" exclaimed Mr. Llewellyn John. "He is a dictator in embryo."

"He happens also to be a patriot," said Sage quietly.

"Wait until you meet him," said the Prime Minister grimly.

"I have met him," said Sage quietly. "I trod on his toe last night at 'Chu Chin Chow.' We had quite a pleasant little chat about it. I think that is all I need trouble you with, sir," he concluded.

"And we are to see the thing through?" interrogated Colonel Walton, as Mr. Llewellyn John rose. "There won't be any——"

"No one else knows anything about it except Sir Lyster, Sir Bridgman and Admiral Heyworth. By the way," Mr. Llewellyn John added, "our Canadian friend has an idea that our Secret Service is run by superannuated policemen in regulation boots."

"I know," said Sage, as he followed his chief towards the door.

"Good-bye," cried Mr. Llewellyn John. "I'm sure I shall have to send you to the Tower, Sage, before I've finished with you."

"Then I'll spend the time writing the History of Department Z., sir," was the quiet reply. The two men went out, and Mr. Llewellyn John rang for his secretary.

"You have rather——" began Colonel Walton, but he stopped short. Sage suddenly knocked him roughly with his elbow.

"I have never seen the Mons Star," he said. "Can we go round by Whitehall? The Horse Guards sentries, I believe, wear it."

The two men had reached the top of the steps leading down into St. James's Park. Without a moment's pause Sage turned quickly, and nearly cannoned into a pretty and stylishly dressed girl, who was walking close behind them. He lifted his hat and apologised, and he and Colonel Walton passed up Downing Street into Whitehall. For the rest of the walk back to St. James's Square, Sage chatted about medals.

Seated once more one on either side of Colonel Walton's table, Sage proceeded to light his pipe.

"Clever, wasn't it?" he asked. "She's fairly new, too."

"Who was she?"

"Vera Ellerton, employed as a Temporary Ministry typist," Sage replied drily.

"So that was it," remarked Colonel Walton, cutting the end of a cigar with great deliberation.

"She was following us on the chance of catching any odd remarks that might be useful. On the way back here two others picked us up on the relay system."

"Do you think she knew who we were?" enquired Colonel Walton.

"No, just an off chance. We were callers on the Skipper, and might let something drop. It's a regular thing, picking up the callers, generally when they've got some distance away though."

"They must have learned quite a deal about numismatics," said Colonel Walton drily.

"A constitutional government is a great obstacle to an efficient Secret Service, it imposes limitations," remarked Sage regretfully.

Colonel Walton looked across in the act of lighting his cigar.

"There are six hundred and seventy of them at Westminster. In war-time we require a system of the *lettre-de-cachêt*. And now," said Sage, rising, "I think I'll get a couple of hours' sleep, I've been pretty busy. By the way," he said, with his hand upon the door-handle, "I think we might get the papers of that fellow on the Bergen boat, also a photograph, clothing, and full details of his appearance."

Colonel Walton nodded and Malcolm Sage took his departure.

II

"It's curious."

Malcolm Sage was seated at his table carefully studying several sheets of buff-coloured paper fastened together in the top left-hand corner with thin green cord. In a tray beside him lay a number of similar documents.

He glanced across at a small man with a dark moustache and determined chin sitting opposite. The man made a movement as if to speak, then apparently thinking better of it, remained silent.

"How many false calls did you say?" enquired Sage.

"Nine in five days, sir," was the response.

Malcolm Sage nodded his head several times, his eyes still fixed on the papers before him.

One of his first acts on being appointed to Department Z. was to give instructions, through the proper channels, that all telephone-operators were to be warned to report to their supervisors anything that struck them as unusual, no matter how trivial the incident might appear, carefully noting the numbers of the subscribers whose messages seemed out of the ordinary. This was quite apart from the special staff detailed to tap conversations, particularly call-box conversations throughout the Kingdom.

A bright young operator at the Streatham Exchange, coveting the reward of five pounds offered for any really useful information, had called attention to the curious fact that Mr. Montagu Naylor, of "The Cedars," Apthorpe Road, was constantly receiving wrong calls.

This operator's report had been considered of sufficient importance to send to Department Z. Instructions had been given for a complete record to be kept of all Mr. Montagu Naylor's calls, incoming and out-going. The first thing that struck Sage as significant was that all these false calls were made from public call-boxes. He gave instructions that at the Streatham Exchange they were to enquire of the exchanges from which the calls had come if any complaint had been made by those getting wrong numbers. The result showed that quite a number of people seemed content to pay threepence to be told that they were on to the wrong subscriber.

"What do you make of it, Thompson?" Malcolm Sage looked up in that sudden way of his, which many found so disconcerting.

Thompson shook his head. "I've had enquiries made at all the places given, and they seem quite all right, sir," was his reply. "It's funny," he added after a pause. "It began with short streets and small numbers, and then gradually took in the larger thoroughfares with bigger numbers."

"The calls have always come through in the same way?" queried Malcolm Sage. "First the number and then the street and no mention of the exchange."

"Yes, sir," was the response. "It's a bit of a puzzle," he added.

Malcolm Sage nodded. For some minutes they sat in silence, Sage staring with expressionless face at the papers before him. Suddenly with a swift movement he pushed them over towards Thompson.

"Get out a list of the whole range of numbers immediately, and bring it to me as soon as you can. Tell them to get me through to Smart at the Streatham Exchange."

"Very good, sir;" and the man took his departure.

A minute later the telephone bell rang.

Malcolm Sage took up the receiver. "That you, Smart?" he enquired, "re Z.18, in future transcribe figures in words exactly as spoken, thus double-one-three, one-hundred-and-thirteen, or one-one-three, as the case may be." He jammed the receiver back again on to the rest, and proceeded to gaze fixedly at the finger-nails of his left hand.

A quarter of an hour later Special Service Officer Thompson entered with a long list of figures, which he handed to Malcolm Sage.

"You've hit it, Thompson," said Sage, glancing swiftly down the list.

"Have I, sir?" said Thompson, not quite sure what it was he was supposed to have hit.

"They are — —"

At that moment the telephone bell rang. Malcolm Sage put the receiver to his ear.

"Yes, Malcolm Sage, speaking," he said. There was a pause. "Yes." Another pause. "Good, continue to record in that manner;" and once more he replaced the receiver.

"Vanity, Thompson, is at the root of all error."

"Yes, sir, said Thompson dutifully.

"Those figures," continued Sage, "are times, not numbers."

With a quick indrawing of breath, which with Thompson always indicated excitement, he reached across for the list, his eyes glinting.

"That was Smart on the telephone, another call just come through, three-twenty Oxford Street, not three-two-o, but three-twenty. Make a note of it."

Thompson produced a note-book and hastily scribbled a memorandum.

"At three-twenty this afternoon you will probably find Mr. Montagu Naylor meeting somebody in Oxford Street. Have both followed. If by chance they don't turn up, have someone there at three-twenty every afternoon and morning for a week; it may be the second, third, fourth, or fifth day after the call for all we know, morning or evening."

"It's the old story, Thompson," said Sage, who never lost a chance of pointing the moral, "over confidence. Here's a fellow who has worked out a really original means of communication. Instead of running it for a few months and then dropping it, he carries on until someone tumbles to his game."

"Yes, sir," said Thompson respectfully. It was an understood thing at Department Z. that these little homilies should be listened to with deference.

"It's like a dog hiding a bone in a hat-box," continued Sage. "He's so pleased with himself that he imagines no one else can attain to such mental brilliancy. He makes no allowance for the chapter of accidents."

"That is so, sir."

"We mustn't get like that in Department Z., Thompson."

Thompson shook his head. Time after time Sage had impressed upon the staff of Department Z. that mentally they must be elastic. "It's only a fool who is blinded by his own vapour," he had said. He had pointed out the folly of endeavouring to fit a fact by an hypothesis.

"That's all," and Malcolm Sage became absorbed in the paper before him. As he closed the door behind him Thompson winked gravely at a print upon the wall of the corridor opposite. He was wondering how it was possible for one man to watch the whole of Oxford Street for a week.

CHAPTER IV.
GINGERING-UP THE ADMIRALTY

"Boss in?"

Mr. Blair started violently; he had not heard John Dene enter his room.

"Er—yes, Mr. Dene," he replied, "I'll tell him." He half rose; but before he could complete the movement John Dene had opened the door communicating with Sir Lyster's private room.

Mr. Blair sank back in his chair. He was a man who assimilated innovation with difficulty. All his life he had been cradled in the lap of "as it was in the beginning." He was a vade-mecum on procedure and the courtesies of life, which made him extremely valuable to Sir Lyster. He was a gentle zephyr, whereas John Dene was something between a sudden draught and a cyclone.

Mr. Blair fixed his rather prominent blue eyes on the door that had closed behind John Dene. He disliked colonials. They always said what they meant, and went directly for what they wanted, all of which was in opposition to his standard of good-breeding.

As he continued to gaze at the door, it suddenly opened and John Dene's head appeared.

"Say," he cried, "if that yellow-headed girl comes, send her right in," and the door closed with a bang.

Inwardly Mr. Blair gasped; it was not customary for yellow-haired girls to be sent in to see the First Lord.

"The difference between this country and Can'da," remarked John Dene, as he planted upon Sir Lyster's table a large, shapeless-looking parcel, from which he proceeded to remove the wrapping, "is that here every one wants to know who your father was; but in Can'da they ask what can you do. I got that pound of tea," he added inconsequently.

"The pound of tea!" repeated Sir Lyster uncomprehendingly, as he watched John Dene endeavouring to extract a packet from his pocket with one hand, and undo the string of the parcel with the other.

"Yes, for that yellow-headed girl. I ran into her in the corridor and smashed her teapot yesterday. I promised I'd get her some more tea. Here it is;" and John Dene laid the package on the First Lord's table. "If she comes after I'm gone, you might give it to her. I told her to run in here and fetch it. This is the pot," he added, still struggling with the wrappings.

Presently he disinterred from a mass of paper wound round it in every conceivable way, a large white, pink and gold teapot.

Sir Lyster gazed from the teapot, terrifying in the crudeness of its shape and design, to John Dene and back again to the teapot.

"Like it?" asked John Dene, as he looked admiringly at his purchase. "Ought to cheer those girls up some."

Sir Lyster continued to gaze at the teapot as if fascinated.

"I told her to run in here and fetch it," continued John Dene, indicating the packet of tea. "She doesn't know about the pot," he added with self-satisfaction.

"In here," repeated Sir Lyster, unwilling to believe his ears.

"Sure," replied John Dene, his eyes still fixed admiringly upon the teapot, "at eleven o'clock. It's that now," he added, looking at his watch.

As he did so Mr. Blair entered and closed the door behind him. He was obviously embarrassed.

"A young person——" he began.

"Send her right in," cried John Dene.

Mr. Blair glanced uncertainly from Sir Lyster to John Dene, then back again to his chief. Seeing no contradiction in his eye, he turned and held open the door to admit Dorothy West.

"Ah! here you are," cried John Dene, rising and indicating that the girl should occupy his chair. "There's your pound of tea," pointing to the package lying before Sir Lyster, "and there's a new teapot for you," he added, indicating that object, which seemed to flaunt its pink and white and gold as if determined to brazen things out.

The girl looked at the teapot, at Sir Lyster and on to John Dene, and back to the teapot. Then she laughed. She had pretty teeth, John Dene decided.

"It's very kind of you," she said, "but there wasn't a pound of tea in the teapot you broke yesterday, and—and——"

"Never mind," said John Dene, "you can keep the rest. Now see here, I want someone to take down my letters. You're a stenographer?" he asked.

The girl nodded her head.

"Speeds?" enquired John Dene.

"A hundred and twenty——" was the response.

"Typing?"

"Sixty-five words——"

"You'll do," said John Dene with decision. "In future you'll do my work only. Nine o'clock, every morning."

The girl looked enquiringly at Sir Lyster, who coughed slightly.

"We will take up your references, Miss—er——"

"Oh! cut it out," said John Dene impatiently, "I don't want references."

"But," replied Sir Lyster, "this is work of a confidential nature.".

"See here," cried John Dene. "I started life selling newspapers in T'ronto. I never had a reference, I never gave a reference and I never asked a reference, and the man who can get ahead of John Dene had better stay up all night for fear of missing the buzzer in the morning. That girl's straight, else she wouldn't be asked to do my letters," he added. "Now, don't you wait," he said to Dorothy, seeing she was embarrassed at his remark; "nine o'clock to-morrow morning."

"I think it will be necessary to take up references," began Sir Lyster as John Dene closed the door on Dorothy.

John Dene span round on his heel. "I run my business on Canadian lines, not on British," he cried. "If you're always going to be around telling me what to do, then I'll see this country to hell before they get my *Destroyer*. The man who deals with John Dene does so on his terms," and with that he left the room, closing the door with a bang behind him.

For a moment he stood gazing down at Mr. Blair. "Can you tell me," he asked slowly, "why the British Empire has not gone to blazes long ago?"

Mr. Blair gazed at him, mild surprise in his prominent eyes.

"I am afraid I don't—I cannot——" he began.

"Neither can I," said John Dene. "You're all just about as cute as dead weasels."

John Dene walked along the corridor and down the staircase in high dudgeon.

"Ha! Mr. Dene, what's happened?" enquired Sir Bridgman, who was mounting the stairs as John Dene descended.

"I've been wondering how it is the British Empire has hung together as long as it has," was the response.

"What have we been doing now?" enquired Sir Bridgman.

"It's my belief," remarked John Dene, "that in this country you wouldn't engage a janitor without his great-grandmother's birth-certificate."

"I'm afraid we are rather a prejudiced nation," said Sir Bridgman genially.

"I don't care a cousin Mary what you are," responded John Dene, "so long as you don't come up against me. I'm out to win this war; it doesn't matter to me a red cent who's got the most grandmothers, and the sooner you tell the First Lord and that prize seal of his, the better we shall get on;" and John Dene abruptly continued on his way.

Sir Bridgman smiled as he slowly ascended the stairs.

"I suppose," he murmured, "we are in the process of being gingered-up."

The rest of the day John Dene devoted to sight-seeing and wandering about the streets, keenly interested in and critical of all he saw.

The next morning he was at the Admiralty a few minutes to nine, and was conducted by an attendant to the room that had been assigned to him. He gave a swift glance round and, apparently satisfied that it would suit his purpose, seated himself at the large pedestal table and took out his watch. As he did so, he noticed an envelope addressed to him lying on the table. Picking it up he tore off the end, extracted and read the note. Just as he had finished there came a tap at the door.

"Come," he called out.

The door opened and Dorothy West entered, looking very pretty and business-like with a note-book and pencil in her hand.

"Good morning," she said.

"Mornin', Miss West," he replied, gazing at her apparently without seeing her. He was obviously thinking of something else.

She seated herself beside his table and looked up, awaiting his signal to begin the day's work.

"There are some things in this country that get my goat," he remarked.

John Dene threw down the letter he was reading, twirled the cigar between his lips and snorted his impatience, as he jumped from his chair and proceeded to stride up and down the room.

"There are quite a lot that get mine," she remarked demurely, as she glanced up from her note-book.

"A lot that get yours," he repeated, coming to a standstill and looking down at her.

"Things that get my goat." There was the slightest possible pause between the "my" and the "goat."

Then John Dene smiled. In Toronto it was said that when John Dene smiled securities could always be trusted to mount at least a point.

"Well, listen to this." He picked up the letter again and read:

"DEAR MR. DENE, —

"Sir Lyster desires me to write and express it as his most urgent wish that you will pay special regard to your personal safety. He fears that you may be inclined to treat the matter too lightly, hence this letter.

"Yours truly,
"REGINALD BLAIR."

"If that chap hadn't such a dandy set of grandmothers and first cousins, he'd be picking up cigarette-stubs instead of wasting his time telling me what I knew a year ago."

"But he's only carrying out Sir Lyster's instructions," suggested Dorothy.

"There's something in that," he admitted grudgingly, "but if they're going to be always running around warning me of danger I know all about——" He broke off. "Why," he continued a moment later, "I was shot at on the steamer, nearly hustled into the docks at Liverpool, set on by toughs in Manchester and followed around as if I was a bell-mule. I tell you it gets my goat. This country wants gingering-up." John Dene continued his pacing of the room.

"Couldn't you wear a red beard and blue glasses and——"

"What's that?" John Dene span round and fixed his eyes on the girl.

"I mean disguise yourself," said Dorothy, dropping her eyes beneath his gaze.

"Why?" The interrogation was rapped out in such a tone as to cause the girl to shrink back slightly.

"They wouldn't know and then it wouldn't——" she hesitated.

"Wouldn't what?" he demanded.

"Get your goat," said Dorothy after a moment's hesitation.

He continued to gaze intently at Dorothy, who was absorbed in a blank page of her note-book.

"Here, take this down;" and he proceeded to dictate.

"MY DEAR MR. BLAIR,—

"I am in receipt of yours of to-day's date. Will you tell Sir Lyster that I have bought a machine-gun, a blue beard, false eyebrows, and Miss West and I are going to do bayonet drill every morning with a pillow.

"With kind regards,
"Yours sincerely."

For a few moments Dorothy sat regarding her book with knitted brows. "I don't think I should send that, if I were you, Mr. Dene," she said at length.

"Why not?" he demanded, unaccustomed to having his orders questioned.

"It sounds rather flippant, doesn't it?"

John Dene smiled grimly, and as he made no further comment, Dorothy struck out the letter from her note-book.

All through the morning John Dene threw off letters. The way in which he did his dictating reminded Dorothy of a retriever shaking the water from its coat after a swim. He hurled short, sharp sentences at her, as if anxious to be rid of them. Sometimes he would sit hunched up at his table, at others he would spring up and proceed feverishly to pace about the room.

As she filled page after page of her note-book, Dorothy wondered when she would have an opportunity of transcribing her notes. Hour after hour John Dene dictated, in short bursts, interspersed with varying pauses, during which he seemed to be deep in thought. Once Sir Bridgman looked in, and Dorothy had a space in which to breathe; but with the departure of the First Sea Lord the torrent jerked forth afresh.

At two o'clock Dorothy felt that she must either scream or faint. Her right hand seemed as if it would drop off. At last she suggested that even Admiralty typists required lunch. In a flash John Dene seemed to change into a human being, solicitous and self-reproachful.

"Too bad," he said, as he pulled out his watch. "Why, it's a quarter after two. You must be all used up. I'm sorry."

"And aren't you hungry as well, Mr. Dene?" she asked, as she closed her note-book and rose.

"Hungry!" he repeated as if she had asked him a surprising question. "I've no use for food when I'm hustling. Where do you go for lunch?"

"I go to a tea-shop," said Dorothy after a moment's hesitation.

"And what do you eat?" demanded John Dene, with the air of a cross-examining counsel.

"Oh, all sorts of things," she laughed; "buns and eggs and — and — —"

"That's no good," was the uncompromising rejoinder.

"They're really quite nourishing," she said with a smile. At the Admiralty it was not customary for the chiefs to enquire what the typists ate.

"You'd better come with me and have a good meal," he said bluntly, reaching for his hat.

Dorothy flushed. The implication was too obvious to be overlooked. Drawing herself up slightly, and with her head a little thrown back, she declined.

"I'm afraid I have an engagement," she said coldly.

John Dene looked up, puzzled to account for her sudden hauteur. He watched her leave the room, and then, throwing down his hat, reseated himself at his table and once more became absorbed in his work.

Dorothy went to the Admiralty staff-restaurant and spent a week's lunch allowance upon her meal. It seemed to help her to regain her self-respect. When she returned to John Dene's room some forty minutes later, determined to get some of her notes typed before he returned, she found him still sitting at his table. As she entered he took out his watch, looked at it and then up at her. Dorothy crimsoned as if discovered in some illicit act. She was angry with herself for her weakness and with John Dene—why, she could not have said.

"You've been hustling some," he remarked, as he returned the watch to his pocket.

"We've both been quick," said Dorothy, curious to know if John Dene had been to lunch.

"Oh, I stayed right here," he said, still gazing up at her.

Dorothy felt rebuked. He had evidently felt snubbed, she told herself, and it was her fault that he had remained at work.

"See here," said John Dene, "I can't breathe in this place. It's all gold braid and brass buttons. I'm going to rent my own offices, and have lunch sent in and we'll get some work done. You can get a rest or a walk about three. I don't like breaking off in the midst of things," he added, a little lamely, Dorothy thought.

"Very well, Mr. Dene," she said, as she resumed her seat.

"Do you mind? Say right out if you'd hate it." There was a suspicion of anxiety in his tone.

"I'm here to do whatever you wish," she said with dignity.

With a sudden movement John Dene sprang up and proceeded to pace up and down the room.

From time to time he glanced at Dorothy, who sat pencil and note-book ready for the flood of staccatoed sentences that usually accompanied these pacings to and fro. At length he came to a standstill in the middle of the room, planted his feet wide apart as if to steady the resolution to which he had apparently come.

"Say, what's all this worth to you?" he blurted out.

Dorothy looked up in surprise, not grasping his meaning.

"Worth to me?" she queried, her head on one side, the tip of her pencil resting on her lower lip.

"Yes; what do they pay you?"

"Oh! I see. Thirty-five shillings a week and, if I become a permanent, a pension when I'm too old to enjoy it," she laughed. "That is if the Hun hasn't taken us over by then."

"That'll be about nine dollars a week," mumbled John Dene, twisting his cigar round between his lips. "Well, you're worth twenty dollars a week to me, so I'll make up the rest."

"I'm quite satisfied, thank you," she said, drawing herself up slightly.

"Well, I'm not," he blurted out. "You're going to work well for me, and you're going to be well paid."

"I'm afraid I cannot accept it," she said firmly, "although it's very kind of you," she added with a smile.

He regarded her in surprise. It was something new to him to find anyone refusing an increase in salary. His cigar twirled round with remarkable rapidity.

"I suppose I'm getting his goat," thought Dorothy, as she watched him from beneath lowered lashes.

"Why won't you take it?" he demanded.

"I'm afraid I cannot accept presents," she said with what she thought a disarming smile.

"Oh, shucks!" John Dene was annoyed.

"If the Admiralty thought I was worth more than thirty-five shillings a week, they would pay me more."

"Well, I'm not going to have anyone around that doesn't get a living wage," he announced explosively.

"Does that mean that I had better go?" she inquired calmly.

"No, it doesn't. You just stay right here till I get back," was the reply, and he opened the door and disappeared, leaving Dorothy with the conviction that someone was to suffer because, in John Dene's opinion, she was inadequately paid.

As she waited for John Dene's return, she could not keep her thoughts from what an extra forty-five shillings a week would mean to her. She could increase the number and quality of the little "surprises" she took home with her to the mother in whose life she bulked so largely. Peaches could be bought without the damning prefix "tinned"; salmon without the discouraging modification "Canadian"; eggs that had not long since forgotten what hen had laid them and when. She could take her more often to a theatre, or for a run in a taxi when she was tired. In short, a hundred and seventeen pounds a year would buy quite a lot of rose-leaves with which to colour her mother's life.

Whilst Dorothy was building castles in Spain upon a foundation of eleven dollars a week, John Dene walked briskly along the corridor leading to Sir Lyster's room. Mr. Blair was seated at his desk reading with calm deliberation and self-evident satisfaction a letter he had just written for Sir Lyster to one of his constituents. He had devoted much time and thought to the composition, as it was for publication, and he was determined that no one should find in it flaw or ambiguity. The morning had been one of flawless serenity, and he was looking forward to a pleasant lunch with some friends at the Berkeley.

"Here, what the hell do you mean by giving that girl only nine dollars a week?"

Suddenly the idyllic peaceful ness of his mood was shattered into a thousand fragments. John Dene had burst into the room with the force of a cyclone, and stood before him like an accusing fury.

"Nine dollars a week! What girl?" he stuttered, looking up weakly into John Dene's angry eyes. "I—I——"

"Miss West," was the retort. "She's getting nine dollars a week, less than I pay an office boy in T'ronto."

"But I—it's nothing to do with me," began Mr. Blair miserably. He had become mortally afraid of John Dene, and prayed for the time to come when the Hun submarine menace would be ended, and John

Dene could return to Toronto, where no doubt he was understood and appreciated.

"Well, it ought to be," snapped John Dene, just as Sir Bridgman North came out of Sir Lyster's room.

"Good morning, Mr. Dene," he cried genially. "What are you doing to poor Blair?"

John Dene explained his grievance. "I'd pay the difference myself, just to make you all feel a bit small, only she won't take it from me."

"Well, I think I can promise that the matter shall be put right, and we'll make Blair take her out to lunch by way of apology, shall we?" he laughed.

"I'd like to see him ask her," said John Dene grimly. "That girl's a high-stepper, sir. Nine dollars a week!" he grumbled as he left the room to the manifest relief of Mr. Blair.

"You're being gingered-up, Blair," said Sir Bridgman; "in fact, we're all being gingered-up. It's a bit surprising at first; but it's a great game played slow. You'll get to like it in time, and it's all for the good of the British Empire."

Mr. Blair smiled weakly as Sir Bridgman left the room; but in his heart he wished it were possible to have a sentinel outside his door, with strict injunctions to bayonet John Dene without hesitation should he seek admittance.

"I've fixed it," announced John Dene, as he burst in upon Dorothy's day dream. "You'll get twenty dollars in future."

She looked up quickly. "You're very kind, Mr. Dene," she said, "but is it—is it——?" she hesitated.

"It's a square deal. I told them you wouldn't take it from me, and that I wasn't going to have my secretary paid less than an office boy in T'ronto. I gingered 'em up some. Nine dollars a week for you!"

The tone in which the last sentence was uttered brought a slight flush to Dorothy's cheeks.

"Now you can get on," he announced, picking up his hat. "I'm going to find offices;" and he went out like a gust of wind.

Dorothy typed steadily on. Of one thing she had become convinced, that the position of secretary to John Dene of Toronto was not going to prove a rest-billet.

At a little after four Marjorie Rogers knocked at the door and, recognising Dorothy's "Come in," entered stealthily as if expecting someone to jump out at her.

"Where's the bear, Wessie?" she enquired, keeping a weather eye on the door in case John Dene should return.

"Gone out to buy bear-biscuits," laughed Dorothy, leaning back in her chair to get the kink out of her spine.

"Do you think he'll marry you?" enquired the little brunette romantically, as she perched herself upon John Dene's table and swung a pretty leg. "They don't usually, you know."

"He'll probably kill you if he catches you," said Dorothy.

"Oh, if he comes I'm here to ask if you would like some tea," was the airy reply.

"You angel!" cried Dorothy. "I should love it."

"Has he tried to kiss you yet?" demanded the girl, looking at Dorothy searchingly.

"Don't be ridiculous," cried Dorothy, conscious that she was flushing.

"I see he has," she said, regarding Dorothy judicially and nodding her head wisely.

Dorothy re-started typing. It was absurd, she decided, to endeavour to argue with this worldly child of Whitehall.

"They're all the same," continued Marjorie, lifting her skirt slightly and gazing with obvious approval at the symmetry of her leg. "You didn't let him, I hope," continued the girl. "You see, it makes it bad for others." Then a moment later she added, "It should be chocs. before kisses, and they've got to learn the ropes."

"And you, you little imp, have got to learn morals." Dorothy laughed in spite of herself at the quaint air of wisdom with which this girl of eighteen settled the ethics of Whitehall.

"What's the use of morals?" cried the girl. "I mean morals that get in the way of your having a good time. Of course I wouldn't— —" She paused.

"Never mind what you wouldn't do, Brynhilda the Bold," said Dorothy, "but concentrate on the woulds, and bring me the tea you promised."

The girl slipped off the table and darted across the room, returning a few minutes later with a cup of tea and a few biscuits.

"I can't stop," she panted. "Old Goggles has been giving me the bird;" and with that she was gone.

It was a quarter to seven before John Dene returned. Without a word he threw his hat on the bookcase and seated himself at his table. For the next quarter of an hour he was absorbed in reading the lists and letters Dorothy had typed. At seven o'clock Dorothy placed the last list on the table before him.

"Is there anything more, Mr. Dene?" she enquired. She was conscious of feeling inexpressibly weary.

"Yes," said John Dene, without looking up. "You're coming out to have some dinner."

"I'm afraid I can't, thank you," she said. "My mother is waiting."

"Oh shucks!" he cried, looking up quickly.

"But it isn't!" she said wearily.

"Isn't what?" demanded John Dene.

"Shucks!" she said; then, seeing the absurdity of the thing, she laughed.

"We'll send your mother an express message or a wire. You look dead beat." He smiled and Dorothy capitulated. It would be nice, she told herself, not to have to go all the way to Chiswick before having anything to eat.

"But where are you taking me, Mr. Dene?" enquired Dorothy, as they turned from Waterloo Place into Pall Mall.

"To the Ritzton."

"But I'm—I'm——" she stopped dead.

"What's wrong?" he demanded, looking at her in surprise.

"I—I can't go there," she stammered. "I'm not dressed for——" She broke off lamely.

"That'll be all right," he said. "It's my hotel."

"It may be your hotel," said Dorothy, resuming the walk, "but I don't care to go there in a blouse and a skirt to be stared at."

"Who'll stare at you?"

"Not at me, at my clothes," she corrected.

"Then we'll go to the grill-room," he replied with inspiration.

"That might be——" She hesitated.

"You're not going home until you have something to eat," he announced with determination. "You look all used up," he added.

Dorothy submitted to the inevitable, conscious of a feeling of content at having someone to decide things for her. Suddenly she remembered Marjorie Rogers' remarks. What was she doing? If any of the girls saw her they would—— She had done the usual thing, sent a telegram to her mother to say she should be late, and was dining out with her chief on the first day—— Oh! it was horrible.

"Would you—would you?"—she turned to John Dene appealingly,—"would you mind if I went home," she faltered. "I'm not feeling—very well." She gulped out the last words conscious of the lie.

"Why sure," he said solicitously. "I'm sorry."

To her infinite relief he hailed a taxi.

"I'll come along and see you safe," he announced in a matter-of-fact tone.

"Oh, please no," she cried, "I'd much sooner——" She broke off distressed.

Without a word he handed her into the taxi.

"Where am I to tell him?" he enquired.

"Douglas Mansions, Chiswick, please," gasped Dorothy, and she sank back in the taxi with a feeling that she had behaved very ridiculously.

CHAPTER V.
JOHN DENE LEAVES WHITEHALL

I

"Come," shouted John Dene irritably.

The door opened and Mr. Blair entered. John Dene swung round from his table and glared at him angrily.

"I tried to telephone," began Mr. Blair.

"Well, you can't," snapped John Dene, "receiver's off. Your boys have been playing dido all morning on my 'phone."

"I'm sorry if——"

"That don't help any. Why don't you stop 'em? Seem to think I'm a sort of enquiry bureau."

Dorothy bent low over her notes to hide the smile she could not restrain at the sight of the obvious wretchedness of Mr. Blair.

"Sir Lyster would like you to step round——"

"Well, I won't; tell him that," was the irascible reply.

"He wants you to meet Sir Harold Winn, the chief naval constructor," explained Mr. Blair.

"Tell him to go to blazes and take his constructions with him. Now vamoose."

Mr. Blair hesitated, glanced at John Dene, seemed about to speak, then evidently thinking better of it withdrew, closing the door noiselessly behind him.

As John Dene swung round once more to his table, he caught Dorothy's eye. She smiled.

With a little grumble in his throat John Dene became absorbed in his papers. Dorothy decided that he was a little ashamed of his outburst.

All the day he had shown marked irritability under the constant interruptions to which he had been subjected.

They worked on steadily for a quarter of an hour. Presently there was a gentle tap at the door. With one bound John Dene was out of his chair and across the room. A second later he threw open the door, ready to annihilate whoever might be there, from the First Lord downwards.

"Oo—er!"

Marjorie Rogers stood there, her pretty eyes dilated with fear as John Dene glared at her. His set look relaxed at the sight of the girl.

"Is—is—Miss West here?" she enquired timidly.

"Sure, come right in," he said.

Dorothy was surprised at the change produced by the appearance of Marjorie Rogers.

The girl came a few steps into the room, then seeing Dorothy tripped over to her and, turning to John Dene, said, still a little nervously:

"I—I came to ask Miss West if she would like some tea." She smiled up at John Dene, a picture of guileless innocence.

"Sorry if I scared you," he said awkwardly.

"Oh, you didn't frighten me," she said, regaining confidence at the sight of John Dene's embarrassment.

"Perhaps Mr. Dene would like a cup of tea too, Rojjie," suggested Dorothy.

"Oh, would you?" cried the girl eagerly.

"Why, sure," said John Dene and he smiled, for the first time that day, Dorothy mentally noted.

In a flash Marjorie disappeared.

"I'm—I'm sorry," said John Dene to Dorothy. "I didn't know she was a friend of yours."

"She's in the room I used to be in, and—she's very sweet and brings me tea."

He nodded comprehendingly. "They do a lot of that here, don't they?"

"A lot of what?" asked Dorothy.

"Drinking tea."

"We only have it in the afternoon, and — —"

At that moment Marjorie entered with a small tray containing three cups of tea and a plate of biscuits. These she placed on John Dene's table.

Dorothy gasped at the sight of the three cups, wondering what John Dene would think.

"I brought mine in to have with you," said Marjorie with perfect self-possession, as she handed Dorothy her cup, then turning to John Dene she smiled. He nodded, as if she had done a most ordinary thing.

Perching herself upon the corner of John Dene's table, Marjorie chatted brightly, having apparently quite overcome her fears.

"You know, Mr. Dene," she said, "we're all dreadfully intrigued about you."

John Dene looked at her with a puzzled expression.

"All the other girls are terribly afraid of you," she continued. "I'm not."

"Of me?" He looked at her in surprise, as if he regarded himself as the last person in the world to inspire fear.

"They say you glare at them." She smiled a wicked little smile that she called "the rouser." As John Dene did not reply Marjorie continued: "They call you 'the bear.'"

"Rojjie!" gasped Dorothy in horror.

"The bear?" repeated John Dene. "Why?"

"Oh, but I am going to tell them you're not," said Marjorie, nibbling at a biscuit and looking across at John Dene appraisingly. "I think you're really rather nice."

John Dene glanced across at Dorothy, as if unable quite to classify the girl before him.

"Of course they don't know that you can smile like that," added Marjorie.

John Dene was about to make some remark when there came another knock.

"Come," he cried, and a moment later the door opened and Sir Lyster entered, followed by a tall, sedate-looking man with a bulging forehead and ragged moustache.

For a moment the two regarded the scene, Sir Lyster having recourse to his monocle.

Marjorie slipped down from the table, all her self-possession deserting her at the sight of Sir Lyster's disapproving gaze. Dorothy bent over her notes, conscious of her burning cheeks, whilst John Dene rose with entire unconcern.

"I'm afraid we've interrupted you, Mr. Dene," said Sir Lyster.

"It's the one thing they do well in this shack," was John Dene's uncompromising retort.

Sir Lyster gazed a little anxiously at his companion.

Taking advantage of the diversion, Marjorie slipped out and Dorothy, deciding that she would not be wanted for at least a few minutes, followed her.

"I want to introduce you to Sir Harold Winn," said Sir Lyster.

"Pleased to meet you," said John Dene, shaking Sir Harold vigorously by the hand. "Take a seat."

John Dene and the Chief Naval Constructor were soon deep in the intricacies of submarine-construction. When at length Sir Harold rose to go, there was something like cordiality in John Dene's voice, as he bade him good-bye. Sir Harold had been able to meet him on common ground, and show an intelligent and comprehensive interest in his work.

Immediately they had gone, Dorothy, who had been waiting in the corridor, slipped back to her chair, first removing the tea tray from John Dene's table. Soon she was busily taking down notes.

While she was thus occupied, Sir Lyster was narrating to Sir Bridgman North the latest John Dene outrage, first his open flouting of the Chief Naval Constructor by refusing to see him, secondly the interrupted tea, and the girl perched upon John Dene's table.

Sir Bridgman laughed loudly, as much at the expression on Sir Lyster's face as at the occurrence itself.

"Such incidents," said Sir Lyster, "are, I think, very undesirable."

"It looks as if John Dene were a dark horse," suggested Sir Bridgman. "Was the other girl pretty?"

"I really didn't notice," said Sir Lyster stiffly. "I thought perhaps you might"—he hesitated for a fraction of a second—"just drop him a hint," he added.

"And be gingered-up as high as our own aerials," laughed Sir Bridgman. "No, my dear Grayne," he added, "I find 'gingering-up' intensely interesting in its application to others. Get Blair to do it."

"But I'm afraid it may create a scandal," said Sir Lyster.

"Oh! another little scandal won't do us any harm," laughed Sir Bridgman. "Now I must be off. By the way," he said, as he reached the door, "what time did this little tea-fight take place?"

"It was about four o'clock when Winn and I——"

"Right," said Sir Bridgman, "I'll drop in about that time to-morrow and see what's doing," and the door closed behind him.

A moment later he put his head round the door. "One of these days you'll be finding Blair with a girl on each knee," he laughed, and with that he was gone.

John Dene's reason for wishing to have offices somewhere away from the Admiralty had been twofold. For one thing he did not desire those he knew were closely watching should see him in close association with Whitehall; for another he felt that he could breathe more freely away from gold braid and those long dreary corridors, which seemed so out of keeping with the headquarters of a Navy at war. He now determined to get out at once. The constant interruptions to which he found himself subjected, rendered concentration impossible. He therefore informed Dorothy that at nine o'clock next morning they would start work in the new offices he had taken in Waterloo Place. They consisted of two rooms, one leading off the other. The larger room John Dene decided to use himself, the smaller he handed over to Dorothy.

With a celerity that had rather surprised John Dene the telephone had been connected and a private wire run through to the Admiralty.

"The thing about a Britisher," he remarked to Dorothy, "is that he can hustle, but won't."

She allowed the remark to pass unchallenged.

"Now things will begin to hum," he said, as he settled himself down to his table. Throwing aside his coat, he set to work. There was little over three weeks in which to get everything organised and planned. Long lists of stores for the *Destroyer* had to be prepared, the details of the structural alterations to the *Toronto*, the name given to the mother-ship that was to act as tender to the *Destroyer*, instructions to the Canadian crew that was coming over, and a thousand and one other things that kept them busily occupied. He arranged to have luncheon sent in from the Ritzton. After the first day the ordering of these meals was delegated to Dorothy. John Dene's ideas on the subject of food proved original, resulting in the ordering of about five times as much as necessary.

Dorothy came to look forward to these dainty meals, which she could order with unstinted hand, and she liked the tête-à-tête half-hours during their consumption. Then John Dene would unbend and tell her of Canada, about his life there and in America, how he had planned and built the *Destroyer*. He seemed to take it for granted that she could be trusted to keep her own counsel.

The night after John Dene's entry into his new offices the place was burgled. In the morning when he arrived he found papers tossed about in reckless disorder. The fourth set of plans of German U-boats had disappeared.

With grim humour he drew a fifth set from his pocket, and placed it in the safe, which he did not keep locked, as it contained nothing of importance. John Dene's method was to burn every paper or duplicate that was no longer required, and to have sent over to the Admiralty each day before five o'clock such documents as were of importance.

For the first time in her life Dorothy felt she was doing something of national importance. John Dene trusted her, and took her patriotism as a matter of course. Sometimes he would enquire if she were tired, and on hearing that she was not he would nod his approval.

"You're some worker," he once remarked casually, whereat Dorothy had flushed with pleasure. Later she remembered that this was the first word of praise she had heard him bestow on anything or anybody British.

At first a buttons had called from the Ritzton each morning and afternoon for orders; but after the second day he had been superseded by a waiter. One morning, after the order had been given, John Dene enquired of Dorothy if she had ever tasted lobster à l'Americaine.

"Typists don't eat lobster à l'Americaine in England, Mr. Dene," she had replied. "It's too expensive."

Whereupon he had told her to ring up the Ritzton and order lobster à l'Americaine for lunch in place of the order already given. Ten minutes later a ring came through from the hotel to the effect that there must be some mistake, as there was no lunch on order for Mr. John Dene. Dorothy protested that they had been supplied with lunch each day for the last four days. The management deprecatingly suggested that there had been a mistake, as after the first two days the order had been cancelled. Dorothy repeated the information to John Dene, who then took the receiver.

"If you didn't supply lunch yesterday, who the blazes did?" he demanded, and a suave voice answered that it did not know who it was that had that honour, but certainly it was not the Ritzton.

John Dene banged back the receiver impatiently. "We'll wait and see what happens at twelve o'clock," he exclaimed, as he turned once more to the papers on his table. "Somebody's feeding us," he muttered.

"Perhaps it's the ravens," murmured Dorothy to herself.

At twelve o'clock a waiter entered with a tray. At the sound of his knock, John Dene revolved round in his chair.

"Here, where do you come from?" he demanded, glaring as if he suspected the man of being of German parentage.

The man started violently and nearly dropped the tray.

"I obey orders," he stammered.

"Yes; but whose orders?"

For a moment the man hesitated.

"Do you come from the Ritzton?" demanded John Dene aggressively.

"I obey orders," repeated the man.

John Dene looked from the tray to Dorothy, and then to the man; but said nothing, contenting himself with waving the man out with an impatient motion of his hand.

After the meal he picked up his hat, lighted a cigar and told Dorothy he would be back in a quarter of an hour. Five minutes later he burst in upon Mr. Blair.

"Here, what the hell's all this about my meals?" John Dene seemed to take a delight in descending upon Sir Lyster's secretary.

Mr. Blair turned towards him with that expression he seemed to keep expressly for John Dene. "Your meals," he stammered.

"Yes," replied John Dene, blowing volumes of acrid smoke towards the sensitive nostrils of Mr. Blair. "Why was my order to the Ritzton cancelled? That sort of thing rattles me."

"I'm afraid that I know nothing of this," said Mr. Blair, "but I will enquire."

"Well, I'd like somebody to put me wise as to why he interferes with my affairs," and John Dene stamped out of the room and back to Waterloo Place.

II

"Shucks!" cried John Dene irritably. "You make me tired."

"I doubt if you appreciate the seriousness of the situation," was Colonel Walton's quiet retort.

"I appreciate the seriousness of a situation that turns my 'phone into a sort of elevator-bell, and makes my office like a free-drink saloon at an election."

Colonel Walton smiled indulgently, Dorothy kept her eyes upon her note-book.

"You get your notion about spies from ten cent thrillers," continued John Dene scornfully. "Don't you worry about me. If there's a hungry dog I believe in feeding it," he added enigmatically. "I might as well be a lost baggage office. Every mutt that has ten minutes to waste seems to blow in on me. You're the tenth this a.m."

"At that rate you will soon have exhausted all the Government Departments," said Colonel Walton with a smile. "I doubt if any will venture a second visit," he added quietly.

John Dene glanced across at him quickly. "Say, I didn't mean to make you mad," he said in a conciliatory tone; "but all this rattles me. I can't get along with things while they're playing rags on my 'phone. It makes me madder'n a wet hen."

"I quite understand, Mr. Dene," said Colonel Walton, with that imperturbable good-humour that was the envy of his friends. "You are rather valuable to us, you see, and if we err on the side of over-caution— —" He paused.

"Sure," cried John Dene, thawing under the influence of Colonel Walton's personality, then after a pause he added. "See here, your boys seem to have a notion that I'm particular green goods. You just let one of 'em try and corral me one of these nights, and when you've explained things to the widow, you can just blow in here and tell me how she took it."

"It's the insidious rather than the overt act," began Colonel Walton.

"The what?" John Dene looked at him with a puzzled expression.

Instead of replying Colonel Walton drew from his right-hand pocket something in a paper bag, such as is used by confectioners. This he placed upon the table. He then extracted from his other pocket a small package rolled in newspaper, which he laid beside the paper bag.

John Dene stared at him as if not quite sure of his sanity.

"Perhaps you will open those packets."

With his eyes still on his visitor John Dene picked up the paper bag and, turning it upside down, shook out upon the table a brown and white guinea-pig—dead. Dorothy drew back with a little cry.

"This some of your funny work?" demanded John Dene angrily.

"There's still the other parcel," said Colonel Walton, his eyes upon the small roll done up in newspaper.

Very gingerly John Dene unrolled the paper, Dorothy watching from a safe distance with wide-eyed curiosity.

"Gee!" he muttered, as a large dead grey rat lay exposed, its upper lip drawn back from his teeth, giving it a snarling appearance. He looked interrogatingly at Colonel Walton.

"There; but for the grace of God lies John Dene of Toronto," he remarked quietly, nodding in the direction of the two rodents.

"Here, what the hell— —!" began John Dene, then catching sight of Dorothy he stopped suddenly.

"Two days ago you ordered for lunch ris de veau and apple tart—among other things. The rat is the victim of the one, the guinea-pig of the other."

Dorothy gave a little cry of horror. John Dene looked across at her quickly, then back to Colonel Walton.

"You mean——" he began.

"That a certain Department has assumed the responsibility of catering for a distinguished visitor," was the quiet reply. "It is but one of the pleasant obligations of empire."

John Dene sat gazing at the dead animals as if fascinated. With distended eyes and slightly parted lips Dorothy looked from the table to Colonel Walton, and then back to the table again, as if unable to comprehend the full significance of what was taking place.

"I would suggest," said Colonel Walton, "that you never take food regularly at any one hotel or restaurant. Avoid being out late at night, particularly raid-nights."

"Raid-nights!"

"You might be knocked on the head and removed as a casualty."

John Dene nodded, Dorothy gasped.

"Never take food or drink of any sort in your room at the hotel, and don't travel on the Tube or Underground, at least never stand on the edge of the platform, and don't use taxis."

"And what about a nurse?" demanded John Dene.

"If you observe these points I scarcely think one would be necessary," was the quiet rejoinder. "It would also be advisable," continued Colonel Walton, "for Miss West to be particularly careful about making chance acquaintances."

Dorothy drew herself up stiffly.

"During the last few days," continued Colonel Walton, "a number of attempts have been made by women as well as men."

"How did you know?" she cried in surprise.

"We have sources of information," smiled Colonel Walton. "For instance, the day before yesterday, at lunch, a pleasant-spoken old lady asked you to go with her to the theatre one Saturday afternoon."

Dorothy gasped.

"You very rightly declined. A few days ago a man ran after you just as you had left the Tube train at Piccadilly Circus, saying that you had left your umbrella."

"How funny that you should know!" cried Dorothy. "Such a number of people have spoken to me lately. First it was men, and now it's always women."

"Make no acquaintances at all, Miss West," said Colonel Walton.

"I'll remember," she said, nodding her head with decision.

"Well, Mr. Dene, I fear I mustn't take up any more of your time," said Colonel Walton, rising, with that air of indolence which with him invariably meant that something important was coming. "If you will not allow us to be responsible for your own safety, we must at least provide for that of Government servants."

"What's that?"

"We should not like anything to happen to Miss West."

To Colonel Walton's "Good-day" John Dene made no response, he seemed unaware that he had left the room.

"Gee!" he muttered at length, then swinging round to Dorothy with a suddenness that caused her to start, "You had better vamoose," he cried.

"Vam——" she began. "How do I do it?"

"Quit, clear out of here." He sprang from his chair and proceeded to pace up and down the room.

"Does that mean that I'm discharged?" she enquired, smiling.

"You heard what he said. They're up to their funny work. They missed us this time and got the rat and guinea-pig. They're always at it. I don't make a fuss; but I know. There'll be a bomb in my bed one of these nights. You'd better call a halt right here."

"Shall we get on with the letters, Mr. Dene?" said Dorothy quietly. "Father was a soldier."

For a moment he looked at her with his keen penetrating eyes, then swinging round to his table caught sight of the two dead rodents.

"Here, what the blazes does he want to leave these things here for," he cried irritably and, seizing a ruler, he swept them into the waste-paper basket.

For the rest of the day Dorothy was conscious that John Dene's heart was not in his work. Several times, when happening to look up unexpectedly, she found his eyes on her, and there was in them an anxiety too obvious to be dissimulated. John Dene was clearly worried.

"It's an extraordinary thing," Sage remarked later that afternoon to Colonel Walton, "that apparently no one has ever thought of encouraging a taste for apple-tart in guinea-pigs."

CHAPTER VI.
MR. MONTAGU NAYLOR OF STREATHAM

Whilst John Dene was preparing interminable lists for the Victualling and Stores Departments of the Admiralty, Department Z. was making discreet and searching enquiries regarding Mr. Montagu Naylor of Streatham. Among other things it discovered that he was essentially English. The atrocities in Belgium and Northern France rendered him almost speechless with indignation. Wherever he went, and to whomsoever he met, he proclaimed the German an enemy to civilisation. It was his one topic of conversation, and in time his friends and acquaintance came to regard the word "Hun" as a danger signal.

Mr. Naylor had arrived at Streatham towards the end of 1909, coming from no one knew whither; but according to his own account from Norwich. He was of independent means, without encumbrances beyond a wife, a deaf servant, registered as a Swiss, and a particularly fierce-dispositioned chow, an animal that caused marked irregularity in the delivery of his milk, newspapers and letters. Sometimes the animal chose to resent the approach of all comers, and after the postman had lost a portion of his right trouser-leg, he had decided that whatever might happen to His Majesty's mails, the postman's calf was sacred. Thenceforth he never delivered letters when James was at large.

Without participating in the postman's mishap, the paper-boy and milkman had adopted his tactics. The dustman point-blank refused to touch the refuse from "The Cedars" unless it were placed on the pavement, and the gate securely closed.

Sometimes the readings of the electric and gas meters were formally noted by officials, whose uniform began and ended with their caps; sometimes they were not. Everything depended upon the geographical position of James at the moment of the inspector's call.

The baker who supplied Mr. Naylor had, as a result of a complaint from his man, made a personal call of protest; but he had succeeded only in losing his temper to Mr. Naylor and the seat of his trousers to James. Thenceforth "The Cedars" had to seek its bread elsewhere. Incidentally the master-baker obtained a new pair of trousers at Mr. Naylor's expense.

Why Mr. Naylor continued to keep James was a puzzle to all the neighbours, who, knowing him as a champion of the rights of man, votes for women, the smaller nations, and many other equally uncomfortable things, were greatly surprised that he should keep a dog that was clearly of a savage and dangerous disposition.

About Mr. Naylor himself there was nothing of the ferocity of his dog. He was suave, with a somewhat deprecating manner, a ready, almost automatic smile, in which his eyes never seemed to join, a sallow complexion, large round glasses, a big nose and ugly teeth. He had a thick voice, thick ears and a thick skin—when it so served his purpose.

His love for England was almost alien, and he was never tired of motoring from one part of the country to another, that is before the war. His car had been something unique, as in a few seconds it could be turned into a moderately comfortable sleeping apartment. Thus he was independent of hotels, or lodgings.

Mrs. Naylor was a woman of negative personality. She looked after the house, fed James and never asked questions of Mr. Naylor, thus justifying her existence.

Susan, the maid, was also negative, from her stupid round, moist face to the shapeless feet that she never seemed to be able to lift from the floor. She had acquired great dexterity in shuffling out of the way just before Mr. Naylor appeared. This she seemed to have reduced to a fine art. If Mr. Naylor were going upstairs and Susan was about to descend, by the time he was halfway up she would have disappeared as effectively as if snatched away by some spirit agency. Susan was dumb; but her sense of sound was extremely acute. It seemed as if, conscious of her inability to hold her own verbally with her employer, she had fallen back upon the one alternative, disappearance.

The Naylors were possessed of few friends, although Mr. Naylor had many acquaintances, the result of the way in which he had identified himself with local clubs and institutions. It was largely due to him that the miniature rifle-range had been started. He was one of the governors of the Cranberry Cottage Hospital. He always subscribed to the annual Territorial sports, patronised the boy scouts, openly advocated conscription, and the two-power standard for the Navy. There were times when Streatham found it almost embarrassing to be possessed of a patriot in its midst.

Never had a breath of scandal tarnished the fair name of Mr. Montagu Naylor. He was what a citizen should be and seldom is. When war broke out his activities became almost bewildering. He joined innumerable committees, helped to form the volunteers, and encouraged every one and everything that was likely to make things uncomfortable for the enemy. Later, he became a member of the local exemption tribunal, and earned fame by virtue of his clemency. It was he who was instrumental in obtaining exemption for some of James's most implacable enemies. The baker, who had lost the whole of his temper and a portion of his trousers, probably owed his life to the manner in which Mr. Naylor championed his claim that bread is mightier than the sword.

Before the war the Naylors received twice each month, once their friends and once their relatives. Never were the two allowed to meet. "Our friends we make ourselves, our relatives are given to us," Mr. Naylor had explained with ponderous humour, "I hate to mix the two." It was noticed that the relatives stayed much longer than the friends, and some commiseration was felt for the Naylors by their immediate neighbours.

There had been one curious circumstance in connection with these social functions. Whenever the friends were invited, James was always in the front garden, restrained by a chain that allowed of the guests carrying their calves into the hall with an eighteen inch margin of safety. When, however, it was the turn of the relatives to seek the hospitality of "The Cedars," James was never visible. A cynic might have construed this into indicating that from his relatives Mr. Naylor had expectations.

Within his own home Mr. Naylor was a changed man. He ruled Mrs. Naylor, Susan and James with an iron hand. They all fawned upon him, vainly inviting the smiles that when others were present seemed never to fail in the mechanical precision with which they illumined his features at appropriate moments. They gave the impression of being turned on, as if controlled by a tap or switch. Never was this smile seen once the hall door was passed. Then Mr. Naylor's jaw squared, and his whole attitude seemed to become more angular.

A knock at the door would cause him to look up quickly from whatever he was doing, just as a gamekeeper might look up at the report of a gun. By his orders Mrs. Naylor and Susan between them kept a complete list of all callers, even hawkers, if they were sufficiently courageous to risk an encounter with the redoubtable James.

Mr. Naylor was a tall man of broad build, with a head that would persist in remaining square, in spite of his best endeavours to grow the hair upon it in such a way as to soften its angularity. His eyes were steely, his forehead low, his mouth hard and his manner furtive. That was within doors. The breath of heaven, however, seemed to mitigate all these unamiable characteristics, and it was only on very rare occasions that, once beyond his own threshold, an observer would see the harshness of the man. He smiled down at children, sometimes he patted their heads, he was never lacking in a tip, appropriate or inappropriate, he was the smoother out of discordant situations, he nodded to all the tradespeople, smiled genially at his inferiors, and saluted his superiors and equals. In short he was an ideal citizen.

The outbreak of war in August, 1914, was responsible for two changes in the Naylor ménage. First the at-home days were discontinued, secondly James was more than ever in evidence. Nobody, however, noticed the changes, because in Streatham such things are not considered worthy of notice.

Mr. Naylor received few letters, for which the postman was grateful to providence. Had Streatham been a little more curious, it would have noticed that Mr. Naylor's comings and goings were fraught with some curious and interesting characteristics. For one thing he appeared constitutionally unable to proceed direct to a given point. For instance, if Hampstead were his object, he would in all probability go to Charing Cross, take a 'bus along Strand, the tube to Piccadilly Circus, a taxi to Leicester Square, tube to Golders Green and 'bus to Hampstead.

Another curious circumstance connected with Mr. Naylor was the number of people who seemed to stop him to enquire their way, obviously people who found it difficult to pronounce the names and addresses of those they sought, for they invariably held in their hands pieces of paper, which Mr. Naylor would read and then proceed to direct them. This would occur in all parts of London.

To the casual observer interested in the details of Mr. Naylor's life, it would have appeared that London waited for his approach, and then incontinently made a bee-line for him to enquire its way. With smiling geniality Mr. Naylor would read the paper offered to him, make one or two remarks, then with a wave of his hand and a further genial smile proceed on his way.

His courtesy was almost continental. He would take great pains to direct the enquirer, sometimes even proceeding part of the way with him to ensure that he should not go astray.

Since the war Mr. Naylor had patriotically given up his car, handing it over to the Red Cross, and receiving from the local secretary a letter of very genuine thanks and appreciation. There had also been a paragraph in *The Streatham Herald* notifying this splendid act of citizenship.

In nothing was Mr. Naylor's sense of Christian charity so manifest as in the patience with which he answered the number of false rings he received on the telephone. It was extraordinary the way in which wrong numbers seemed to be put through to him; yet his courtesy never forsook him. His reply was always the same. "No; I am Mr. Montague Naylor of Streatham." It frequently happened that shortly after such a call Mr. Naylor would go out, when James would be left in the front garden.

Mrs. Naylor had particular instructions always to make a note of any rings that came on the telephone during Mr. Naylor's absence, no matter whether they were for him or for anyone else. She was to take down every word that was said, and always say in response that the subscriber was on to Mr. Naylor of Streatham.

One morning whilst John Dene was giving down letters to Dorothy in his customary jerky manner, Mr. Naylor sat at breakfast, his attention equally divided between the meal and the morning paper. Opposite sat Mrs. Naylor, watching him as a dog watches a master of uncertain temper. She was a little woman with a colourless face, from which sparse grey hair was drawn with puritan severity. In her weak blue eyes was fear—fear of her lord and master, and in her manner deprecation and apology.

The only sound to be heard were the champing of Mr. Naylor's jaws, and the occasional rustle of the newspaper. Mr. Naylor was a hearty eater and an omnivorous reader of newspapers. In the front garden James gave occasional tongue, protesting against the existence of some passer-by.

After a particularly vigorous bout of barking on James's part, Mr. Naylor looked up suddenly and, fixing Mrs. Naylor with astern eye, demanded, "Any post?"

"I haven't heard the post-woman yet," faltered Mrs. Naylor apologetically. She was at heart a pacifist in the domestic sense.

"Go and see," was the gruff retort, as Mr. Naylor thrust into his mouth a large piece of bread, which he had previously wiped round his plate to absorb the elemental juices of the morning bacon.

Mrs. Naylor rose meekly and left the room. A few moments later she returned, carrying in her hand two envelopes. Mr. Naylor looked up over his spectacles.

"They were on the path," she explained timidly. "James is in the garden."

The post-woman had tacitly carried on the tradition of her predecessor, the postman. If James were about, the letters went over the garden gate; if James were not about, they went into the letter-box.

With a grunt Mr. Naylor snatched the letters from Mrs. Naylor's hand and looked at them keenly. One bore a halfpenny stamp, and was consequently of no particular importance. This he laid beside his plate. The other, however, he subjected to a rigorous and elaborate examination. He scrutinised the handwriting, examined carefully the postmark, turned it over and gazed at the fastening. Then taking a letter-opener from his pocket, he slowly slit the top of the envelope, and taking out a sheet of notepaper unfolded it.

"Gott——" He bit off the phrase savagely, and looked up fiercely at Mrs. Naylor, as if she was responsible for his lapse. Instinctively she shrank back. From the garden James's vigorous barking swelled out into a fortissimo of protest.

"Stop that dog," he shouted, whereat Mrs. Naylor rose and left the room.

With scowling eyebrows Mr. Naylor read his letter, and ground his teeth with suppressed fury.

"Der mann muss verrückt 'sein."

He re-read the letter, then placing it in his pocket looked across the table, seeming for the first time to notice that Mrs. Naylor had left the room. Going to the door he opened it and shouted a peremptory "Here!"

As Mrs. Naylor entered with obvious trepidation, he fixed her with a stern disapproving eye.

"There's somebody coming this afternoon at four," he said. "I'll see him in the study," and with that he once more drew the letter from his pocket and read it for the third time, whilst Mrs. Naylor withdrew.

The letter which was typewritten, even to the signature, ran:

'DEAR MR. NAYLOR, —

"I hope to call upon you on Thursday afternoon at four o'clock. I regret that unforseen circumstances have prevented me from giving myself this pleasure before.

"Yours very truly,
"J. VAN HELDER."

With a grumble in his throat Mr. Naylor walked out of the dining-room, across the hall and into his study. Closing and locking the door he went over to his writing-table, and seemed to collapse into rather than sit on the chair. He was oblivious to everything except the scrap of paper before him. The cloud upon his brow seemed to intensify, his face became more cruel. The Mr. Naylor of Streatham, patriot, philanthropist and good citizen, had vanished, giving place to a man in whose heart was anger and fear.

At the end of five minutes he drew towards him a small metal tray. Taking a match from a stand, he struck it and deliberately setting light to the paper, held it while it burned. When the flame seared his fingers, he placed the whole upon the metal dish, scowling at the paper as it writhed and crackled in its death agony. He then proceeded to burn the envelope. When both were reduced to twisted shapes of carbon, he opened a drawer, took from it a duster and pressed it down upon the metal plate, reducing the contents to black powder.

Picking up the tray he carried it over to the grate, emptied the powder into the fireplace, wiped the tray and replaced it upon the table, thrusting the duster back into the drawer. He then sank once more into his chair, conscious that the morning had begun ill.

Ten minutes later he rose, unlocked the door and went out into the hall. He took his hat from the stand and brushed it carefully. Picking up his gloves and umbrella, he gave a final look round, then composing his features for the outside world, he opened the door and passed out into Apthorpe Road.

For such of his neighbours as he encountered he had a cheery word, a lifting of his hat, or a wave of the hand. Housewives would sigh enviously as they saw Mr. Naylor pass genially on his way. He was always the same, they told themselves, remembering with a little pang the vagaries of their own husbands.

Before his return to "The Cedars" for lunch, Mr. Naylor with unaccustomed emphasis foretold the doom of the Government unless it immediately rushed a measure through Parliament for the internment of all aliens. He was nothing if not thorough.

CHAPTER VII.
MR. NAYLOR RECEIVES A VISITOR

I

"Height five feet six and a half inches."

"Five feet eight, sir."

"Chest thirty-eight."

"Thirty-eight and a half, sir."

"Weight eleven stone nine."

"Twelve stone, sir."

"Near enough."

"Yes, sir," replied Thompson.

"You've got everything?"

"Down to his under-wear, sir," was the response.

"The ring?"

"Yes, sir."

Malcolm Sage looked up from the buff-coloured paper before him, then picking up a photograph from the table, proceeded to study it with great intentness.

"Yes," he said, "Finlay can do it."

At that moment Colonel Walton strode into the room, smoking the inevitable cigar. Thompson straightened himself to attention, Malcolm Sage nodded, then once more became absorbed in the photograph.

"I hear Finlay's here," said Colonel Walton.

Sage looked up and nodded. "We've just been checking his measurements," he said.

"With that Bergen fellow's?"

Sage nodded.

"It's a considerable risk," said Colonel Walton.

"Finlay likes 'em," retorted Sage without looking up. "I'd give a good deal to solve that little mystery."

The mystery to which Malcolm Sage referred was the arrest of a man on a Bergen-Hull boat some ten days previously. Although his passport and papers were in order, his story when he had been interrogated was not altogether satisfactory. It had been decided to deport him; but Malcolm Sage, who had subjected him to a lengthy cross-examination, had decided that it would be better to detain him for the time being, and the suspect was consequently lodged in the Tower. Both Malcolm Sage and Colonel Walton were convinced that he had been sent over on a special mission.

"Where's Finlay?" asked Colonel Walton.

"He's painting the lily," said Sage with a glint in his eye.

"In other words?" enquired Colonel Walton.

"Seeing how near he can get to this Bergen fellow. I took him down to the Tower to see the men together."

Colonel Walton nodded.

Malcolm Sage regarded disguise as exclusively the asset of the detective of fiction. A disguise, he maintained, could always be identified, although not necessarily penetrated. Few men could disguise their walk or bearing, no matter how clever they might be with the aid of false beards and wigs.

"You remember the lost code-book?" Sage queried.

"I do," said Colonel Walton.

"A remarkable piece of work of Finlay's," continued Sage. "It wasn't a disguise, it was an alteration; trim of moustache, cut and colour of hair, darkened skin and such trifles."

"And the black eye, sir," interpolated Thompson.

"That was certainly a happy stroke," cried Colonel Walton.

"It takes a good deal of moral courage to black your own eye," said Sage quietly. "I tried it once myself."

"How do you plan to proceed?" It was Colonel Walton who spoke.

"If Naylor is really the man we're after and this Bergen fellow is on a secret mission, then it's pretty sure they were intended to get into touch." Sage paused for a moment, then added: "Anyhow, it's worth trying. It's a risk, of course. Naylor may have met him before."

"The risk will be mainly Finlay's," said Colonel Walton drily, as he smoked meditatively.

"It would be yours or mine, chief, only nature cast us in a different mould."

For some moments Colonel Walton did not reply.

"I don't like sending a man on a——" He paused.

"There's no question of sending Finlay; it's more a matter of holding him back. By the way," he continued casually, "Thompson burgled John Dene's place last night, got a set of plans, the chit signed by Sir Lyster and the Skipper, and one or two other papers that should be useful."

"I don't quite like it, Sage." Colonel Walton knitted his brows.

"It's giving the Yard something to do," was Sage's indifferent retort. "They're buzzing about John Dene like flies to-day. He's expressing himself to them in choice Canadian too, so Thompson tells me."

Thompson gave an appreciative grin.

"I dropped in there this morning, sir, and——" He did not conclude his sentence; but his look was one of keen appreciation. "He's got some words, has Inspector Bluggers," he added, "but Mr. Dene left him standing."

"We've just been going over the points of Finlay and the Bergen man," explained Sage. "They're pretty well in agreement. Personally I believe there's a lot in that ring. We stripped the other fellow of his clothes, Finlay insisted on having them baked. Fussy sort of chap in things like that," he added, "but that ring. Men don't generally wear turquoises set in an eccentric pattern. Ha!" He looked up suddenly.

Colonel Walton looked across at him interrogatingly.

"You remember the initials inside, chief?"

Colonel Walton nodded.

"D.U.A. weren't they?"

"What about Deutsches über alles?"

"A bit obvious," suggested Colonel Walton.

"The Hun always is."

There was a knock at the door.

"Come in," called Colonel Walton.

A moment later there entered a man of foreign appearance, with dark well-brushed hair, sallow skin and the deprecating manner of one who is in a country where he is not quite sure either of the customs or of the language. For a moment he stood smiling.

Malcolm Sage caught Colonel Walton's eye. Upon Thompson's face there spread a grin of admiration.

"Wonderful, Finlay," said Colonel Walton. "Wonderful."

"You think it is like?" enquired he who had been addressed as Finlay.

"Wonderful," repeated Colonel Walton, "but," he added a moment after, "it's a dangerous game."

Finlay shrugged his shoulders in a manner that was almost aggressively un-English. He possessed one remarkable characteristic, once he had assumed a personality, he continued to be that man until he finally relinquished the part.

"He'll put you to sleep if you make a mistake," said Sage with uncompromising candour.

Again the shrug of the shoulders.

"That ring," said Sage, pointing to a flat gold band on the third finger of the left hand in which were set three turquoises in the form of a triangle. "What do you make of the inscription?"

"I do not know," said Finlay with the finnicking inflection of one talking in a strange tongue.

"What about Deutsches über alles?" suggested Walton.

"Ah! you have discovered."

"Perfect," said Sage, "absolutely perfect. You're a genius, Finlay."

With a smile and a half-shrug of his shoulders, Finlay deprecated the compliment.

"Where are you going to stay?" enquired Colonel Walton.

"At the Ritzton with John Dene, same floor if possible," said Sage. "He starts from the Tower to-morrow. Released, you know."

Colonel Walton nodded. "By the way, Thompson, you didn't happen to drop any finger prints about in Waterloo Place?"

"Rubber gloves, sir," said Thompson with a smile.

Malcolm Sage nodded.

"It would embarrass us a bit if you got lodged in Brixton prison," said Colonel Walton.

"No chance of that, sir," was the confident retort.

"The account will be in the papers this afternoon, I understand."

Malcolm Sage nodded.

"Well, Finlay," said Walton, "off you go and the best of luck. If you bring this off you ought to get a C.B.E."

"Gott in himmel!" cried Finlay in such tragic consternation, that both Colonel Walton and Sage were forced to smile.

"No, sir," said Sage drily, "we must guard Department Z. against the Order of the British Empire; it deserves well of the country.

"When does he go to Streatham?" enquired Colonel Walton.

"I go now," responded Finlay, "if I find the place. These suburbs!" He rolled his eyes expressively.

Malcolm Sage smiled grimly.

II

For some time Mr. Naylor had sat staring in front of him, immobile but for the movement of his eyes and the compression of his pouch-like lips as he swallowed. Irritation or anxiety always caused him to swallow with a noisy gulp-like sound.

Since lunch he had scowled impartially upon everything. Mrs. Naylor, Susan, James, the paper, his food, all seemed to come under the ban of his displeasure. From time to time he muttered under his breath. He made several efforts to concentrate upon the newspaper before him, but without success. His eyes would wander from the page and scowl into vacancy. The heavy jowls seemed to mould his face into a brutal square, which with his persistent swallowing gave him the appearance of a toad.

His original anger at the threatened advent of a visitor seemed to have changed into irritation at his non-arrival. From time to time he looked at his watch. A step echoing in the street brought him to a listening attitude. When at last a ring sounded at the bell, followed by a peremptory "rat-tat," he started violently. He listened intently to the pad of Mrs. Naylor's footsteps along the passage, to the murmur of voices that followed, and the sound of steps approaching.

When the door opened, the scowl had fled from Mr. Naylor's features, the jowls had lifted, the set frown had passed from his brows. His mouth was pursed up into a smile only one degree less repellent than the look that it had replaced. Mr. Naylor had assumed his best public-meeting manner.

"Mr. Van Helder?" he queried, as he shook hands and motioned his visitor to a seat.

"We shall not be overheard, no?" interrogated Van Helder.

Mr. Naylor shook his head, transferring his eyes from a paper-weight before him to his visitor's face and back again to the paper-weight.

"These London suburbs!" exclaimed Van Helder, as he drew a silk handkerchief from his pocket and proceeded to wipe his face. "I seem to have pursued you to everywhere. I crossed from Bergen on the 21st," he added with a smile.

"The 21st," repeated Mr. Naylor.

"Just ten days ago," continued Van Helder. "I came not before because— —" He raised his eyes suddenly and looked straight at Mr. Naylor, who smiled; but there was guile behind the momentary exposure of his yellow teeth.

"The crossing," continued Van Helder, "three times the alarm of U-boats." He smiled a crafty little smile. "The Germans they make the sea unsafe." Again he smiled.

"So you have been in London since the 21st." Mr. Naylor's tone was casual; but his eyes glinted.

Van Helder nodded indifferently.

"Where are you staying?" Mr. Naylor's eyes never left his visitor's face.

"At the Ritzton."

"You have been comfortable?" The tone was conversational.

Again Van Helder shrugged his shoulders.

"You have been seeing the sights?" Again the tone was casual; but in Mr. Naylor's eyes there was a crafty look.

"It is as I have been told," said Van Helder with a smile. "Always cautious. You are fond of dogs," he added irrelevantly, "I heard one."

"James does not like strangers." This with a sinister smile.

"No?" continued the other; taking a cigarette-case from his pocket and offering it to Mr. Naylor who declined. "I may smoke?"

Mr. Naylor nodded.

Van Helder lighted a cigarette and proceeded to blow smoke rings with quiet content. He wanted to think. It was obvious to him that something was wrong, something lacking. There was the suggestion in his host's manner of a cat watching a mouse, watching and waiting.

"You are becoming, how do you call it, ungeschickt," he said with a disarming smile, as he blew three rings in rapid succession.

"You think so?" Mr. Naylor smiled amiably.

"Yes, how do you call it, awkward, clumsy. You have lived long in England," he continued a little contemptuously, as he ejected more smoke-rings.

"You find London interesting?" asked Mr. Naylor, with ominous calm. He was determined to pick up the thread of conversation that had been snatched from his hand.

"You are a fool." Van Helder turned just as he emitted a smoke-ring. At the calm insolence of his tone Mr. Naylor started slightly, but quickly recovered himself.

"What do you mean?"

"I have been in the Tower." For the fraction of a second Van Helder's eyes sought those of Mr. Naylor. Was it relief that he saw? The change was only momentary, just a flash.

Van Helder continued to blow smoke-rings as if entirely indifferent alike to his host's presence and emotions. "I was released yesterday morning. They apologised for my detention."

"And you came here?" f Mr. Naylor's voice was even and devoid of inflection.

Deliberately Van Helder took from his pocket a gold ring set with three turquoises in the form of a triangle. It was his last card.

"Ah! I see you look at my ring," he said, seeing Mr. Naylor's eyes fix greedily upon it. "It was given to me by one whom I serve." Deliberately he drew it from his finger again and handed it to Mr. Naylor, who took it casually and proceeded to examine it. The other watched him closely. Yes; he was looking at the inscription on the inside.

"They are not my initials," said Van Helder.

Mr. Naylor looked up quickly. "No," he said, returning the ring.

The other shrugged his shoulders without replying. Mr. Naylor's manner had undergone a change.

"And now about John Dene. Ah!" as one smoke-ring passed through another.

"John Dene!"

"Yes, of Toronto," continued Van Helder, smiling and continuing to blow rings with apparent enjoyment. "He is staying at the Ritzton, too."

"London is full of visitors."

"My friend, we waste time. There is such a thing as over-caution. As I say you are ungeschickt. There was that affair of John Dene's lunch. Such things will not please those——" He shrugged his shoulders.

For fully a minute Naylor gazed at him quietly, searchingly.

"There was then the chocolates and the girl."

"I do not understand." Mr. Naylor looked across at him craftily.

"We waste time, I know. I will tell you. The secretary, you make your woman offer her chocolates at a tea-shop, and to go for a ride in a taxi. The chocolates——" He shrugged his shoulders expressively. "She refuses. You are clumsy."

The contemptuous insolence of his visitor seemed to impress Mr. Naylor. The look of suspicion in his eyes became less marked.

"How did you know?" he asked, still wary.

"We waste time," was the response with a wave of the hand.

For a few moments Mr. Naylor sat watching Van Helder as he continued to blow rings with manifest content.

"Listen," continued Van Helder. "John Dene has brought over here an invention, a submarine that is to end the war. He has given it to the Admiralty."

"Given it!" involuntarily repeated Mr. Naylor.

"Given it. There are patriots even in England. You think he is trying to sell it, therefore you try to remove him."

"Not selling it." Mr. Naylor leaned slightly forward.

"He gives it on condition that he commands it with his own men. It makes easy the matter."

"Then it is true what— —" Mr. Naylor stopped.

"How did you learn this?" He slobbered his words slightly as he spoke.

"I know things, it is my duty," was the response.

"But what proof— —?"

With great deliberation Van Helder drew from his pocket a large envelope; extracting a single sheet of paper he handed it across the table. Mr. Naylor snatched it eagerly and proceeded to devour it with his eyes. "I also got a set of plans of a submarine; but it was one of our own. He is clever, this man."

"How did you get it?"

Van Helder smiled. "How did you get the copy?" he enquired.

"The copy! How did you know?"

Mr. Naylor stared at him, his jaw a little dropped. He swallowed noisily.

"You have been clumsy," repeated Van Helder. "You try to kill the cock that lays the eggs of gold." He shrugged his shoulders contemptuously.

Mr. Naylor flushed angrily. "And you?" he almost snarled.

"I am here to watch." He looked across at Mr. Naylor with a cunning smile. He was at last sure of his ground.

"Watch who?"

Van Helder shrugged his shoulders, and proceeded to light a new cigarette from the burning end of the old one.

"You must not kill—yet," he said, gazing at the end of his cigarette to see that it was well alight.

"What then?" demanded Mr. Naylor. His jowls had returned and the yellow of his teeth was visible between his slightly parted lips.

"Wait and watch," was the reply.

"And let him go North," sneered the other.

"If you kill, where are the plans? Do as you would," he continued indifferently. "There will be The Day for you, too. Now I go." He made a movement to rise; but Mr. Naylor motioned him back into his chair.

Two hours later Mr. Naylor himself let out his visitor. Closing the front door, he returned to his study, where for an hour he sat at his table gazing straight in front of him. Mr. Naylor was puzzled.

Conscious that he was being followed by a small man in a grey suit with shifty eyes, James Finlay made his way leisurely to the High Road where he took a 'bus bound for Piccadilly Circus.

CHAPTER VIII.
DOROTHY WEST AT HOME

"Mother mine," cried Dorothy West, as she withdrew the pins from her hat, "John Dene's a dear, and I think his passion for me is developing."

"Dorothy!" cried Mrs. West, a tiny white-haired lady whose face still retained traces of youthful beauty.

"You needn't be shocked, lovie; John Dene is as worthy as his namesake in *Evangeline*." She laughed lightly. "Now I must eat. John Dene's like sea air, he's so stimulating;" and she began to eat the dinner that Mrs. West always prepared with such care.

For some minutes she watched with a smile of approval her daughter's healthy appetite.

"I think I should like Mr. Dene, Dorothy," she said at length. "I have always heard that Canadians are very nice to women. You must ask him to call."

"Oh, you funny little mother!" she laughed. "You forget that we have come down in the world, and that I'm a typist."

"A secretary, dear," corrected Mrs. West gently.

"Well, secretary, then; but even a secretary doesn't invite her employer to tea, even when the tea is as mother makes it. It's not done, so the less that's said of John, I think, the better," she quoted gaily. "Oh! by the way," she added, "you might get his goat; Sir Lyster does."

"His goat, dear!" Mrs. West looked up with a puzzled expression.

Dorothy explained the allusion. She went on to tell of some of the doings of John Dene, his impatience, his indifference to and contempt for constituted authority. In short she added a few vivid side-lights to the picture she had already given her mother of how John Dene had come and carried all before him.

"I think," she said in conclusion, screwing up her pretty features, "that John Dene is rather a dear." Then after a pause she added, "You see, he is also a man."

"A man, my dear," questioned Mrs. West, looking at her daughter with a smile.

"Yes, mother, he's so intensely masculine. I get so fed up with——"

"Dorothy!" expostulated Mrs. West.

"Yes, I know it's trying, mother, but I get so weary of the subaltern and junior naval officer. Of course they're splendid and brave; but they don't seem men."

"But think of how they have given their lives," began Mrs. West.

"Yes; but we see those who haven't, mother, and very few of them have chevrons on their sleeves. Now John Dene is quite different. He always seems to be a man; yet he never forgets that you are a woman, although he never appears to be conscious of your being a woman."

Dorothy caught her mother's eye, and laughed.

"Of course it sounds utterly ridiculous I know; but there it is, and then think of what——" She suddenly broke off.

"Yes, dear," said Mrs. West gently.

"I was nearly letting out official secrets, mother. Of course I mustn't do that, must I?"

"Of course not, dear," said Mrs. West.

"Yes," continued Dorothy, her head on one side, "I like John Dene. It must be ripping to be able to bully a First Lord of the Admiralty," she added irrelevantly.

"Bully a First Lord," said Mrs. West. Mrs. West seemed to be in a perpetual state of repeating in a bewildered manner her daughter's startling statements.

"He doesn't care for anybody. He calls Mr. Blair, that's Sir Lyster's secretary, the prize seal, and I'm sure he takes a delight in frightening the poor man. That's the best of being a Canadian, you see you don't care a damn——"

"Dorothy!" There was horror in Mrs. West's voice.

"I'm so sorry, mother dear; but it slipped out, you know, and really it's such an awfully convenient word, isn't it? It's so different from not caring a bother, or not caring a blow. Anyway, when you're a Canadian you don't care a—well you know, for anybody. If a man happens to be a lord or a duke, you're rude to him just to show that you're as good as he is. Sometimes, mother, I wish I were a Canadian," said Dorothy pensively. "I should so like to 'ginger-up' Sir Lyster."

"Your language, my dear," said Mrs. West gently.

"Oh, that's John Dene," said Dorothy airily. "That's his favourite expression, 'ginger-up.' He came over here to 'ginger-up' the Admiralty, and in fact 'ginger-up' anybody who didn't very strongly object to being 'gingered-up,' and those who did, well he gingers them up just the same. You should see poor Mr. Blair under the process." Dorothy laughed as she thought of Mr. Blair's sufferings. "The girls call him 'Oh, Reginald!' and he looks it," she added.

Mrs. West smiled vaguely, finding it a little difficult to follow her daughter along these paths of ultra-modernism.

"You see, if Sir Lyster says to me 'go,' I have to go," continued Dorothy, "and if he says to me 'come,' I have to come; but if he says to John Dene 'go,' he just says 'shucks.'"

"Says what, Dorothy?"

"Shucks!" she repeated with a laugh, "it means go to—well, you know, mother."

"And does he say that to Sir Lyster?" enquired Mrs. West in awe-struck voice.

Dorothy nodded vigorously.

"The only one that seems to understand him is Sir Bridgman North, and he never stands on his dignity, you know. If I were in the Navy," said Dorothy meditatively, "I should like to be under Sir Bridgman, he's really rather a dear."

"But why do——" began Mrs. West, "why does Sir Lyster allow——"

"Allow," broke in Dorothy. "It doesn't matter what you allow with John Dene. If you agree with him he just grunts; if you don't he says 'shucks,' or else he questions whether you've got any head-filling."

"Any what?" asked Mrs. West.

"Head-filling, that means brains. Oh, you've got an awful lot to learn," she added, nodding at her mother in mock despair. "I think John Dene very clever," she added.

"Dorothy, you mustn't call him 'John Dene.'"

"He's always called 'John Dene,'" said Dorothy. "You can't think of him as anything but John Dene, and do you know, mother, all the other girls are so intrigued. They're always asking me how I get on with 'the bear,' as they call him. That's because he doesn't take any notice of them, except Marjorie Rogers, and she's as cheeky as a robin."

"But he isn't a bear, is he, Dorothy?"

"A bear? He's the most polite creature that ever existed," said Dorothy—"when he remembers it," she added after a moment's pause. "You see they all expect me to marry him."

"Dorothy!"

"I'm not so sure that they're wrong, either," she added naïvely. "You see, he's got plenty of money and——"

"I don't like to hear you talk like that, dear," said Mrs. West gravely.

"Oh, I'm horrid, aren't I?" she cried, running over to her mother and putting her arm round her neck. "What a dreadful thing it must be for you, poor mother mine, to have such a daughter! She outrages all the dear old Victorian conventions, doesn't she?"

"You mustn't talk like that, Dorothy dear," said Mrs. West. There was in her voice that which told her daughter she was in earnest.

"All right, mother dear, I won't; you know my bark is worse than my bite, don't you?"

"Yes, but dear——"

"You see, way down, as John Dene would say, in his own heart there is chivalry, and that is very, very rare nowadays among men. He is much nicer to me than he would be to Lady Grayne, or Mrs. Llewellyn John, or to the Queen herself, I believe. I'm sure he likes me," added Dorothy half to herself. "You see," she added, "he broke my teapot, and he owes me something for that, doesn't he?"

"Dorothy, you are very naughty." There was no rebuke in Mrs. West's voice.

"And you're wondering how it came about that such a dear, sweet, conventional, lovely, Victorian symbol of respectability and convention should have had such a dreadfully outrageous daughter as Dorothy West. Now confess, mother, aren't you?"

Mrs. West merely smiled the indulgent smile that Dorothy always interpreted into forgiveness for her lapses, past, present and to come.

"You see, mother, John Dene has got it into his head that we're hopelessly out of date," she said. "He's quite sincere. He thinks we're fools, Sir Lyster, Sir Bridgman and the whole lot of us, and as for poor Mr. Blair, he knows he's a fool. He thinks that Mr. Llewellyn John is almost a fool, in fact he's sure in his own mind that unless you happen to be born a Canadian you're a fool and can't help it. He's quite nice about it, because it really isn't your fault."

"I'm afraid he must be very narrow-minded," said Mrs. West gently.

"No, he isn't, that's where it's so funny, it's just his idea. He looks upon himself as a heaven-sent corrective to the British Government. I'm afraid poor John Dene is going to have a nasty jar before he's through, as he would say himself."

"How do you mean, Dorothy?" enquired Mrs. West.

"I mustn't say any more, because I should be divulging official secrets. The other girls are so curious to know what is happening. Bishy, that's Miss Bishcroft, asked me whether John Dene made love to me, and Rojjie is sure that he kisses me." Dorothy rippled off into laughter.

"How impertinent of her!" Mrs. West was shocked.

"It wasn't impertinence, mother, it was funny. If you could only see John Dene, and imagine him making love to anyone. It really is funny. Sometimes I sit and wonder if he knows how to kiss a girl."

"Dorothy, you are — —" began Mrs. West.

"Why shouldn't we be frank and open about such matters? Every man kisses a girl at some time during his life, except John Dene," she added. "In Whitehall it's nothing but minutes and kisses. Why shouldn't we talk about it? It's helping to win the war. It's so silly to hide everything in that silly Victorian way of ours. If a nice girl meets a nice man she wants him to kiss her, and she's disappointed if he doesn't. Now isn't she?" challenged Dorothy as she perched herself upon the arm of her mother's chair and looked down at her, her eyebrows and mouth screwed up, impertinent and provocative.

"I wish you wouldn't talk like that, dear," said Mrs. West, as she regarded her daughter's pretty features.

"Why, mother?" she enquired, bending and brushing a swift kiss upon her mother's white hair.

"It—it doesn't seem——" she paused, then added rather weakly, "it doesn't seem quite nice."

Dorothy jumped up and stood before her mother, smiling mischievously.

"And so you don't think I'm quite nice, Mrs. West?" She made an elaborate curtsey. "Thank you very much indeed. At the Admiralty there are quite a lot of young men, and some old ones, too, who don't agree with you," she added, returning to her chair.

"But you mustn't say such—such things," protested Mrs. West weakly.

"But, mother, when you were a girl and knew a nice man, didn't you want him to kiss you?"

"We never thought about such things. We——"

"Didn't you want father to kiss you?" persisted Dorothy.

"We were engaged, my dear, and your dear father was so——"

"But before you were engaged. Suppose father had tried to kiss you. What would you have done?"

The girl's eyes were on her mother, mischievous and challenging. A faint blush tinged Mrs. West's cheeks.

"I'll tell you what you'd have done, you dear, naughty little mother. You'd have pretended to be shocked, but in your heart you would have been glad, and you'd have lain awake all night thinking what an awful rip you had been." She nodded her head wisely.

"Sometimes," said Mrs. West after a pause, "I wish it had not been necessary for you to work. Girls seem so different nowadays from what they were when I was young."

"We are, you dear little mouse," smiled Dorothy. "We know a lot more, and to be forewarned is to be forearmed. I'm glad I didn't live when you had to faint at the sight of a mouse, or swoon when you were kissed. It would be such a waste," she added gaily.

Mrs. West sighed, conscious that a new age of womanhood had dawned with which she was out of touch.

"Mother," said Dorothy presently, "what made you love father?"

Mrs. West looked up in surprise at her daughter, but continued to fold her napkin and place it in her ring before replying.

"Because your father, Dorothy, was——" she hesitated.

"My father," suggested Dorothy.

Mrs. West smiled; but there was a far-away look in her eyes. "Everybody loved your father," she went on a moment later.

"Yes, mother, but everybody didn't marry him," she said practically.

"Noooo——" hesitated Mrs. West.

"But you mean to say that everybody would have liked to marry him."

"He was very wonderful," said Mrs. West, a note of sadness creeping into her voice.

"But you haven't answered my question," persisted Dorothy. "Why is it that we women love men?"

Mrs. West was not conscious of the quaint phrasing of her daughter's remark.

"We don't love men, Dorothy," she cried, "we love a man, the right man."

"But," persisted Dorothy, "why do we do it? They're not pretty and they're not very interesting," she emphasised the "very," "and only a few of them are clever. Sometimes in the Tube coming home I see a girl and a man holding hands. What is it that makes them want to hold hands?"

"It's natural to fall in love," said Mrs. West gently.

"But that's not falling in love," protested Dorothy scornfully. "If I fell in love with a man I shouldn't want to hold his hand in a train. I should hate him if he expected it."

"It's a question of class," said Mrs. West a little primly.

"Oh! mother, what an awful snob you are," cried Dorothy, jumping up and going round and giving her mother a hug. "Let's go into the drawing-room and be comfy and have a chat."

When they were seated, Mrs. West in an armchair and Dorothy on a stool at her feet, the girl continued her interrogations. "Now suppose," she continued, "I were to fall in love with a man who was ugly, ill-mannered, badly dressed, with very little to say for himself. Why should I do it?" Dorothy looked challengingly up at her mother.

"But you wouldn't, dear," said Mrs. West with gentle conviction.

"Oh, mother, you're awfully trying you know," she cried in mock despair. "You've got to suppose that I have, or could. Why should I do it?" Mrs. West gazed at her daughter a little anxiously, then shook her head.

"Now I can quite understand," went on Dorothy, half to herself, "why a man should fall in love with me. I'm pretty and bright, wear nice things, particularly underneath——"

"Dorothy!" broke in Mrs. West in a tone of shocked protest.

She laughed. "Oh, mother, you're a dreadful prude. Why do you think girls wear pretty shoes and stockings, and low cut blouses as thin as a cobweb?"

"Hush! Dorothy, you mustn't say such things." There was pain in Mrs. West's voice.

"I wish we could face facts," said Dorothy with a sigh. "You see, mother dear," she continued, "when you're in a government office, with heaps of other girls and men about, you get to know things, see things, and sometimes you get to hate things."

"I have always regretted," began Mrs. West sadly.

"You mustn't do that, mother dear," cried Dorothy; "it has been an education. But what I want to know is, what is it in a man that attracts a girl?"

"Goodness, honour and——" began Mrs. West.

"No, it isn't," said Dorothy, "at least they don't attract me."

Mrs. West looked pained but said nothing.

"You see," continued Dorothy, "there are such a lot of good men about, and honourable men, and—and—they're so dreadfully dull and monotonous. I couldn't marry that sort of man," she added with conviction.

"But——" began Mrs. West. "You wouldn't——"

Then she paused.

"I can't explain it, mother," she said, "but I should hate to be doing the same thing always."

"But we are doing the same things always, Dorothy," said Mrs. West.

"Oh! no we're not," protested Dorothy. "I never know until I get home on Saturday where I'm going to take you. Now if I had a husband, a good and honourable husband, he would begin about Thursday saying that on Saturday afternoon we would go to Hampstead, or to Richmond, or to—oh! anywhere. Then when Saturday came I should hate the very name of the place he had chosen. Then on Sunday we should go to church in the morning, for a walk in the afternoon, pay a call or two, then church or a cinema in the evening. That's good and honourable married life," she concluded with decision.

Mrs. West looked down with a puzzled expression on her face.

"Wait a minute, mother," said Dorothy. "Now we'll imagine the real me married to a good and honourable man. At twelve-thirty on the Saturday that he has arranged to lose himself and me at the maze at Hampton Court, I telephone to say that we're going to Brighton, and that he's to meet me at Victoria at half-past one, and I'll bring his things. Now what do you think he'd do?" With head on one side she gazed challengingly at her mother.

"I—I don't know," faltered Mrs. West.

"I do," said Dorothy with conviction. "He'd have a fit. Then if I wanted him to come for a 'bus ride just as he was going to bed," went on Dorothy, "he'd have another fit; and if one fine morning, just as he was off to the office, I were to ask him not to go, but to take me to Richmond instead, he'd have a third fit, and then I should be a widow."

"A widow!" questioned Mrs. West. "What are you talking about?"

"Third fits are always fatal, mother," she said wisely. Then with a laugh she added, "Oh, there's a great time in store for the man who marries Dorothy West. He will have to have a strong heart, a robust constitution and above all any amount of stamina," and she gave a mischievous little chuckle of joy. Then a moment after, looking gravely at her mother she said, "You must have been very wicked, lovie, or you'd never have had such a daughter to plague you. I'm your cross;" but Mrs. West merely smiled.

CHAPTER IX.
DEPARTMENT Z. AT WORK

"Naylor isn't satisfied then." Colonel Walton glanced across at Malcolm Sage, who was gazing appreciatively at his long, lender fingers.

"He's the shyest bird I've ever come across," said Sage without looking up. "He gave Finlay a rare wigging for that call. Now he's having him watched."

"I expected that," said Colonel Walton, engrossed in cutting the end of a cigar.

"I think it's jealousy," continued Sage. "He's afraid of the special agent getting all the kudos—and the plunder," he added. "It was a happy chance getting that Bergen chap."

"I'm rather concerned about Finlay," said Colonel Walton.

"Good man, Finlay." There was a note of admiration in Sage's voice. "He's quite cut adrift from us. He's nothing if not thorough. I can't get in touch with him."

"Of course he knows?"

"That he's being watched? Yes."

"Who's looking after him?"

"Hoyle." Sage drew his pipe from his pocket and proceeded to charge it from a chamois-leather tobacco-pouch. "I've had to call Thompson off, I think they linked him up with us."

"That's a pity," said Colonel Walton, gazing at the end of his cigar. "He's a better man than Hoyle."

"It's that little chap they've got," continued Sage, "lives at Wimbledon, retired commercial-traveller, clever devil." Malcolm Sage never grudged praise to an opponent.

"How about John Dene?"

"He's not taking any risks," said Sage, as he applied a match to his pipe. "But they'll never let him go north."

"Then we must prevent him."

"Perhaps you'd like to take on that little job, chief." There was a momentary suspicion of a twinkle in Sage's eye before a volume of tobacco smoke blotted it out.

"I'm afraid it'll force our hand," said Colonel Walton.

"That burglary business complicated things," said Sage, as he sucked in his lips, with him a sign of annoyance. "It was a mistake to keep it dark."

"That was Sir Lyster."

"It made Naylor suspicious."

"Has Finlay seen him since?" enquired Colonel Walton.

"Naylor must have given him the secret-code. They've met several times; but I believe Naylor is determined to act on his own. He's a weird creature. I wish I could get in touch with Finlay, however."

"Why not try the taxi?"

"I've had Rogers following him round all the time; but Finlay hasn't once taken a taxi."

"I'm afraid he's taking a big risk——" began Colonel Walton. "That Naylor fellow——" He paused.

Sage nodded.

During the previous ten days Department Z. had learned a great deal about the comings and goings of Mr. Montagu Naylor of Streatham. It had become manifest to Sage that he had to do with a man who had reduced cunning and caution to a fine art. His every act seemed to have been carefully thought out beforehand, not only in relation to himself, but to what might grow directly out of it.

During a walk he would sometimes turn suddenly and proceed swiftly in the direction from which he had come, as if he had forgotten something, looking keenly at every one he passed. At others he would step into a shop, where he could be seen keeping a careful watch through the window. A favourite trick was to walk briskly round a corner, then stop and look in some shop window with a small mirror held in the palm of his hand.

From the first Malcolm Sage had realised that the conventional methods of shadowing a suspect would be useless for his purpose. Those in whom Department Z. were interested would be old hands at the game, and to set a single person to watch them would inevitably result in the discovery of what was afoot. He therefore set at least three men, or women, to dog the footsteps of the suspect.

These would follow each other at intervals of from twenty-five to a hundred yards, according to the district in which they were operating. At a signal that the first in the line was dropping out, the trail would be taken up by number two, who in turn would relinquish the work to number three. Sometimes as many as six were allocated to one shadowing.

This method had the additional advantage of enabling the Department to assure itself that the watchers were not in turn being watched.

It was no uncommon thing for a suspect to arrange to have himself shadowed in order to ascertain whether or no there were any one on his track. This was a favourite device with Mr. Naylor.

For nearly two years Department Z. had been endeavouring to solve the problem of a secret organisation, with the offshots of which they were constantly coming into contact. The method this organisation adopted was one of concentration upon a single object. At one time it would be at the sailing of vessels from home ports, at another the munitions output, or again the anti-aircraft defences of London.

Malcolm Sage was convinced that somewhere there was at work a controlling mind, one that weighed every risk and was prepared for all eventualities. Individuals had been shadowed, some had been arrested, much to Sage's disgust. The efforts of the organisation had frequently been countered and its objects defeated; but Department Z. had hitherto been unable to penetrate beyond the outer fringe. The most remarkable thing of all was that no document of any description had been discovered, either on the person of those arrested, or through the medium of the post.

Scotland Yard stoutly denied the existence of the organisation. They claimed to have made a clean sweep of all secret service agents in their big round-up on the outbreak of war. Whatever remained were a few small fry that had managed to slip through the meshes of their net. Malcolm Sage merely shrugged his shoulders and worked the harder.

When it had been discovered that the famous Norvelt aeroplane, which was to give the Allies the supremacy of the air, had been copied by the Germans, the War Cabinet regarded the matter as one of the gravest setbacks the Allied cause had received. Mr. Llewellyn John had openly reproached Colonel Walton with failure. Again when time after time a certain North Sea convoy was attacked, the Authorities knew that it could be only as a result of information having leaked out to the enemy. A raid into the Bight of Heligoland had been met in a way that convinced those who had planned it that the enemy had been warned, although the utmost secrecy had been observed. All these things had tended to cause the War Cabinet uneasiness, and Department Z. had been urged to redouble its efforts to find out the means by which information was conveyed to the enemy.

"We must watch and wait, just hang about on the outer fringe. When we find the thread it will lead to the centre of things," Sage had remarked philosophically. In the meantime he worked untiringly, keeping always at the back of his mind the problem of this secret organisation.

Day by day the record of Mr. Montagu Naylor's activities enlarged. With him caution seemed to have become an obsession. As Malcolm Sage went through the daily reports of his agents he was puzzled to account for many of Mr. Naylor's actions other than by the fact that circumlocution had become with him a habit.

Among other things that came to light was Mr. Naylor's fondness for open spaces, and the frequency with which he got into conversation with strangers. He would wander casually into Kew Gardens, or Waterlow Park, or in fact anywhere, seat himself somewhere on a bench, and before he had been there ten minutes, someone would inevitably select the same bench on which to rest himself or herself, with the result that they would soon drift into desultory conversation with Mr. Naylor.

The same thing would happen at a restaurant at which Mr. Naylor might be lunching, dining or taking tea. With strangers his manner seemed irresistible.

It would sometimes happen that he would keep one of the telephone appointments, pass through the thoroughfare indicated, and proceed either to a park or a tea-shop, where later he would find himself in casual conversation with someone who, curiously enough, had been in that particular thoroughfare when he passed through it.

For some time Malcolm Sage was greatly puzzled by the fact that even when the name of a long thoroughfare were indicated in one of the telephone messages, such as Oxford Street, Marylebone Road, or even the Fulham Road, Mr. Naylor never experienced any difficulty in locating the whereabouts of his subordinate. Sage gave instructions for the exact position of each thoroughfare to be indicated. As a result he discovered that contact was always established in the neighbourhood of the building numbered 10.

"It's the German mind," remarked Sage one day to Colonel Walton. "It leaves nothing to chance, or to the intelligence of the other fellow."

As each one of Mr. Naylor's associates was located, he or she was continuously shadowed. In consequence the strain upon the resources of Department Z. became increasingly severe. It was like an army advancing into an enemy country, and having to furnish the lines of communication from its striking force. Sometimes Sage himself was engaged in the shadowing, and once or twice even Colonel Walton.

"By the time we've finished, there won't be even the office cat left," Thompson one day remarked to Gladys Norman, a typist whom Malcolm Sage had picked out of one of the Departments through which he had passed during his non-stop career. She had already shown marked ability by her cleverness and resource, to say nothing of her impudence.

"Never mind, Tommy," she had replied. "It's all experience, and after the war, when I marry you and we start our private inquiry bureau— —" She nodded her head knowingly. "Why, I've got enough facts from my own department to divorce half the officers on the staff," she added.

The work of shadowing Mr. Naylor was not without its humours. Sometimes Department Z. was led away on false scents. On one occasion a week was spent in tracking a venerable-looking old gentleman, he turned out to be a quite respectable pensioned civil servant, who, out of the kindness of his own heart, had passed the time of day with Mr. Naylor.

The plan decided upon by Colonel Walton and Malcolm Sage was carefully to watch all Mr. Naylor's associates and, at a given time, make a clean sweep of the lot. To achieve this effect a zero hour was to be established on a certain day. Each was to be arrested as soon after that time as it was possible. This was mainly due to Malcolm Sage's suspicion that some scheme of warning existed between the various members of the combination, whereby any danger threatening one was quickly notified to all the others.

"In all probability we shall get a few harmless birds into the net," Malcolm Sage had remarked. "Probably the sister of an M.P., or the head of a department in one of the new Ministries; but that can't be helped."

"Still I should prefer that it didn't happen," Colonel Walton had said drily. "You know the Skipper hates questions in the House."

"By the way," said Malcolm Sage to Colonel Walton one day, "Thompson sent in an interesting report this morning."

"Naylor?" queried Colonel Walton.

Malcolm Sage nodded.

"He's having a sort of small greenhouse arrangement fitted in the window of the front-room of the basement. It may be for flowers or for salad."

"Or— —?" interrogated Colonel Walton.

Malcolm Sage merely shrugged his shoulders as he proceeded to dig the ashes out of his pipe.

The work of Department Z. continued quietly and unostentatiously. John Dene was never permitted out of sight, except when in some private place. This meant the constant changing of those responsible for keeping him under observation.

The necessity of this was not more evident to Department Z. than to John Dene himself. In spite of his scornful manner, he was not lacking in caution, as soon became obvious to Malcolm Sage. At the hotel he was careful, taking neither food nor drink in his room. He never dined two consecutive nights at the same restaurant, and he consistently refused all overtures from strangers.

It soon became evident to Malcolm Sage that John Dene realised how great was the danger by which he was threatened.

The ransacking of his room at the Ritzton left John Dene indifferent. The fact that he never locked the small safe he kept at his office at Waterloo Place was not without its significance for Malcolm Sage.

In the course of the next few weeks Malcolm Sage learned a great deal about John Dene of Toronto. Although proof against the wiles of confidence men, always on the look-out for the colonials, he fell an easy victim to the plausible beggar. He never refused a request for assistance, and the record of his unostentatious charities formed a no inconsiderable portion of the rapidly increasing dossier at Department Z.

Many were the incidents recorded of John Dene's kindness of heart. A child smiling up into his eyes would cause him to stop, bend down and ask its name, or where it lived. Whilst the little one was sucking an embarrassed finger John Dene would be feeling in his pocket for a coin that a moment later would cause the youngster to gaze after him in speechless wonder, clutching in his grimy hand a shilling or a half-a-crown.

Once he was observed leading a tearful little girl of about five years old up the Haymarket. The child had apparently become lost, and John Dene was seeking a policeman into whose care to consign her. It became obvious to Malcolm Sage that John Dene's weak points were children and "lame dogs."

Thompson, who first had charge of the guarding of John Dene, reported that one of the most assiduous of those who seemed to interest themselves in the movements of the Canadian, was a little man in a grey suit, with a pair of shifty eyes that never remained for more than a second on any one object.

"He's clever, sir," Thompson had remarked to Sage, "clever as a vanload of monkeys, and he takes cover like an alien," he added grinning, at his own joke.

"Has he linked up with Naylor yet?"

Thompson shook his head. "The old bird's too crafty for that, sir," he said. "He only comes up against the small fry. This little chap in the grey suit is something bigger."

The officials at Department Z. soon discovered that the chiefs of the organisation, against which they were working, never came into contact with each other. Communication was established verbally by subordinates. Another thing that added to the difficulties of Sage's task was that a man, who had for some days been particularly active, would suddenly drop out, apparently being superseded by someone else with whom he had not previously been in contact. Later, the man who had dropped out would pick up an entirely different thread. This meant innumerable loose ends, all of which had to be followed up and then held until they began to develop along new lines.

"It's a great game played slow, Gladys," Thompson remarked one day to Gladys Norman as they sat waiting for Malcolm Sage.

"Slow," cried the girl. "If this is slow, what's fast?"

"Her initials are G. N.," was the reply.

Malcolm Sage entered at the moment when Gladys had succeeded in making her colleague's hair look like that of an Australian aborigine.

CHAPTER X.
JOHN DENE GOES TO KEW

"And now we'll go to Kew and say how-do-you-do to the rhododendrons," cried Dorothy, as she rolled up her napkin and slipped it into the silver ring that lay beside her plate. "I'll go and make myself smart; and mother"—she paused at the door—"mind you put on your new hat that makes you look so wicked."

Mrs. West smiled what Dorothy called her "Saturday afternoon smile."

Half an hour later Dorothy was gazing at herself in the looking-glass over the dining-room mantelpiece. With a sigh half of content, half of rebelliousness she turned as Mrs. West entered. For a moment she stood looking enquiringly at her daughter.

"Shall I do?" she demanded impudently. "I've put on my very best, undies and all."

"But why, Dorothy?" began Mrs. West.

"Oh, I just wanted to feel best to-day. I wonder if John Dene notices legs, mother," she added inconsequently.

"Really, Dorothy!" began Mrs. West, with widening eyes.

"Well, I've got rather nice legs, and—Oh! but I'm sure he doesn't. We had fillets of sole done up in a most wonderful way the other day, and he asked if it was cod. He's got cod on the brain, poor dear." With a sigh she turned once more to regard herself in the looking-glass. "If he could see me in this hat, it would be all 'u.p.' with Honest John;" and she laughed wickedly as she caught her mother's eye.

"I wish you wouldn't use such expressions," protested Mrs. West gently, "and—and——" She stopped and looked appealingly at her daughter.

"I know I'm a horrid little beast," she cried, turning quickly, "and I say outrageous things, don't I?" Then with a sudden change of mood she added: "But why shouldn't a girl be pleased because she's got nice legs, mother?"

"It's not nice for a young girl to talk about legs," said Mrs. West a little primly, making the slightest possible pause before the last words.

"But why, mother?" persisted Dorothy.

"It's—it's not quite nice."

"Well, mine are, anyway," said Dorothy with a little grimace. "Now we must be off."

Mrs. West merely sighed, the sigh of one who fails to understand.

"Mother dear," said Dorothy, observing the sigh, "if I didn't laugh I'm afraid I should cry." All the brightness had left her as she looked down at her mother. "I wonder why it is?" she added musingly.

To Mrs. West, Saturday afternoons were the oases in her desert of loneliness. During the long and solitary days of the week, she looked forward with the eagerness of a child to the excursions Dorothy never failed to plan for her entertainment. If it were dull or wet, there would be a matinee or the pictures; if fine they would go to Kew, Richmond, or the Zoo. It was an understood thing that Mrs. West should know nothing about the arrangement until the actual day itself.

"I think," remarked Dorothy, as they walked across Kew Bridge, "that I must be looking rather nice to-day. That's the third man who has given me the glad-eye since——"

"Oh, Dorothy! I wish you wouldn't say such dreadful things," protested Mrs. West in genuine distress.

Slipping her arm through her mother's, the girl squeezed it to her side.

"I know I'm an outrageous little beast," she said, "but I love shocking you, you dear, funny little mother, and—and you know I love you, don't you?"

"But suppose anyone heard you, dear, what would they think?" There was genuine concern in Mrs. West's voice.

"Oh, I'm dreadfully respectable with other people. I never talk to John Dene about legs or glad-eyes, really." Her eyes were dancing with mischief as she looked down at her mother. "Now I'll promise to be good for the rest of the day; but how can a girl say prunes and prisms with a mouth like mine. It's too wide for that, and then there are those funny little cuts at the corners; they are what make me wicked," she announced with a wise little nod.

Mrs. West sighed once more; she had learned that it was useless to protest when her daughter was in her present mood.

They entered the Gardens, and for an hour walked about absorbing their atmosphere of peace and warmth, sunlight and shadow and the song of birds; the war seemed very far away.

Presently they seated themselves by the broad walk leading to the large tropical greenhouse, and gazed idly at the stream of passers-by.

"I wish I were a girl bird," said Dorothy dreamily, as she listened to the outpourings of a blackbird fluting from a neighbouring tree.

Mrs. West smiled. She was very happy.

"It would be lovely to be made love to like that," continued Dorothy, "so much nicer than— — Mother, darling, look!" she broke off suddenly, clutching Mrs. West's arm. "There's John Dene."

Following the direction of her daughter's eyes, Mrs. West saw a rather thick-set man with hunched-up shoulders, looking straight in front of him, a cigar gripped aggressively between his teeth. He was walking in the direction that would bring him within a few feet of the seat on which they sat.

"He'll never see us," whispered Dorothy excitedly. "He never sees anything, not even a joke. Oh! I wish he would," she added. "I should so like you to meet him."

Mrs. West did not speak; she was gazing with interest at the approaching figure.

"Mother dear, do you think you could faint?" Dorothy's eyes were shining with excitement.

"Faint!" echoed Mrs. West.

"Yes, then I could call for help and John Dene would come, and you would get to know him. I'm sure he'll never see us."

"Hush, dear, he might hear what you are saying," said Mrs. West.

When John Dene was within a few feet of them, Dorothy's sunshade fell forward, seeming to bring him back with a start to his surroundings. Instinctively he stepped forward, picked up the sunshade and lifting his hat handed it to Dorothy. For a moment there was a puzzled expression in his eyes, followed instantly by one of recognition; and then John Dene smiled, and Mrs. West liked him.

"You see, I found my way," he said to Dorothy when she had introduced him to her mother, and for some reason she blushed.

"We often come here," said Dorothy lamely, conscious that her mother's eyes were upon her.

"It's fine. I've just been looking around," he remarked, as he took a seat beside Mrs. West. "We haven't anything like this in Can'da," he added generously.

"I suppose you have parks, though," said Mrs. West conversationally.

"Sure," he replied; "but this is way beyond anything we've got."

"You don't think it wants gingering-up then, Mr. Dene," asked Dorothy demurely.

"Dorothy!" expostulated Mrs. West in shocked tones; but John Dene merely looked at her, at first without understanding and then, seeing the point of her remark, he smiled right into her eyes, and again Dorothy blushed and dropped her eyes.

"You see," he said, turning to Mrs. West, "we're a new country and it doesn't matter a bean to us how a thing was done yesterday, if some one comes along and tells us how we can do it better to-morrow, and we don't mind its getting known. That's what she meant," he added, nodding in Dorothy's direction.

"You must all feel delightfully free," murmured Mrs. West tactfully.

"Free," echoed John Dene in a tone of voice that seemed to suggest that in no place of the world was freedom so well understood as in the Dominion. "In Can'da we're just about as free as drinks at an election."

Dorothy giggled; but John Dene seemed to see nothing strange in the simile.

"You see, mother, Mr. Dene thinks we're all hopelessly old-fashioned," said Dorothy with a mischievous side-glance at John Dene; then, as he made no response, she added, "Mr. Dene can do three or four different things at the same time and—and——"

She broke off and began to poke holes in the gravel with the point of her sunshade.

"And what?" he demanded peremptorily.

"Well, we're not all so clever," she concluded, angry to feel herself flushing again. "Oh— —"

Suddenly Dorothy started forward. A little boy who had been playing about in front of them for some time past, had tripped and fallen on his face. In an instant she was down on her knees striving to soothe the child's frightened cries, and using her dainty lace-edged handkerchief to staunch the blood that oozed from a cut on his cheek.

John Dene, who had risen also, stood watching her, his usual expression changed to one of deep concern. He looked from the child to Dorothy, obviously struck by the change in her. There was knowledge and understanding of children in the way in which she handled the situation, he decided. He also noticed that she seemed quite oblivious of the fact that she was kneeling on the rough gravel to the detriment of her pretty frock.

When eventually the mother of the child had led it away pacified by the attentions of Dorothy and the largesse of John Dene, he turned to the girl.

"You like them?" he asked, nodding in the direction of the retreating infant.

"I love them," she said softly, with a dreamy look. Then catching John Dene's eye she blushed, and John Dene smiled.

For the next half-hour Mrs. West and John Dene talked, Dorothy remaining a listener. The sympathy and gentleness of Mrs. West led John Dene to talk in a way that surprised Dorothy, accustomed to his habitual suspicion of strangers—British strangers.

"Say, does this bother you any?" he enquired presently of Mrs. West, indicating the cigar from which he was puffing clouds of smoke.

"Not at all," said Mrs. West, striving to keep from choking. "I—I like smoke."

Dorothy tittered in spite of herself at the expression of martyrdom on her mother's face. John Dene turned to her enquiringly; she developed her giggle into a cough.

"But you like England, Mr. Dene?" asked Mrs. West by way of bridging the slight gulf that Dorothy's giggle had caused.

"Sure," said John Dene; "but I don't seem to be able to figure things out here as I did at T'ronto. Over there we're just as dead keen on winning this war as we are on keeping alive; but here——" He filled in the hiatus with a volume of cigar smoke.

"And don't you think we want to win the war, Mr. Dene?" asked Dorothy.

"Well, some of those dancing lizards up at the Admiralty have a funny way of showing it," was the grim rejoinder.

"Please, Mr. Dene, what is a dancing lizard?" asked Dorothy demurely, developing a design that she was making in the gravel with the end of her sunshade.

"Dorothy!" expostulated Mrs. West, and then without giving him an opportunity of replying, she continued: "but, Mr. Dene, I'm sure they are all extremely patriotic and—and——"

"Perhaps it's because I don't understand Englishmen," he conceded. "Why, the other day, when Sir Lyster took me along to see Mr. Llewellyn John about one of the biggest things that's ever likely to come his way, what do you think he talked about?"

Mrs. West shook her head, with a smile that seemed to say it was not for her to suggest what First Lords talked of.

"Pelicans!" Into that simple and unoffending word John Dene managed to precipitate whole dictionaries of contempt and disapproval.

"Pelicans!" repeated Mrs. West in surprise, whilst Dorothy turned aside to hide the smile that was in danger of becoming a laugh.

"Sure," replied John Dene. "Birds with beaks like paddle-blades," he added, as if to leave no room for misunderstanding.

"But didn't Nero fiddle while Rome burned?" enquired Dorothy mischievously.

"Maybe," was the reply, "but I'll auction it didn't put the fire out."

Dorothy laughed.

"You see, Mr. Dene," said Mrs. West gently, "different countries have different traditions——"

"I've no use for traditions," was the uncompromising rejoinder. "It seems to me that in this country every one's out to try and prevent every one else from knowing what they're thinking. I've a rare picnic to find out what Sir Lyster's thinking when I'm talking to him." He bit savagely into the end of his cigar, when turning suddenly to Mrs. West he said, "Here, will you and your daughter come and have some tea with me? I suppose we can get tea around here?" he enquired, apparently of the surrounding landscape.

"It's very kind of you, Mr. Dene," said Mrs. West sweetly. "We should be delighted, shouldn't we, Dorothy?"

"Yes, mother," said Dorothy without enthusiasm.

John Dene turned suddenly and looked at her. Again he smiled.

"Why, I hadn't thought of that," he said.

"Thought of what?" she asked.

"Why, you see enough of me all the week without my butting in on your holidays."

"Oh, Mr. Dene!" cried Dorothy reproachfully, "how can you be so unkind? Now we shall insist upon your taking us to tea, won't we, mother?"

Mrs. West smiled up at John Dene who had risen. "I'm afraid we can't let you off now, Mr. Dene," she said sweetly.

"Well, I take it, I shan't be tugging at the halter," he said, as they walked towards where the pagoda reared its slim, un-English body above the trees.

Having found a table and ordered tea, John Dene looked about him appreciatively.

"We haven't got anything like this in T'ronto," he repeated, as if anxious to give full justice to the old country for at least one unique feature.

"Thank you for that tribute," said Dorothy demurely.

"But it's true," said John Dene, turning to her.

"But you don't always say a thing just because it's true, do you?" she enquired.

"Sure," was the uncompromising response.

"But," continued Dorothy, "suppose one day I was looking very plain and unattractive, would you tell me of it?"

"You couldn't."

This was said with such an air of conviction that Dorothy felt her cheeks burn, and she lowered her eyes. John Dene, she decided, could be extremely embarrassing. His conversation seemed to consist of one-pound notes: he had no small change.

For some time she remained silent, again leaving the conversation to John Dene and her mother. He was telling her something of his early struggles and adventures, first in Canada, then in America and finally in Canada again. How he had lost both his parents when a child, and had been adopted by an uncle and aunt who, apparently, made no attempt to disguise the fact that they regarded him as an expensive nuisance. At twelve he had run away, determined to carve out his own career, "And I did it," he concluded.

"But how did you manage to do it in the time?" asked Mrs. West.

"I was thirty-seven last fall. I began at twelve. You can do a rare lot in twenty-five years—if you don't happen to have too many ancestors hanging around," he added grimly.

"I think you are very wonderful," was Mrs. West's comment, and John Dene knew she meant it.

"If I'd been in this country," he remarked with a return of his old self-assertiveness, "I'd probably be driving a street-car, or picking up cigarette-stubs."

"Why?" enquired Mrs. West, puzzled at the remark.

"You can't jump over a wall when you're wearing leaden soles on your boots," was the terse rejoinder.

"And haven't you sometimes missed not having a mother?" enquired Mrs. West gently, tears in her sympathetic eyes at the thought of this solitary man who had never known the comforts of a home. "She would have been proud of you."

"Would she?" he enquired simply, as he crumbled his cake and threw it to a flurry of birds that was hopefully fluttering on the fringe of the tables.

"A son's success means more to a mother than anything else," said Mrs. West.

"I seem to have been hustling around most of my time," said John Dene. "I'm always working when I'm not asleep. Perhaps I haven't felt it as much — —"

He left the sentence uncompleted; but there was a look in his eyes that was not usually there.

Mrs. West sighed with all a mother's sympathy for a lonely man.

"Do you like birds, Mr. Dene?" asked Dorothy.

"Why, sure," he replied, "I like all animals. That's what I don't understand about you over here," he continued.

"But we love animals," said Mrs. West.

"I mean stag and fox-hunting." There was a hard note in his voice. "If I had a place in this country and anyone came around hunting foxes on my land, there'd be enough trouble to keep the whole place from going to sleep for the next month."

"What should you do?" enquired Dorothy wickedly.

"Well, if anything had to be killed that day it wouldn't be the fox."

"I'm afraid you wouldn't be very popular with your neighbours," said Dorothy.

"I don't care a pea-nut whether I'm popular or not," he said grimly; "but they'd have to sort of learn that if they wanted to run foxes, they must go somewhere else than on my land."

Dorothy decided that the English county that opened its gates to John Dene would have an unexpectedly exciting time. Mentally she pictured him, a revolver in each hand, holding up a whole fox-hunt, the sudden reining in of horses, the shouting of the huntsman and the master, whilst the dogs streamed across the country after their quarry. Perhaps it was as well, she decided, that John Dene had no intention of settling in England.

"This has been fine," said John Dene after a long silence, during which the three seemed content to enjoy the beauty of the afternoon. "I wonder if you — —" Then he paused, as he looked across at Mrs. West.

"You wonder if I would what, Mr. Dene?" she asked with a smile.

"I was just going to invite you to dine with me," continued John Dene, "only I remembered that your daughter probably has enough of me——"

"If you word all your invitations like that," said Dorothy, "we shall accept every one, shan't we, mother?"

Mrs. West smiled.

"Say, that's bully," he cried. "We'll get a taxi and drive back. I'd hate to spoil a good day by dining alone;" and he called for his bill.

"That's the third time I've seen that little man this afternoon," said Dorothy, lowering her voice as a man in a blue suit and light boots paused a few yards in front of them to read the label on a tree. "Isn't it funny how one runs across the same person time after time?"

"Sure," said John Dene. There was in his voice a note of grimness that neither Dorothy nor Mrs. West seemed to detect.

At the main gates they secured a taxi. As they hummed eastward, Dorothy noticed that the heavy preoccupied look, so characteristic of John Dene's face had lifted. He smiled more frequently and looked about him, not with that almost fierce penetrating glance to which she had been accustomed; but with a look of genuine interest.

"If it wouldn't bother you any," said John Dene, suddenly leaning across to Mrs. West, "I'd like to get an automobile, and perhaps you'd show me one or two places I ought to see. I'd be glad if——" He looked at her and smiled.

"It's very kind of you——" began Mrs. West.

"Of course I don't want to butt-in," he said a little hastily.

"Am I included in the invitation?" asked Dorothy quietly.

"Sure," he replied, looking at her a little surprised. Then, seeing the twitching at the corners of her mouth, he smiled.

"Then that's fixed up," he said. "I'll have an automobile for next Saturday, and you shall arrange where we're to go."

"But you mustn't joy-ride," said Dorothy, suddenly remembering D.O.R.A. and all her Don't's.

"Mustn't what?" demanded John Dene, in the tone of a man who finds his pleasures suddenly threatened from an unexpected angle.

"It's forbidden to use petrol for pleasure," she explained.

John Dene made a noise in his throat that, from her knowledge of him, Dorothy recognised as a sign that someone was on the eve of being gingered-up.

"I'll get that automobile," he announced; and Dorothy knew that there was trouble impending for Mr. Blair.

"And we'll have a picnic-hamper, shall we?" she cried excitedly.

"Sure," replied John Dene, "I'll order one."

"Oh, won't that be lovely, mother!" she cried, clapping her hands.

Mrs. West smiled her pleasure.

"Where are you taking us to dinner?" enquired Dorothy of John Dene.

"The Ritzton," he replied.

"Oh, but we're not dressed for that!"

"It's war time and I never dress," he announced, as if that settled the matter.

"But—" began Mrs. West hesitatingly.

"Perhaps you'd rather not come?" he began tentatively, his disappointment too obvious to disguise.

"Oh, but we want to come!" said Mrs. West, "only we're not in quite the right clothes for the Ritzton, are we?"

"Don't you worry," he reassured her; then a moment later added, "that's what I'm up against in this country. Everybody's putting on the clothes they think other people expect them to wear. If people don't like my clothes, they can look where I'm not sitting. We're not going to win this war by wearing clothes," he announced.

Then Dorothy started to gurgle. The picture of endeavouring to win the war without clothes struck her as comical.

"Dorothy!" admonished Mrs. West.

"I—I was just thinking, mother."

"Thinking of what?" asked John Dene.

"I was just wondering how Sir Lyster would look trying to win the war without clothes," and she trailed off into a splutter of laughter.

"Dorothy!" Mrs. West turned to John Dene with a comical look of concern. "I'm afraid my daughter is in one of her wilful moods to-day, Mr. Dene," she explained.

"She'll do as she is," he announced with decision

And again Dorothy felt her cheeks burn.

"I like Mr. Dene," announced Mrs. West that night as she and Dorothy sat at the open window of the drawing-room before going to bed.

"So you approve of your future son-in-law, mother mine, I'm so glad," said Dorothy.

"You mustn't say such things, my dear," expostulated Mrs. West.

"I'm afraid I shall have to do the proposing though," Dorothy added.

"It was very strange, meeting Mr. Dene to-day," remarked Mrs. West half to herself.

"Very," remarked Dorothy, and she hastened to talk of something else.

That night John Dene dreamed he was a little boy again, and had fallen down and hurt himself, and a beautiful lady had knelt beside him and kissed him. He awakened with a start just as the lady had turned into Dorothy, with her note-book, asking if there were any more letters.

CHAPTER XI.
THE STRANGENESS OF JOHN DENE

"Here, I'm being trailed."

Mr. Blair looked up from his writing-table with a startled expression as John Dene burst into his room. In entering a room John Dene gave the impression of first endeavouring to break through the panels, and appearing to turn the handle only as an afterthought.

"Trailed," repeated Mr. Blair in an uncomprehending manner.

John Dene stood looking down at him accusingly, as if he were responsible.

"Yes, trailed, watched, tracked, shadowed, followed, bumped-into, trodden-on," snapped John Dene irritably. He was annoyed that a man occupying an important position should not be able to grasp his meaning without repetition. "You know anything about it?" he demanded.

Mr. Blair merely shook his head.

"He in?" John Dene jerked his head in the direction of Sir Lyster's room.

"He's—he's rather busy," began Mr. Blair.

"Oh, shucks!" cried John Dene, and striding across to the door he passed into Sir Lyster's room. "Morning," he cried, as Sir Lyster looked up from his table. "Someone's following me around again," he announced, "and I want to know whether it's you or them."

"Me or who?" queried Sir Lyster.

"Whether it's some of your boys, or the other lot."

After a moment's reflection Sir Lyster seemed to grasp John Dene's meaning. "I'll make enquiry," he said suavely.

"Well, you might suggest that it doesn't please me mightily. I don't like being trailed in this fashion, so if it's any of your boys just you whistle 'em off."

"I doubt if you would be aware of the fact if we were having you shadowed, Mr. Dene," said Sir Lyster quietly, "and in any case it would be for your own safety."

"When John Dene can't take care of himself," was the reply, "he'd better give up and start a dairy."

"How is the *Destroyer* progressing?" enquired Sir Lyster with the object of changing the conversation.

"Fine," was the reply. "Your man had better be ready on Friday. One of my boys'll pick him up, Jim Grant's his name."

"Sir Goliath Maggie has appointed Commander Ryles," said Sir Lyster.

"Well, let him be ready by Friday. Grant'll pick him up on his way north. Your man can't mistake him, little chap with red hair all over him. Don't forget to call off your boys;" and with that John Dene was gone.

Ten minutes later Sir Bridgman North found the First Lord sitting at his table, apparently deep in thought.

"I can see John Dene's been here," laughed Sir Bridgman. "You and Blair both show all the outward visible signs of having been 'gingered-up.'"

Sir Lyster smiled feebly. He felt that Sir Bridgman was wearing the joke a little threadbare.

"He's been here about one of his men picking up Ryles on his way to Auchinlech," said Sir Lyster. "A little man with red hair all over him was his description."

"That seems pretty comprehensive," remarked Sir Bridgman. "He'd better go right through and pick up Ryles at Scapa. They'll probably appreciate him there. It's rather dull for 'em."

"I take it that Mr. Dene will follow in a day or two. It——" Sir Lyster paused; then, seeing that he was expected to finish his sentence, he added, "It will really be something of a relief. He quite upset Rickards a few days ago over some requisitions. I've never known him so annoyed."

"Profane, you mean," laughed Sir Bridgman. "What happened?"

"Apparently he objected to being called a dancing lizard, and told to quit his funny work." Sir Lyster smiled as if finding consolation in the fact that another had suffered at the hands of John Dene.

"It's nothing to what he did to poor old Rayner," laughed Sir Bridgman. "A dear old chap, you know, but rather of the old blue-water school."

Sir Lyster nodded. He remembered that Admiral Rayner seemed to take a delight in reminding him of his civilian status. With Sir Lyster he was always as technical in his language as a midshipman back from his first cruise.

"Rayner wanted to fit up the Toronto with an Archie gun, and John Dene told him to cut it out. Rayner protested that he was the better judge and all that sort of thing. John Dene ended by telling poor old Rayner that next time he'd better come in a dressing-gown, as he'd be damned if gold bands went with the colour of his skin. Rayner hasn't been civil to anyone since;" and Sir Bridgman laughed loudly.

"I think my sympathies are with Rayner," smiled Sir Lyster, as Sir Bridgman moved towards the door. "Frankly, I don't like John Dene."

"Don't like him! Why?"

"Well," Sir Lyster hesitated for the fraction of a second, "he will persist in treating us as equals."

"Now I call that damned nice of him;" and Sir Bridgman left the First Lord gazing at the panels of the door that closed behind him.

Whilst Sir Lyster and Sir Bridgman were discussing his unconventional methods with admirals, John Dene had returned to his office and was working at high pressure. Sometimes Dorothy wondered if his energy were like the widow's cruse. Finishing touches had to be put to everything. Instructions had to be sent to Blake as to where to pick up Grant and Commander Ryles, and a hundred and one things "rounded-off," as John Dene phrased it.

During his absence, Dorothy was to be at the office each day until lunch time to attend to any matters that might crop up. If John Dene required anything, it was arranged that he would wireless for it, and Dorothy was to see that his instructions were carried out to the letter.

The quality about John Dene that had most impressed Dorothy was his power of concentration. He would become so absorbed in his work that nothing else seemed to have the power of penetrating to his brain. A question addressed to him that was unrelated to what was in hand he would ignore, appearing not to have heard it; on the other hand a remark germane to the trend of his thoughts would produce an instant reply. It appeared as if his mind were so attuned as to throw off all extraneous matter.

His quickness of decision and amazing vitality Dorothy found bewildering, accustomed as she was to the more methodical procedure of a Government department. "When you know all you're likely to know about a thing, then make up your mind," he had said on one occasion. He had "no use for" a man who would wait until to-morrow afternoon to see how things looked then. "I sleep on a bed, not on an idea," was another of his remarks that she remembered, and once when commenting upon the cautiousness of Sir Lyster Grayne he had said, "The man who takes risks makes dollars."

Gradually Dorothy had fallen under the spell of John Dene's masterful personality. She found herself becoming critical of others by the simple process of comparing them with the self-centred John Dene.

She would smile at his eccentricities, his intolerance, his supreme belief in himself, and his almost fanatical determination to "ginger-up" any and every one in the British Empire whose misfortune it was to exist outside the Dominion of Canada.

At odd moments he told her much about Canada, and how little that country was understood in England. How blind British statesmen were to the fact that the eyes of many Canadians were turned anxiously towards the great republic upon their borders; how in the rapid growth of the U.S.A. they saw a convincing argument in favour of a tightening of the bonds that bound the Dominion to the Old Country.

When on the subject he would stride restlessly up and down the room, snapping out short, sharp sentences of protest and criticism. His Imperialism was that of the enthusiast. To him a Canada lost to the British Empire meant a British Empire lost to itself. His great idea was to see the Old Country control the world by virtue of its power, its brain and its justice.

His memory was amazing. If Dorothy found her notes obscure, and to complete a sentence happened to insert a word that was not the one he had dictated, John Dene would note it as he read the letter with a little grunt, sometimes of approval, sometimes of doubt or correction.

There were times when she felt, as she expressed it to her mother, as if she had been dining off beef essence and oxygen. Sometimes she wondered where John Dene obtained all his amazing vitality. He was a small eater, seeming to regard meals as a waste of time, and he seldom drank anything but water.

At the end of the day Dorothy would feel more tired than she had ever felt before; but she had caught something of John Dene's enthusiasm, which seemed to carry her along and defy the fatigues of the body. Had it not been for the Saturday afternoons, and the whole day's rest on Sunday, she felt that she would not have been able to continue.

In his intolerance John Dene was sometimes amusing, sometimes monotonous; but always uncompromising. One day Dorothy ventured a word of expostulation. He had just been expressing his unmeasured contempt for Mr. Blair.

"You mustn't judge the whole British Navy by Mr. Blair," she said, looking up from her note-book with a smile.

"One fool makes many," he had snapped decisively.

"So that if I prove a fool," continued Dorothy quietly, "it convicts you of being a fool also."

"But that's another transaction," he objected.

"Is it?" she asked, and became absorbed in her notes.

For some time John Dene had continued to dictate. Presently he stopped in the middle of a letter. "I hadn't figured it out that way," he said.

Dorothy looked up at him in surprise, then she realised that he was referring to her previous remark, and that he was making the amende honorable.

His manner frequently puzzled Dorothy. At times he seemed unaware of her existence; at others she would, on looking up from her work, find him regarding her intently. He showed entire confidence in her discretion, allowing her access to documents of a most private and confidential nature.

For week after week they worked incessantly. Dorothy was astonished at the mass of detail requisite for the commissioning of a ship. Indents for stores and equipment had to be prepared for the Admiralty, reports from Blake read and replied to, requisitions for materials required had to be confirmed, samples obtained, examined, and finally passed, and instructions sent to Blake. Strange documents they seemed to Dorothy, rendered bewildering by their technicalities, and flung at her in short, jerky sentences as John Dene strode up and down the room.

"If you could only see John Dene prancing, mother mine," said Dorothy one day to Mrs. West, "and the demure Dorothy taking down whole dictionaries of funny words she never even knew existed, you'd be a proud woman."

Mrs. West had smiled at her daughter, as she sat at her favourite place on a stool at her feet.

"You see, what John Dene wants is managing," continued Dorothy sagely, "and no one understands how to do it except Sir Bridgman and me. With us he'll stand without hitching."

"Stand without what, dear," asked Mrs. West.

"Without hitching," laughed Dorothy. "That's one of his phrases. It means that he's so tame that he'll eat out of your hand;" and she laughed gaily at the puzzled look on her mother's face.

"Mr. Dene has been very kind," said Mrs. West presently. "I should miss him very much if he went away." There was regret in her voice.

"Now, mother, no poaching," cried Dorothy. "John Dene is mine for keeps, and if I let you come out with us and play gooseberry, you mustn't try and cut me out, because," looking critically at her mother, "you could if you liked. Nobody could help loving my little Victorian white mouse;" and she hugged her mother's knee, missing the faint flush of pleasure that her words had aroused.

Finding his welcome assured, John Dene had taken to joining Dorothy and her mother on their Saturday and Sunday excursions. The picnic had proved a great success, and Dorothy had been surprised at the change in John Dene's manner. The hard, keen look of a man who is thinking how he can bring off some deal was entirely absent. He seemed always ready to smile and be amused. Once he had almost laughed. She was touched by the way in which he always looked after her mother, his gentleness and solicitude.

"Wessie, darling," Marjorie Rogers had said one day, "you're taming the bear. He'll dance soon; but, my dear, his boots," and the comical grimace that had accompanied the remark had caused Dorothy to laugh in spite of herself.

"If ever I marry a man," continued Marjorie, "it will be because of his boots. Let him have silk socks and beautiful shoes or boots, and I am as clay in his hands. For such a man I would sin like a 'temporary.'"

"Marjorie, you're a little idiot," cried Dorothy.

"I saw John Dene a few days ago," continued Marjorie.

"Did you?"

"Yes, and I stopped him."

"You didn't, Marjorie." There was incredulity in Dorothy's voice.

"Didn't I, though," was the retort. "I gave him a hint, too."

"A hint." Dorothy felt uncomfortable. The downrightness of Marjorie Rogers was both notorious and embarrassing.

"Well," nonchalantly, "I just said that at the Admiralty men always kept their secretaries well-supplied with flowers and chocolates."

"You little beast!" cried Dorothy, remembering the chocolates and flowers that had recently been reaching her. "I should like to slap you."

"Why not give me one of the chocolates instead," said Marjorie imperturbably. "I saw the box directly I came in," nodding at a large white and gold box that Dorothy had unsuccessfully striven to hide beneath a filing-cabinet as Marjorie entered. "If it hadn't been for me you wouldn't have had them at all," she added. Presently she was munching chocolates contentedly, whilst Dorothy found herself hating both the chocolates and flowers.

At the end of the fifth week Blake wrote that the *Destroyer* would be ready for sea on the following Wednesday. The effect of the news upon John Dene was curious. Instead of appearing elated at the near approach of the fruition of his schemes, he sat at his table for fully half an hour looking straight in front of him. When at last he spoke, it was to enquire of Dorothy if she liked men in uniform.

That afternoon he worked with unflagging industry. It seemed to Dorothy that he was deliberately calling to mind every little detail that had for some reason or other temporarily been put aside. He seemed to be determined to leave no loose ends. Such matters as he was unable to clear up himself, he gave elaborate instructions to Dorothy that would enable her to act without reference to him. At half-past five, after a final glance round the room, he leaned back in his chair.

"I shall sleep some to-night," he remarked.

"Don't you always sleep?" enquired Dorothy.

"I sleep better when there are no loose ends tickling my brain," was the reply.

As Dorothy left the office a few minutes after six he called her back.

"If I've forgotten anything you'd best remind me."

"Mother," she remarked, when she got home that evening, "John Dene's the funniest man in all the world."

"Is he, dear?" said Mrs. West non-committally.

Dorothy nodded her head with decision. "He wastes an awful lot of time, and then he hustles like—like—well, you know."

"How do you mean, dear?" queried Mrs. West.

"Well, he'll sit sometimes for an hour looking at nothing. It's not complimentary when I'm there," she added.

"Perhaps he's thinking," suggested Mrs. West.

"Oh, no!" Dorothy shook her head with decision. "He thinks while he's eating. You can see him do it. That's why he thinks salmon is pink cod. No; John Dene is a very remarkable man; but he'd be very trying as a husband."

Dorothy spoke lightly; but during the last few days she had been asking herself what she would do when John Dene was gone. Sometimes she would sit and ponder over it, then with a movement of impatience she would plunge once more into her work. What was John Dene to her that she should miss him? He was just her employer, and in a few months he would go back to Canada, and she would never see him again. One morning she awakened crying from a dream in which John Dene had just said good-day to her and stepped on a large steamer labelled "To Canada." That day she was almost brusque in her manner, so much so that John Dene had asked her if she were not well.

The next morning when Dorothy arrived at the office, she found John Dene sitting at his table. As she entered, he looked round, stared at her for a moment and then nodded, and as if as an after-thought added, "Good morning."

Dorothy passed into her own room. She was a little puzzled. This was the first morning that John Dene had been there before her.

As she came out with her note-book she looked at him closely, conscious of something in his manner that was strange, something she could not altogether define. His voice seemed a little husky, and he lacked the quick bird-like movements so characteristic of him.

She made no remark, however, merely seating herself in her customary place and waited for letters.

He drew from his pocket some notes and began to dictate.

Never before had he used notes when dictating. Several times she glanced at him, and noted that he appeared to be reading from the manuscript rather than dictating; but she decided that he had probably written out rough drafts in order to assure accuracy. His voice was very strange.

"Did you sleep well last night, Mr. Dene?" she enquired during a pause in the dictation.

"Sleep well," he repeated, looking up at her, "I always sleep well."

Dorothy was startled. There was something in the glance and the brusque tone that puzzled her. Both were so unlike John Dene. She had mentally decided that he spoke to her as he spoke to no one else. She had compared his inflection when addressing her with that he adopted to others, even so important a person as Sir Bridgman North. Now he spoke gruffly, as if he were irritated at being spoken to.

Apparently he sensed what was passing through her mind, for he turned to her again and said:

"I'm not feeling very well this morning, Miss West, I——" Then he hesitated.

"Perhaps you didn't sleep very well," she suggested mischievously.

"No, I'm afraid that's what it was," he acknowledged Dorothy's eyes opened just a little in surprise. A minute ago he had stated that he always slept well. Either John Dene was mad or ill; and Dorothy continued to take down, greatly puzzled. Had he been drugged? The thought caused her to pause in her work and glance up at him. He certainly seemed vague and uncertain, and then he looked so strange.

When he had dictated for about half an hour, John Dene handed her a large number of documents to copy, telling her that there would not be any more letters that day. To her surprise he picked up his hat and announced that he would not be back until five o'clock to sign the letters. Never before had he missed lunching at his office. Dorothy was now convinced that something was wrong. Everything about him seemed strange and forced.

Once or twice she caught him looking at her furtively; but immediately she raised her eyes, he hastily shifted his, as if caught in some doubtful act.

At twelve o'clock lunch arrived, and Dorothy had to confess to herself that it was a lonely and unsatisfactory meal.

At five o'clock John Dene returned and signed the letters with a rubber stamp, which he had recently adopted.

"When are you going away, Mr. Dene?" asked Dorothy.

"I don't know," he responded gruffly.

"I merely asked because two people on the telephone enquired when you were going away."

"And what did you say?"

"Oh, I just said what you told me. A man called this afternoon also with the same question."

For a moment he looked at her, then turning on his heel said "good evening," and with a nod walked out.

Dorothy had expected him to make some remark about these enquiries. She knew that John Dene had no friends in London, and the questions as to when he was going away had struck her as strange.

The next day was a repetition of the first. A few letters were dictated, a sheaf of documents handed to her to copy, and John Dene disappeared. Again lunch was brought for her, which she ate alone, and at five o'clock he came in and signed the letters.

By this time Dorothy was convinced that he was ill. The strain of the past few weeks had evidently been telling on him. When he had signed the last letter she bluntly enquired if he felt better.

"Better?" he interrogated. "I haven't been ill."

"I thought you didn't seem quite well," said Dorothy hesitatingly; but he brushed aside the enquiry by picking up his hat and bidding her "good evening."

Dorothy was feeling annoyed and a little hurt; and preserved an attitude of businesslike brevity in all her remarks to John Dene. If he chose to adopt the attitude of the uncompromising employer, she on her part would humour him by becoming an ordinary employee. Still she had to confess to herself that the old pleasure in her work had departed. Hitherto she had looked forward to her arrival at the office, the coming of John Dene, their luncheons together and the occasional little chats that were sandwiched in between her work.

She had become deeply interested in the *Destroyer* and what it would achieve in the war. She had been flattered by the confidence that John Dene had shown hi her discretion, and had felt that she was "doing her bit." Again, the sense of being behind the scenes pleased her. She was conscious of knowing secrets that were denied even to Cabinet Ministers. The members of the War Cabinet knew less than she did about the *Destroyer* and what was expected of it.

John Dene was a man who did everything thoroughly. If he trusted anyone, he did it implicitly; if he distrusted anyone, he did it uncompromisingly. Where he liked, he liked to excess; where he disliked, he disliked to the elimination of all good qualities. Half measures did not exist for John Dene of Toronto.

When Dorothy discovered that all the old intimacy had passed away, and John Dene had become merely an employer, treating her as a secretary, she was conscious that the glamour had fallen from her work. Somehow or other the *Destroyer* had receded into something impersonal, whereas hitherto it had appeared to her as if she had been in some way or other intimately associated with it.

It was all very strange and very puzzling, she told herself. Sometimes she wondered if she had done anything to annoy him. Then she told herself that there was something more than personal pique in his manner. His whole bearing seemed to have changed, as if he had decided to regard her merely as a piece of mechanism, just as he did the typewriter, or his office chair.

It was at this period of her reasoning that Dorothy discovered her dignity. From that time her attitude was that of the injured woman, yet perfect secretary. Her sense of humour had deserted her, and she arrived at the office and left it very much upon her dignity. Even Mrs. West noticed the difference in her manner, and at last enquired if anything were wrong, or if she were unwell; but Dorothy reassured her with a hug and a kiss, and for the rest of that evening had been particularly bright and vivacious.

When Mrs. West mentioned the name of John Dene, Dorothy did not pursue the topic, although Mrs. West failed to notice that she was switched off to other subjects.

At the end of the week she noticed that John Dene handed her the week's salary in notes. Hitherto it had been his custom to place the money in an envelope and put it on her table. She concluded that this new method was to impress upon her that she was a dependent, and that the old relationship between them had been severed. That evening, Dorothy was always paid on the Friday evening, she held her head very high when she left the office. If Mr. John Dene required decorum, then he should have it in plenty from his secretary.

The next morning and the Monday following, Dorothy was very much on her dignity. She seemed suddenly to have become imbued with all the qualities of the perfect secretary. No hint of a smile was allowed to wanton across her features, she was grave, ceremonial, efficient. She worked harder than ever and, when she had finished the tasks John Dene set her, she manufactured others so that her time should be fully occupied.

For a day and a half she laboured to show John Dene that she was offended; but apparently he was oblivious, not only of having offended her, but of the fact that she was endeavouring to convey to him the change that had come about in their relations.

On the Monday evening he did not return to sign his letters until nearly six. By that time Dorothy was almost desperate in her desire to show this obtuse man that she was annoyed with him. She felt at the point of tears when he bade her good night and left the office, just as Big Ben was booming out the hour.

She would go home and forget all about the stupid creature, Dorothy decided, as she hastily put on her coat and dug the hat-pins through her hat. On reaching the street she saw John Dene standing at the corner of Charles Street. For a moment she thrilled. Was he waiting for her? No, he was looking in the opposite direction, apparently deep in thought. She saw a taxi draw up beside him. The driver, a little man with a grey moustache, Dorothy remembered to have seen him several times "crawling" about on the look-out for fares. The taxi stopped and the man bent towards John Dene. Dorothy stood and watched. John Dene was right in her line of route to the Piccadilly Tube, and she did not wish him to see her.

For a moment John Dene seemed to hesitate, then with a word to the driver he opened the door and got in. Suddenly Dorothy remembered Colonel Walton's warning. Impulsively she started forward, just as the taxi started and a moment later whizzed swiftly past her. John Dene was evidently in a hurry. At that moment her attention was distracted by shouts and a smash. A small run-about car had suddenly dashed across Regent Street from the west side of Charles Street and crashed into the forepart of another taxi. A crowd gathered, a policeman arrived, and she had a vision of an angry taxi-driver, another man pointing to the roadway, as if the blame lay there, whilst the passenger from the taxi was running towards the Florence Nightingale statue shouting and waving his arms at the vehicles passing along Pall Mall.

Slowly Dorothy turned and pursued her way up Regent Street. She was tired and—and, oh! it was so stupid, going on living.

That night as she was undressing she remembered the passenger from the second taxi. Why had he been so interested in the taxi that was bearing John Dene away, and why had he tried to signal to other vehicles passing along Pall Mall? He had seemed greatly excited. Above all, why had John Dene taken a taxi when he had been warned against it?

CHAPTER XII.
THE DESTROYER READY FOR SEA

James Blake stood in the bows of the *Toronto* gazing down at the long, cigar-shaped object that lay like a huge grey cocoon reposing in her bowels. The morrow would see the *Destroyer* floated out to carry her three hundred odd feet of menace into the blues and greys of the ocean.

Blake was a man upon whom silence had descended as a blight; heavy of build, slow of thought, ponderous of movement, he absorbed all and apparently gave out nothing. His most acute emotion he expressed by fingering the right-hand side of his ragged beard, whilst his eyes seemed to smoulder as his thoughts slowly took shape.

As he gazed down at the grey shape of the *Destroyer's* hull, there was in his eyes a strange look of absorption. For nearly two years he had lived for the *Destroyer*. It had been wife and family to him, home and holiday, labour and recreation, food and drink. Nothing else mattered, because nothing else was. The war existed only in so far as it was concerned with the *Destroyer*. It was the *mise en scêne* for this wonder-boat. It was to be her setting, just as a stage is the setting for a play.

As he gazed down at her, he fumbled in the pocket of his pilot-jacket and drew forth a cigar, one of a box that John Dene had sent him. Slowly and deliberately he pulled out his jack-knife, cut off the end and, taking a good grip of the cigar with his teeth, lighted it, all without once raising his eyes from the *Destroyer*.

As he puffed clouds of smoke for the breeze to pick up and scurry off with to the west, he thought lovingly of the work of the last two years, of the last month in particular. Never had men worked as had James Blake and his "boys." It was not for country or for gain that they slaved and sweated; it was not patriotism or pride of race that caused them to work until forced, by sheer inability to keep awake, to lie down for a few hours' sleep, always within sound of their comrades' hammers, often beside the *Destroyer* herself. It was "the Boss" for whom they worked. They were his men, and this was their boat. Every time John Dene wrote to Blake, there was always a message for "the boys." "I know the boys will show these Britishers what Canada can do," he would write, or, "see that the boys get all they want and plenty to smoke." Remembering was John Dene's long suit; and his men would do anything for "the Boss."

Blake had not spared himself. When not engaged in the work of overseeing, he had thrown off his coat and worked with the most vigorous. He seemed never to sleep or rest. Every detail of the *Destroyer's* construction he carried in his head. Plans there had been in his shack; but what were the use of plans to a man who had every line, every bolt and nut engraved upon his brain. He had them merely for reference.

And now all was ready. That morning the *Destroyer* had been floated into the *Toronto* to see that everything on the mother-ship was in order. Once floated out again, there remained only the taking on board stores and munitions. These lay piled upon the *Toronto's* deck ready at the word of command to be transferred to the *Destroyer*.

In design the *Destroyer* was very similar to the latest form of submarine: 310 ft. 6 ins. in length, she had a breadth of 26 ft. 6. ins. amidships, tapering to a point fore and aft. She carried two ordinary torpedo tubes and mounted two 3 in. guns; but these were in the nature of an auxiliary armament. Her main armament consisted of eight pneumatic-tubes, two in the bows, two in the stern, one on either bow and one on either beam. These fired small arrow-headed missiles, rather like miniature torpedoes fitted with lance-heads for cutting through nets. They had sufficient power to penetrate the plates of a submarine, and were furnished with an automatic detonator, which caused the bursting charge to explode three seconds after impact. The charge was sufficient to blow a hole in the side of a "U"-boat large enough to ensure its immediate destruction.

These projectiles were rendered additionally deadly by the fact that their heads became automatically magnetic as they sped through the water. Thus the target against which they were launched achieved its own destination. They were fitted with small gyroscopes to keep them straight until the magnetic-heads began to exert a dominating influence.

Amidships was the conning-tower, with its four searchlights, so arranged as to be capable of being used singly or together. Thus it was possible to illuminate the waters for half a mile in every direction. Above the conning-tower were two collapsible periscopes, and beneath it the central ballast, beneath which lay the charge of T.N.T. that John Dene had boasted would send the *Destroyer* to Kingdom Come should she ever be in danger of capture.

Abaft the conning-tower were the engines, a switchboard, and finally the berths of the engine-room staff. For'ard of the conning-tower were the berths of the crew, and still further for'ard were those of John Dene and the officers. John Dene's invention of a new and lighter storage-battery had enabled him to control the *Destroyer* entirely by electricity. She possessed an endurance of fifteen-hundred miles, and as for the most part she held a watching brief, this would mean that she could remain at sea for a month or more.

Her speed submerged was fourteen knots, which gave her a superiority over the fastest German craft, and she could remain submerged for two days. She could then recharge her compressed-air chambers without coming to the surface by means of a tube, through which fresh air could be sucked from the surface, and the foul discharged. These were weighted and floated in various parts in such a manner that they could be thrown out in a diagonal direction. The object of this was to protect the *Destroyer* from depth-charges in the event of her whereabouts being discovered by an enemy ship, which would render it dangerous for her to come to the surface.

"The *Destroyer's* a submarine," John Dene had remarked, "and submarines fight and live under water and not on it."

Consequently in designing the *Destroyer* he had first considered the special requirements entailed by the novelty of the methods she would employ. She had deck-guns, periscopes and torpedo-tubes; but they were in every sense subsidiary to those qualities that rendered her unique among boats capable of submersion, viz., her searchlights and her magnetic projectiles. Under water there were only two dangers capable of threatening her—mines and depth-charges. Properly handled and without mishap, there was no reason why she should ever return to the surface except in the neighbourhood of her own harbour.

Her most remarkable device, however, was the microphone, so sensitive that, with the aid of her searchlights it would enable the *Destroyer* to account for any "U"-boat that came within seven or eight miles of where she was lying.

As Blake stood surveying his handiwork, he was joined by his second-in-command, Jasper Quinton, known among his intimates as "Spotty," a nickname due to the irregularity of his complexion. Quinton was an Englishman who had gone to Canada to make his fortune as a mining-engineer. Soon after war broke out he had successfully applied to John Dene for a job, and had acquitted himself so well that John Dene had taken him into his confidence in regard to the *Destroyer*, and "Jasp," as he called him, had proved "a cinch." John Dene made few mistakes about men and none about women: the one he understood, the other he avoided.

"Spotty" Quint on spat meditatively upon the hull of the *Destroyer*. He was a man to whom words came infrequently and with difficulty; but he could spit a whole gamut of emotions: anger, contempt, approval, indifference, all were represented by salivation. If he were forced to speech, he built up his phrases upon the foundation of a single word, "ruddy"; but apparently with entire unconsciousness that it had its uses as an oath. To "Spotty" Quinton, John Dene was the "ruddy boss," his invention the "ruddy *Destroyer*," the enemy the "ruddy Hun," the ocean the "ruddy water." He served out his favourite adjective with entire impartiality. He no more meant reproach to the Hun than to John Dene. He tacitly accepted them both, the one as a power for evil, the other as a power for good.

As Quinton silently took up a position by his side, Blake turned and looked at him interrogatingly.

"Ruddy masterpiece," exclaimed Quinton, spitting his admiration.

Blake gazed upon the unprepossessing features of his subordinate, and tugging a cigar from his pocket, handed it to him.

Silently "Spotty" took the cigar, bit off the end and spat it together with his thanks into the hold of the *Toronto*. He then proceeded to light the cigar. The two men turned and made their way to the cabin allotted to them as a sort of office of works. Both were thinking of the morrow when the *Destroyer* would be floated out from the parent ship ready for her first voyage. In addition to John Dene and his second-in-command, she would carry Commander Ryles, who had a distinguished record in submarine warfare. He would represent the Admiralty. John Dene had experienced some difficulty at the Admiralty over the personnel of the *Destroyer's* crew; but he had stood resolutely to his guns, and the Authorities had capitulated. This was largely due to Sir Bridgman North's wise counsels.

"When," he remarked, "I have to choose between giving John Dene his head and being gingered-up, I prefer the first. It's infinitely less painful."

Sir Lyster had been inclined to expostulate with his colleague upon the manner in which he gave way to John Dene's demands. Sir Lyster felt that the dignity of his office was being undermined by the blunt-spoken Canadian.

"Do you not think," he had remarked in the early days of the descent of John Dene upon the Admiralty, "that it would be better for us to stand up to Mr. Dene? I think the effect would be salutary."

"For us, undoubtedly," Sir Bridgman had said drily. "Personally I object to being gingered-up. Look at poor Blair. There you see the results of the process. He ceased to be an Imperialist within twenty-four hours of John Dene's coming upon the scene. Now he goes about with a hunted look in his eyes, and a prayer in his heart that he may get through the day without being gingered-up by the unspeakable John Dene."

"I really think I shall have to speak to Mr. Dene about— —" Sir Lyster had begun.

"Take my advice and don't," was the retort. "Blair and John Dene represent two epochs: Blair is the British Empire that was, John Dene is the British Empire that is to be. It's like one of Nelson's old three-deckers against a super-dreadnought, and Blair ain't the dreadnought."

"He is certainly a remarkable man," Sir Lyster had admitted conventionally, referring to John Dene.

"He's more than that, Grayne," said Sir Bridgman, "he's the first genus-patriot produced by the British Empire, possibly by the world," he added drily, proceeding to light a cigarette. "Think of it," he added half to himself, "he could have got literally millions for his invention from any of the big naval powers; yet he chooses to give it to us for nothing, and what's more he's not out for honours. Ginger or no ginger, John Dene's a man worth meeting, Grayne, on my soul he is."

Blake and Quinton seated themselves one on either side of the little wooden table in the cabin of the *Toronto* that answered as an office of works, Blake looking straight in front of him, Quinton absorbed in smoking and expectoration. Presently Blake took from his pocket a large silver watch, gazed at it with deliberation, then raising his eyes nodded to his companion. With a final expectoration, "Spotty" rose and left the cabin, walked over to the starboard side and climbed down into the motor-boat that lay there manned by her crew of three men.

Without a word the man with the boat-hook pushed off, the motor was started and the boat throbbed her way to the entrance to the little harbour. The crew of the *Destroyer* had learned from Blake the virtue of silence. For half an hour the motor-boat tore her way over the waters, heading due south. From time to time Quinton gazed ahead through a pair of binoculars.

"Starb'd," he called to the helmsman as he lowered the glass from his eyes for the twentieth time, then by way of explanation added, "The ruddy chaser." "Steady," he added a moment later.

A few minutes later a cloud of white spray indicated the approach of a small craft travelling at a high rate of speed. Quinton continued to watch the approaching boat until the humped shoulders of a submarine-chaser were distinguishable through the spume. As the boats neared each other he gave a quick command to the engineer, and the speed of the motor-boat decreased. At the same moment the curtain of spray that screened the on-coming chaser died down, her fine and sinister lines becoming discernible.

Dexterously the helmsman brought the motor-boat alongside the larger vessel and, without a word there stepped on board a little man wearing motor-goggles and a red beard of rather truculent shape, and a naval commander whom the stranger introduced to Quinton as Commander Ryles. With a nod to the man with the boathook, and a wave of his arm to those aboard the chaser, James Grant took his seat together with Commander Ryles beside Quinton, the motor-boat pushed off and, with a graceful sweep, turned her nose northwards and proceeded to run up her own track.

Grant and Quinton continued to talk in undertones, Grant asking questions, Quinton answering with great economy of words and prodigious salivation. The chaser, steering a south-westerly course, was soon out of sight.

As the motor-boat entered the little harbour, Grant's eyes eagerly fixed themselves upon the *Toronto*, seeming to take in every detail of her construction.

"Ready for the trial trip?" he enquired of Quinton.

"Sure," was the reply as he spat over the side.

"Jim there?"

Quinton jerked his thumb in the direction of the *Toronto*, for which the motor-boat was making. As they reached her the two men nimbly climbed up the side and, Quinton leading, dived below to the office of works. As they entered Blake was sitting exactly as Quinton had left him an hour and a half previously. At the sight of Grant his eyes seemed to flash; but he made no movement except to hold out his hand, which Grant gripped.

"Through with everything?" he enquired, as he seated himself, and Quinton threw himself on a locker.

"Sure," replied Blake.

"I——" began Grant, then breaking off cast a swift look over his shoulder.

Blake nodded his head comprehendingly, whilst Quinton spat in the direction of the door as if to defy eavesdroppers.

From his pocket Grant drew a map, which he proceeded to unfold upon the table. Quinton walked across and the three bent over, studying it with absorbed interest. Meanwhile Commander Ryles had been shown to his cabin.

CHAPTER XIII.
THE DISAPPEARANCE OF JOHN DENE

"No more Saturday afternoons for you and John Dene, little mother," cried Dorothy with forced gaiety as she rose from the breakfast table.

Mrs. West looked up quickly. "Why?" she asked, a falter in her voice.

"He's going away," announced Dorothy indifferently, as she pinned on her hat.

"To Canada?" asked Mrs. West anxiously.

"No," replied Dorothy in a toneless voice, "he's going away on business."

"Oh!" Mrs. West's relief was too obvious for dissimulation.

"He won't be back for months," continued Dorothy relentlessly, "and I shall spend my time in counting my fingers and flirting with Sir Bridgman. Good-byeeeeee," and brushing a kiss on her mother's cheek she was gone, leaving Mrs. West puzzled, more by her manner than the announcement she had made.

Arrived at the office Dorothy cleared up what remained of the previous night's work, ordered luncheon, tidied things generally, and then sat down to wait. From time to time she glanced at the watch upon her wrist, at first mechanically, then curiously, finally anxiously. For the last few days she had been more concerned than she was prepared to admit by John Dene's strangeness of manner. She was hurt that he should now treat her as if she were a stranger, whereas hitherto he had been so confidential and friendly.

Womanlike she ascribed it to illness. He had been over-working. He was a man of such impulsive energy, so full of ideas, so impatient of delays. He seemed always to want to do everything at the moment he thought of it. Incidentally he expected others to be imbued with his own vitality. He had worn himself out, she decided, or was it that he was being drugged? Time after time the idea had suggested itself to her, only to be dismissed as melodramatic.

Sometimes there would cross her mind a suspicion so strange, so fantastic that she would brush it aside as utterly ridiculous.

Luncheon arrived and no John Dene. Dorothy made an indifferent meal. One o'clock passed, two o'clock came. She had visions of him lying in his room at the hotel too ill to summon assistance. She determined upon action and rang up the Ritzton. To her enquiry as to whether or no Mr. John Dene were in came the reply that he was not. Would they find out at what time he left the hotel? It was his secretary speaking. Yes, they would if Dorothy would hold on.

At the end of what seemed an age came the reply: Mr. John Dene had left the hotel on the previous morning and had not since returned.

With a clatter the receiver fell from Dorothy's hand. It was something worse than illness then that had kept John Dene from his office! This she saw clearly. Probably he was lying dead in some out of the way spot, a victim of the hidden hand. She felt physically sick at the thought. He was such a splendid man, she told herself. Ready to give everything for nothing. The sort of man that made for victory.

Suddenly she remembered the episode of the taxi on the previous evening and became galvanised to action. What a fool she had been. Seizing the receiver of the private line to the Admiralty, she demanded to be put through to Mr. Blair. Presently she heard his mellow, patient voice. No, he had heard nothing of John Dene, nor had he seen him for several days. There was a note of plaintive gratitude in Mr. Blair's voice; but Dorothy was too worried to notice it.

Putting up the receiver, she snatched up her hat, jabbed the pins through it, one of them into her head, and almost throwing herself into her coat, dashed down the stairs and literally ran across Waterloo Place, down the Duke of York's steps into the Admiralty. She passed swiftly in and up to Mr. Blair's room, into which she burst with a lack of ceremony that convinced him she had already imbibed the qualities that made John Dene the terror of his existence.

"I want to see Sir Lyster at once," she panted.

Mr. Blair looked up at her in surprise.

"He's engaged just now, Miss West," he said mildly. "Is there anything I can do?"

"It doesn't matter whether he's engaged, you must go into him at once, Mr. Blair, and tell him I must see him."

Mr. Blair still continued to gaze at her with bovine wonder.

"Oh, you stupid creature!" Dorothy stamped her foot in her impatience. Then with a sudden movement she made for Sir Lyster's door, knocked and entered, leaving Mr. Blair gazing before him, marvelling that so short an association with John Dene should have produced such startling results. However, it was for Sir Lyster to snub her now, and he resumed his work.

Sir Lyster, Sir Bridgman North and Admiral Heyworth were bending over a table on which a large plan lay spread out. Sir Lyster was the first to look up; at the sight of the flushed and excited girl his gaze became fixed. Sir Bridgman and Admiral Heyworth followed the direction of his eyes to where Dorothy stood with heaving breast and fear in her eyes.

"Mr. Dene has disappeared!" she gasped without any preliminary apology.

"The devil!" exclaimed Sir Bridgman.

Admiral Heyworth jumped to his feet. Sir Bridgman rose and placed a chair for Dorothy into which she sank. Then she told her story, concluding with "It's all my fault for not doing something about the taxi." The three men listened without interruption. When she had concluded they looked anxiously from one to the other. It was Sir Bridgman who broke the silence.

"We had better get Walton here."

Sir Lyster nodded and going to the door requested Mr. Blair to ask Colonel Walton to come round at once on a matter of importance. Then it was that Sir Bridgman seemed to notice Dorothy's excited state. With that courtesy that made him a great favourite with women, he poured out a glass of water from a carafe on a side table and handed it to her. With her eyes she thanked him. Sir Bridgman decided that she was an extremely pretty girl. The water seemed to co-ordinate Dorothy's ideas. For the first time she appreciated that she had unceremoniously burst into the private room of the First Lord of the Admiralty.

"I—I'm very sorry," she faltered, "but it seemed so important, and Mr. Blair wouldn't let me come in."

Sir Lyster nodded his approval of her action. "You did quite right, Miss——"

"West," said Dorothy.

"Miss West," continued Sir Lyster. "There are occasions when——" He hesitated for a word.

"John Dene's methods are best," suggested Sir Bridgman.

Sir Lyster smiled; but there was no answering smile in Dorothy's eyes.

"What do you think has happened?" she asked, looking from one to the other.

"It's impossible to say," began Sir Lyster, "it's—it's——"

"Spies," she said with a catch in her voice. "I'm sure of it. They've drugged him. They tried to poison our food."

"Poison your food," repeated Sir Lyster uncomprehendingly.

"Yes," said Dorothy, and she proceeded to tell how it came about that the luncheon and dinners were supplied from an anonymous source.

"That's Walton," said Admiral Heyworth, and the other nodded.

For a few minutes they sat in silence, all waiting for the arrival of Colonel Walton. When the telephone bell rang, Sir Lyster started perceptibly. Taking up the receiver from the instrument he listened for a few seconds.

"Show him in," he said; then, turning to the others, he explained: "Walton is out; but Sage is here."

"Good," said Sir Bridgman, "sometimes Jack is better than his master."

Sir Lyster looked at him meaningly, and then at Dorothy.

With perfect self-possession Malcolm Sage entered, gave a short, jerky bow, and without invitation drew a chair up opposite to where Dorothy was sitting. For a moment he gazed at her and saw the anxiety in her eyes.

"Don't be alarmed," he said quietly, "the situation is well in hand." There was the ghost of a smile about the corners of his mouth.

"Is he safe?" enquired Dorothy, leaning forward, whilst the three men looked at Sage as if not quite sure of his sanity.

"I can only repeat what I have said," replied Sage, "the situation is well in hand."

"But how the devil— —" began Sir Bridgman.

"I should like to ask Miss West a few questions," said Sage.

Sir Bridgman subsided.

"Why did you come here?" he asked, turning to Dorothy.

"Mr. Dene didn't come this morning. I waited until past two, then I rang up the Ritzton," she paused.

"Go on," said Sage.

"They told me he had not been back since yesterday morning."

"And then?" enquired Sage.

"I rang up Mr. Blair. He had heard nothing, so I thought I had better come round and—and—I'm afraid I burst in here very rudely. Mr. Blair— —"

"You did quite right, Miss West," said Sir Lyster. "Why didn't you act before?"

Dorothy felt Sage's eyes were burning through her brain, so intent was his gaze. "I had forgotten about the taxi. I—I—thought he might be unwell," said Dorothy.

"Why?"

"Well," she began, and then paused.

"Go on," said Sage encouragingly.

"He has seemed rather strange for some days," she said, "his memory was very bad. As a rule he has a wonderful memory, and never makes a note."

"How was his memory bad?"

"He seemed to forget what he had written, and was always having letters turned up."

Sage nodded. "Go on," he said.

"Then," she continued, "he seemed to want always to put things off. He was undecided; so unlike his normal self. Most of the things he asked me to attend to."

"And that made you think he was ill," suggested Sage.

"Yes," she said, "that and other things."

"What other things?"

Dorothy screwed up her eyebrows, her head on one side, as if striving to find words to express what was in her mind. "His manner was strange," she began. "It is very difficult to give instances; but previously he had always been so pleasant and — and — —"

"Unconscious of himself, shall we say?" suggested Sage.

"That's it," she said brightly. "He was just Mr. Dene. Afterwards he seemed to be always watching me, as if not quite sure who I was. It was almost uncanny. I thought perhaps — —" She hesitated.

"What?"

"That he was being drugged," she concluded reluctantly.

"When did you first notice this?"

"Let me see," said Dorothy. "This is Tuesday. It was on Thursday morning that I first noticed it. What struck me then was that he said, 'Good morning' when he came in."

"And what did he usually say?" enquired Sage.

"He used to say 'morning,' or what really sounded more like 'morn,'" she said with a smile.

"Thank you," said Sage. "Unless these gentlemen have any further questions to put to you, there is nothing more to be done at present."

"But is he — —" she began, then she paused.

"I should not be unnecessarily alarmed, Miss West, if I were you," said Sage. "Above all, keep your own counsel. Mr. Dene disapproves of people who talk."

"I know," said Dorothy, rising and drawing herself up with dignity.

"I regard your prompt action as highly commendable, Miss West," said Sir Lyster. "You will, of course, continue in attendance at the office until you hear further. If anything unusual transpires, please get into touch with me immediately, even to the extent of — —" he paused a moment.

"Bursting in as you did just now," said Sir Bridgman with a laugh. "It's the real John Dene manner."

"Exactly," said Sir Lyster.

Sir Lyster conducted Dorothy into Mr. Blair's room.

"Mr. Blair," he said, "if Miss West ever wishes to see me urgently, please tell me, no matter with whom I am engaged. If I do not happen to be in, Sir Bridgman will see her, or failing that get through to Colonel Walton, or to Mr. Sage."

Sir Lyster bowed to Dorothy and returned to his room. Mr. Blair blinked his eyes in bewilderment; the influence of John Dene upon the British Admiralty was most extraordinary.

"I don't understand the drift of all your questions, Mr. Sage," said Sir Lyster, resuming his seat.

Malcolm Sage turned his eyes upon the First Lord. "I will explain that later, sir," he said, "but for the present I must ask your indulgence."

"But——" began Sir Lyster.

"I might advance a hundred theories; but until I am sure it would be better for me to keep silence. I must confer with my chief."

Sir Bridgman nodded approval.

"Quite so," said Sir Lyster. "In the meantime what is to be done?"

"Raise the hue and cry," said Sage quietly.

"Good God, man!" exclaimed Sir Bridgman. "It would give the whole game away."

"I propose," said Sage quietly, "that photographs of John Dene be inserted in every paper in the kingdom, that every continental paper likewise has full particulars of his disappearance. That you offer a thousand pounds reward for news that will lead to his discovery, and go on increasing it by a thousand every day until it reaches ten thousand." Malcolm Sage paused; his three listeners stared at him as if he were out of his senses.

"You seriously suggest this publicity?" enquired Sir Lyster in cold and even tones.

"I do," said Sage.

"You know why Mr. Dene is here."

"I do."

"And yet you still advise this course?" asked Sir Lyster.

"I do," responded Sage.

"Well, I'm damned!" said Sir Bridgman.

For a moment a flicker of a smile crossed Malcolm Sage's serious features.

"What are your reasons?" demanded Sir Lyster.

"My reasons are closely connected with my conclusions, sir, and at the present time they are too nebulous to express."

"We will consider this," said Sir Lyster with an air of concluding the interview.

Malcolm Sage rose. "The time is not one for consideration, sir," he said, "but for action. If you hesitate in this publicity, I must ask your permission to see the Prime Minister;" then with a sudden change of tone and speaking with an air of great seriousness he added, "This is a matter of vital importance. The announcement should be made in the late editions of all the evening papers, and the full story must appear in to-morrow's papers. There is not much time. Have I your permission to proceed?"

"No, sir, you have not," thundered Sir Lyster. "I shall report this matter to Colonel Walton."

"That, sir, you are quite at liberty to do," said Sage calmly. "Incidentally you might report that I have resigned from my position at Department Z. I wish you good afternoon, gentlemen," and with that Malcolm Sage left the room.

"Good Lord! Grayne, you've done it now," said Sir Bridgman. "L. J. thinks the world of that chap."

"He's a most impertinent fellow," said Sir Lyster with heat.

"Clever men frequently are," laughed Sir Bridgman. "It seems to me that everybody's getting under the influence of John Dene. I suppose it's Bolshevism," he muttered to himself.

Half an hour later Colonel Walton was seated in earnest conversation with Mr. Llewellyn John.

"It's very awkward, very awkward," said Mr. Llewellyn John; "still, you must act along your own lines. It's no good creating a department and then allowing another department to dictate to it; but it's very awkward," he added.

"It would be more awkward, sir, if Sage were allowed to go," said Colonel Walton.

"Of course, of course," said Mr. Llewellyn John, "that's unthinkable. If I were only told," he muttered, "if I were only told. They keep so much from me." Then after a pause he added, "I'm inclined to blame you, though, Walton, for not—not——" Mr. Llewellyn John hesitated.

"Keeping John Dene under proper observation," suggested Colonel Walton quietly.

"Exactly." Mr. Llewellyn John looked at him quickly.

"He was always guarded."

"Then you——" began Mr. Llewellyn John.

"Our men were tricked."

"Tricked!" Mr. Llewellyn John looked startled.

"Yes," continued Colonel Walton. "McLean was on duty that night. Immediately he saw John Dene hail a taxi, he jumped into his own taxi; but he had hardly started when he was run into by a small runabout, and the other taxi got away."

"But the number of——"

"Fictitious both, the taxi and the run-about. We thought it expedient not to detain the man who ran into McLean," Colonel Walton added.

For nearly a minute Mr. Llewellyn John sat staring at the Chief of Department Z.

"It's most unfortunate, disastrous in fact," he said at length. "We must try and get into touch with Auchinlech by wireless."

"I'm afraid it will be useless," was the response.

"There's the War Cabinet to be considered," murmured Mr. Llewellyn John to himself. "The war does not——" He hesitated.

"Make men tractable," suggested Colonel Walton helpfully.

"Exactly," agreed Mr. Llewellyn John. "They may not take the same view as Sir Lyster and myself with regard to that memorandum of ours to Dene. It's very awkward happening just now," he added, "with all this trouble about interning aliens."

"What am I to do, sir? There is very little time."

"Do," said Mr. Llewellyn John, "why run your department in your own way, Walton."

"I have an absolutely free hand?" enquired Colonel Walton.

"Absolutely," said Mr. Llewellyn John; "but I wish you could tell me more."

"To be quite frank, I'm as much in the dark as you are. Sage is as obstinate as a pack-mule and as sure-footed. He's no respecter of——"

"Prime Ministers or First Lords," suggested Mr. Llewellyn John with a smile.

"Exactly."

"Well, go your own way," said Mr. Llewellyn John; "but I should like to know what it all means. Frankly I'm puzzled. We are cut off entirely from Auchinlech, and without John Dene the *Destroyer* can't sail. We're losing valuable time. It's very unfortunate; it's a disaster, in fact. But," he burst out excitedly, "why on earth does Sage want to advertise our anxiety as to Dene's whereabouts? That's what puzzles me."

"It puzzles me too, sir," said Colonel Walton quietly.

"It's such a confession of weakness," continued Mr. Llewellyn John, "such a showing of our hand. What will people think when we offer ten thousand pounds for news of John Dene of Toronto?"

"They'll probably think that he's an extremely valuable man," was the dry retort.

"That's it exactly," said Mr. Llewellyn John, "and Berlin will congratulate itself upon a master-stroke."

Colonel Walton felt inclined to suggest that was exactly what Malcolm Sage seemed most to desire; but he refrained.

"Very well, Walton, carry on," said Mr. Llewellyn John; "but frankly I don't like it," he added half to himself.

Colonel Walton left No. 110, Downing Street, and ten minutes later Malcolm Sage withdrew his resignation.

Whilst Department Z. hummed and buzzed with energy, and men and women were coming and going continuously, Dorothy sat at the window of John Dene's room gazing out at a prospect of white enamelled bricks punctuated by windows. She had nothing to do. Everything seemed so different. John Dene's impulsive energy had vitalised all about him. Now she felt as if all her faculties had suddenly wilted.

In her own mind she was convinced that he was ill. She could not blot from her mind the strangeness of his manner during the last few days. His sudden loss of memory proved that he was unwell. For a man to forget where the postage stamps are kept, or the position in the room of the letter files, was, in itself, a proof that something very strange had suddenly come over him, the more so in the case of one who was almost aggressively proud of his memory. Then there had been other little details. His movements did not seem the same, that jerkiness and sudden upward glance from his table had disappeared. It was as if he had been drugged. Dorothy wondered if that really were the explanation. Oh! but she was very miserable and horribly lonely.

That night Dorothy and her mother sat up long after midnight talking of John Dene. To both had come the realisation that he stood to them in the light of an intimate friend.

As she said "Good night," Mrs. West put her arm round Dorothy's shoulders, and in a shaky voice said:

"I don't think God would let anything happen to a good man like Mr. Dene;" and Dorothy turned and left the room abruptly.

CHAPTER XIV.
THE HUE AND CRY

The late editions of the evening papers contained no mention of the disappearance of John Dene. For one thing much valuable time had been lost owing to the attitude of Sir Lyster Grayne, for another, Malcolm Sage had decided to make a great display in the morning papers. All that afternoon Department Z. was feverishly busy. Photographs of John Dene had to be duplicated, and the story distributed through the Press Bureau, in order that it might possess an official character.

On the morning following the discovery of John Dene's disappearance, the British public was startled at its breakfast-table by an offer of £10,000 reward for details that would lead to the discovery of the whereabouts of one John Dene, a citizen of Toronto, Canada, who had last been seen at 6 p.m. on the previous Monday outside his offices in Waterloo Place.

The notice drawn up by Department Z. ran:

MISSING

£10,000 REWARD

Where is

JOHN DENE of TORONTO?

"On Monday at 6 p.m., Mr. John Dene, the well-known Canadian inventor and engineer of Toronto, left his offices in Waterloo Place, after bidding his secretary good night. Since then a shroud of mystery seems to have enveloped his movements.

HIS SECRETARY BECOMES ALARMED

"His Secretary, Miss Dorothy West, arrived at the office at the usual time on Tuesday morning. Mr. Dene was most punctual in his habits, invariably reaching his office a few minutes after nine. Miss West waited until two o'clock, then fearing that he might be ill, she rang through to the Ritzton Hotel, where Mr. Dene was staying. To her surprise she was informed that he had not returned to his hotel the night before.

WHERE IS JOHN DENE OF TORONTO?"

Miss West immediately got into communication with the head of a certain Government department with which Mr. Dene was associated; but nothing was known of his whereabouts. The authorities have reason to believe that Mr. Dene has been spirited away by some organisation that has a special object in view.

IS IT FOUL PLAY?

"A reward of £10,000 will be paid to anyone who will give such information as will lead directly to the discovery of Mr. John Dene's whereabouts. It may be added that Mr. Dene is a distinguished engineer and inventor, and it is the duty of every citizen of the British Empire to endeavour to assist the Authorities in tracing the missing man.

THIS IS WHAT HE IS LIKE.

"The following is a description of Mr. John Dene:—Height 5 ft. 5 ins. Clean shaven with grey eyes and a determined expression, invariably carried a cigar in his mouth, very frequently unlighted. Has a peculiar habit of twisting and twirling the cigar in his mouth. Thick set with keen, rather jerky movements, and a habit of looking at people suddenly and piercingly. A square jaw and tightly closed lips. When last seen was wearing a dark grey tweed suit, trilby hat, dark blue tie and brown boots. Spoke with a marked Canadian accent.

"All communications should be addressed to Scotland Yard, S.W."

In addition to the foregoing semi-official particulars, there followed much information that had been gleaned by various reporters. Most of the papers gave a leader, and several hinted at the hidden hand, urging that this new outrage obviously pointed to the necessity for the internment of all aliens. Great emphasis was laid upon the importance of tracing the present whereabouts of John Dene of Toronto, and anyone who had seen a man at all answering to his description, was called upon to communicate with Scotland Yard.

The afternoon papers contained practically the same information, but elaborated and adorned. Several hinted at the fact that John Dene had come to England with a new invention of great importance, and that he had disappeared just on the eve of the fruition of his schemes, with the result that everything was at a stand-still. In support of this theory the writers pointed to the amount of the reward. Ten thousand pounds would not have been offered, they argued, unless there were good reasons for it. One paper went so far as to suggest that the Government itself was offering the reward, although in its next issue it apologised for and contradicted the statement—this was a little stroke of Malcolm Sage's.

Dorothy was besieged by interviewers, until at last she was forced to refrain from answering the succession of knocks at the outer door. Her head was in a whirl.

The prevailing topic of conversation was the disappearance of John Dene. Everybody was asking why such a reward had been offered. Shoals of letters descended upon Scotland Yard. Hundreds of callers lined up in a queue, waiting their turn to be interviewed. Telegrams rained in from the provinces. Apparently John Dene had been seen in places as far distant as St. Andrews and Bournemouth, Aberystwyth and King's Lynn. He had been observed in conversation with men, women and children, some of harmless, some of sinister appearance. He had been seen in trains, 'buses, trams and cars. He had been seen perturbed and calm, hastening and loitering, in uniform and in mufti.

Scotland Yard was almost out of its mind, and the officer in charge of the John Dene investigation rang through to Malcolm Sage, demanding what the funny peter he was to do with the enormous correspondence, and the bewildering queue that already stretched along the Embankment halfway to Charing Cross railway-bridge.

"Burn the telegrams and letters and tell the queue to write," was Sage's laconic response, as he put up the receiver, whereat the officer had sworn heavily into the mouth-piece of the instrument.

The Chief Commissioner was particularly annoyed because all his own correspondence had been engulphed in the epistolary flood, and he was expecting a letter from his wife telling him where to meet her on the following day on her return from a motor tour. Those who knew Lady Wrayle understood the Chief Commissioner's anxiety.

All day long Scotland Yard worked in a conscientious endeavour to sift the mass of evidence that streamed in upon it from all parts of the kingdom. Some of the stories to which weary but patient officials listened were grotesque in the extreme. As the chief expressed it, "Half the idiots and all the damned fools in the country are descending upon us."

The callers were interesting as studies in obtuseness and optimism; but they were as nothing to the telegrams. One man wired from St. Andrews that he was tracking a strange man round the golf course, would Scotland Yard telegraph a warrant for his arrest? Another enquired if the reward would be in cash or war bonds, and if the Government guaranteed the money—this man telegraphed from Aberdeen. Several asked for railway warrants to London that they might lay certain facts before the authorities. Scores telegraphed for photographs, as the pictures in the papers were indistinct. One lady telegraphed from Suffolk that a man with a beard identical with that worn by John Dene in the picture in *The Daily Photo* had that day come to her door begging.

The telegrams were, however, nothing to the letters that followed them. The lady who had telegraphed about a bearded John Dene, wrote to apologise for her mistake, explaining it by saying that the paper boy must have accidentally rubbed the paper before delivering it. She was not to be denied, however, and went on to say that she thought the picture strangely like the man who had begged of her. Did Scotland Yard think that John Dene had disguised himself with a false beard?

Some correspondents wrote bitterly censuring the Government for not interning all aliens, for allowing John Dene out of its sight, for an Imperialistic policy, for plunging the country into war, for offering the reward, and for a thousand and one other irrelevant things. The one thing that no one did was to supply any information that would be remotely useful to the authorities in tracing the missing man.

People waited eagerly for the morrow's papers. They contained another surprise, this time in the form of a two column advertisement, offering £20,000 for information that would lead to the discovery of the whereabouts of John Dene. Clearly somebody was determined that John Dene should be found.

When Mr. Llewellyn John opened the first morning paper he picked up from the pile awaiting him he gasped. Himself a great believer in the possibilities of the press, he felt, nevertheless, that Department Z. was overdoing things, and he telephoned for its chief and Malcolm Sage to call upon him at ten o'clock.

At two minutes to ten, the two presented themselves at No. 110, Downing Street, and were immediately shown into the presence of the Prime Minister.

"Has it struck you," asked Mr. Llewellyn John, indicating one of the advertisements, "that questions will be asked in the House as to whether or no the Government is offering these large rewards?"

"I should think it highly probable, sir," was Sage's response.

"And what are we to say?" demanded Mr. Llewellyn John. He was a keen politician, and saw that the situation might be fraught with considerable difficulties.

"Acknowledge that they are, sir," was the response.

"Acknowledge it!" cried Mr. Llewellyn John.

"Certainly, sir."

"Mr. Sage," said Mr. Llewellyn John severely, "you do not appear to appreciate that this may seriously compromise the Government." Then turning to Colonel Walton he continued: "Hitherto you have been given a free hand, now I must ask you to explain why you are offering these large rewards. You first of all suggested £1,000, rising daily from £1,000 to £10,000. In two days it has amounted to £20,000."

"It won't rise any higher, sir. It has reached the limit."

"That is not the point," said Mr. Llewellyn John. "I want to know why it is that you are advertising to Germany that we want John Dene. It is an obvious confession of weakness." He made a quick nervous movement with his right hand, he was far from easy in his mind.

Malcolm Sage continued to examine his finger-nails with great intentness.

Seeing that he made no indication of replying, Mr. Llewellyn John continued:

"I'm afraid that this cannot go on." There was a suggestion of irritability in his voice.

"Then have it stopped, sir," said Sage calmly, still intent upon the finger-nails of his right hand.

"The mischief is done," said Mr. Llewellyn John. "What is at the back of your mind, Sage?" he demanded.

"I'm working on a hypothesis, sir," was the reply. "I think I'm right, in fact I'm convinced of it; but until I know for certain, I must keep my theories to myself. If you wish it, I'll tell you what I actually know; but I make it a rule never to air theories."

Mr. Llewellyn John smiled. "Well, tell me what you actually know then," he said.

"When Mr. Dene left his office at three minutes past six on Monday evening, he stood for nearly a minute, as if making up his mind in what direction to go. Just as he was about to turn and walk up Regent Street a taxi crawled past him. The driver spoke to him and John Dene got in and drove away."

"Kidnapped!" exclaimed Mr. Llewellyn John.

Malcolm Sage shrugged his shoulders.

"In which direction did he drive?" enquired Mr. Llewellyn John eagerly.

"Along Pall Mall, sir," was the reply. "Colonel Walton told you what happened?"

Mr. Llewellyn John nodded. "And have you informed the police?" he asked.

Malcolm Sage shook his head.

"Why?" enquired Mr. Llewellyn John eagerly.

"If my theory is right," said Sage, "it's unnecessary. If my theory's wrong, it's useless. Believe me, sir, our best course is to continue to boom John Dene's disappearance for all we are worth."

"But the *Destroyer*!" exclaimed Mr. Llewellyn John excitedly.

"You know the conditions, sir, that the island of Auchinlech was to be left severely alone for four months."

"Do you imagine that Dene slipped off to the north to trick the Germans?"

"That wouldn't trick them, sir," said Malcolm Sage quietly. "John Dene would never have been allowed to reach Auchinlech alive. That was settled. I may add that I have every reason to believe that the taxi and its occupant did not go fifty miles from London."

"And that he is a prisoner?" Mr. Llewellyn John jumped from his chair.

Malcolm Sage inclined his head in the affirmative.

"Good heavens!" exclaimed Mr. Llewellyn John, "we must——"

"Depend entirely upon the advertisements," said Sage, rising. "You will of course regard this as strictly confidential, and to be told to no one. I cannot tell you how important it is." There was an unaccustomed note of seriousness in Sage's voice, which did not fail to impress Mr. Llewellyn John.

"But the questions in the House as to why we are offering this reward?" persisted Mr. Llewellyn John. "What reply are we to make?"

"You might fall back on the old cliché, sir: 'Wait and see.'"

Mr. Llewellyn John smiled.

"That phrase," continued Sage, "was a great asset to one party, why should it not be to another?"

"Look at this." Mr. Llewellyn John held out a slip of paper, which Colonel Walton took and read aloud.

"Has the attention of the Home Secretary been drawn to a statement in *The Tribune* to the effect that it is the Government that is offering the reward of £10,000 for information that will lead to the discovery of the whereabouts of Mr. John Dene of Toronto, and if so can it justify the offer of so large a sum of public money?"

"They haven't lost any time," remarked Sage quietly.

"They never do." There was an unaccustomed note of irascibility in Mr. Llewellyn John's voice. "These questions are a scandal."

"Except when one happens to be in opposition, sir," said Sage, apparently absorbed in examining the nails of his left hand.

Mr. Llewellyn John made no response, and Colonel Walton handed back to him the slip, which he tossed upon the table.

"Well," he demanded, looking from Colonel Walton to Sage, "what are we to reply?"

"The answer is in the affirmative, sir," said Malcolm Sage.

For a moment Mr. Llewellyn John looked at him, frowning, then he broke into a smile.

"That's all very well, Sage, but it's not sufficient."

"If I may venture a suggestion— —" began Sage.

"Do—do, that's why I sent for you—both," he added, as if in deference to Colonel Walton.

"I would say that for reasons not unconnected with the prosecution of the war, the discovery of Mr. John Dene's whereabouts is imperative."

"But that would be giving us away more than ever."

"I think it would be desirable to temporise," said Sage.

Mr. Llewellyn John made a movement of impatience.

"You might reply that it is not in the public interest to answer the question," continued Sage.

"But that would be tantamount to acknowledging that we are offering the reward," said Mr. Llewellyn John with a suspicion of irritation in his voice.

Malcolm Sage looked at him steadily, but without speaking.

"There will inevitably be other questions arising out of this," continued Mr. Llewellyn John.

"I was going to suggest, sir, that if we could arrange for some newspaper to make a definite statement that the Government is offering the reward, we could prosecute it under D.O.R.A."

For fully a minute Mr. Llewellyn John gazed at Malcolm Sage, as if not quite sure of his sanity. "But," he began, and then broke off, looking helplessly across at Colonel Walton.

"Of course, sir, I'll relinquish the enquiry if you wish it."

"This is not the time to talk of relinquishing anything, Sage," said Mr. Llewellyn John with some asperity in his tone. "What I want to know is what all this means."

"That's exactly what I'm endeavouring to discover," said Sage evenly. "If I were a stage detective, I should be down on my knees smelling your carpet, or examining Pall Mall with a strong lens; but I'm not. I never carry a magnifying-glass and I know nothing about finger-prints. The solving of mysteries, like the detection of crime, is invariably due to a mistake on the part of somebody who ought not to have made a mistake."

"Then tell me how far you have got." Mr. Llewellyn John glanced across to Colonel Walton, and was conscious of a slight knitting of his brows, then he looked back again at Malcolm Sage, who for some moments remained silent.

"If you were uncertain of my sanity, sir," said Sage quietly, "would you discuss the matter with others, or would you first assure yourself of the accuracy of your suspicions?"

He looked up suddenly, straight into Mr. Llewellyn John's eyes.

"We all know you are hopelessly and irretrievably mad, Sage," said Mr. Llewellyn John with a smile.

"When I know definitely what has become of John Dene, I'll tell you, sir," said Sage. "I'm not spectacular, sir. I can't deduce bigamy from a bootlace, or murder from a meringue. I can tell you this, however"—he paused and both his listeners leaned forward eagerly—"that if my hypothesis is correct, the policy to pursue is to magnify the importance of John Dene's disappearance. Incidentally," he added, "it might result in Mr. John Dene revising his opinion of the incapacity of British officialdom."

"Then you refuse to tell me?"

"It would be highly injudicious on my part to tell you of a mere suspicion which might— —" Malcolm Sage lifted his eye from the nail of his left thumb, and looked straight at Mr. Llewellyn John—"which might dictate your policy, sir."

"But the time we are wasting," protested Mr. Llewellyn John, rising and pacing up and down impatiently.

"Nothing is lost that's wrought with tears, sir," was the enigmatical response.

"Sage," said Mr. Llewellyn John, as he shook hands with Malcolm Sage, "you're the most pig-headed official in the British Empire. Chappeldale can be tiresome; but you're nothing short of an inconvenience. Mind, Walton," he continued, turning to the chief of Department Z., "I shall hold you responsible for Sage. If he lets me down over this Dene business, I shall lose faith in Department Z." The smile that accompanied his words, however, robbed them of any sting they might have contained.

"Why don't you take the Skipper into your confidence, Sage?" enquired Walton, as they walked towards the Duke of York's steps.

"Vanity, chief, sheer vanity," was the response. "We have never failed him yet, and if I started barking up the wrong tree, he'd never again have confidence in Department Z. I suppose," he added irrelevantly, "that some day we shall be taken over altogether by the colonies. It would not be a bad thing for the British Empire, either. John Dene might be our first president."

There was one man who was deeply thankful for the disappearance of John Dene. Mr. Blair went about as if he had received a new lease of life. He became almost sprightly in his demeanour, and no longer looked up apprehensively when the door of his room opened. Sir Bridgman North commented on the circumstance to Sir Lyster Grayne and, as he passed through Mr. Blair's room, openly taxed him with being responsible for the kidnapping of John Dene. Mr. Blair smiled a little wearily; for to him John Dene was no matter for joking.

When Mr. McShane's question with regard to the disappearance of John Dene came up for answer, the Home Secretary replied that for the present at least it was not in the public interest to give the information required.

"That's tantamount to an acknowledgment," cried Mr. McShane, springing to his feet. "It's a scandal that public money — —"

He got no further, as at this point he was called to order by the Speaker.

It was clear that the House was not satisfied. In the lobbies Mr. McShane's question and the answer given were discussed to an extent out of all proportion to their apparent importance. The feeling seemed to be that if John Dene were of such value to the Government, he should have been guarded with a care that would have prevented the possibility of his disappearance. If on the other hand the Government had no interest in the enormous reward offered for information concerning him, then a statement to that effect should have been made. Whatever the facts, the Government was obviously in the wrong. That was the general impression.

The next day several newspapers commented very strongly upon the incident. There seemed to be a determination on the part of the press to make an "affaire John Dene" out of the Canadian's disappearance. The Government was attacked for adopting German bureaucratic methods. "A dark age of bureaucracy is settling down upon the country," said *The Morning Age*. "The real danger of Prussianism is not military, but bureaucratic."

The Government was called upon to lift the curtain of mystery with which it had surrounded itself. If it were responsible for the rewards offered, then let it say so. If, however, these rewards were in no way connected with the Government, then a denial should immediately be made. At the moment everybody regarded the Government as responsible for the tremendous press campaign resulting from John Dene's disappearance.

Malcolm Sage read the newspapers with obvious relish. Mr. Llewellyn John, on the other hand, frowned heavily at finding his administration attacked. The Home Secretary rang up the Deputy-Commissioner at Scotland Yard, telling him that something must be done, and the Deputy-Commissioner had replied with some heat that if the Home Secretary would step across to the Yard, he would see what actually was being done. He further intimated that the whole work of the Yard had been disorganised.

The Prime Minister sent over for Colonel Walton. "Look here, Walton," he cried as the chief of Department Z. entered the room. "This affair is getting rather out of hand, and it looks dangerous. You've seen the papers?"

Colonel Walton nodded. He was a man to whom words came with difficulty.

"Well, I don't like the look of it," continued Mr. Llewellyn John. "Sir Roger has just rung through that he's been urging Scotland Yard to greater efforts."

"They can do no harm," remarked Colonel Walton drily.

"I want Sage to go round and see the Deputy-Commissioner."

"I doubt if he'll do it," was the grim response.

"Not do it!" cried Mr. Llewellyn John, with a note of anger in his voice.

"In fact, I'm quite sure he won't."

"If you tell him that those are my instructions——" began Mr. Llewellyn John.

"It's no use, sir, he'll merely resign. He's as independent as an American boot-boy."

Mr. Llewellyn John flopped down in a chair, and sat gazing at Colonel Walton. "But he's got us into this muddle," he began.

"I've never known Sage's judgment at fault yet," replied Colonel Walton.

"Then you advise— —" began Mr. Llewellyn John.

"I never venture to advise," was the reply.

"Now look here, Walton," said Mr. Llewellyn John persuasively, "this is a very serious matter. It has already been magnified out of all proportion to its actual importance. I want to know what you would do if you were in my place."

"Exactly as Sage advises," was the terse response.

"Why, you're as bad as he is," grumbled Mr. Llewellyn John. "Still, I suppose I must do as you suggest. I don't like the look of things, however. It's invariably the neglected trifle that wrecks a government."

The mysterious disappearance of John Dene was made the subject of special consideration at a meeting of the War Cabinet. It was urged that the curious nature of the circumstances exonerated the Prime Minister and the First Lord of the Admiralty from the personal pledge they had given to John Dene, and that it was a matter of vital national importance that the *Destroyer* should be put into commission with the least possible delay.

Mr. Llewellyn John looked interrogatingly across at Sir Lyster Grayne, who shook his head decisively.

"We have given a personal pledge," he said, "under no circumstances whatever to communicate or endeavour to communicate other than by wireless with the island of Auchinlech for the period of four months from the date of our undertaking. The words 'under no circumstances whatever' admit of only one interpretation."

"But," protested Sir Roger Flynn, the Home Secretary, "Mr. Dene could not have foreseen his own disappearance. Circumstances surely alter the aspect of the case," he urged.

"If you, Flynn, were to promise under no circumstances to move from this room, then fire or flood would not justify you in breaking that promise," said Sir Lyster with decision. He was notorious for his punctiliousness in matters of personal honour. "What was possible to the Roman sentry is imperative with responsible Ministers," he added.

Mr. Llewellyn John nodded, and made a mental note of the phrase.

"Besides," continued Sir Lyster, "Mr. Dene was particularly emphatic on this point. I recall his saying to the Prime Minister, 'When I say under no circumstances, I mean under no circumstances,' and he went on to expound his interpretation of the phrase."

"But," persisted Sir Roger, "if the majority of the War Cabinet take the opposite view, then you and the Prime Minister would be absolved from your promise."

"Nothing can absolve a man from his personal pledge," was Sir Lyster's calm retort. "He can be outvoted politically; but he has always his alternative, resignation."

Mr. Llewellyn John looked up quickly. "I think," he said, "that Grayne is right. Nothing can absolve us from our pledge."

"The point is," said Sir Roger, "what is happening at Auchinlech?" He fixed an almost accusing eye upon Sir Lyster Grayne, who merely shook his head with the air of one who has been asked an insoluble conundrum.

"Here we are," continued Sir Roger indignantly, "with a weapon that would exercise a considerable effect in bringing victory nearer, debarred from using it because —

"The Prime Minister has given his word," interpolated Sir Lyster quietly.

Sir Roger glared at him. "Death nullifies a contract of this description," retorted Sir Roger.

"But the Prime Minister is not yet dead," said Sir Lyster drily.

Mr. Llewellyn John started slightly. He did not like these references to death and resignation.

"In law — —" began Sir Roger.

"This is not a matter of law, but of a private promise." Sir Lyster was insistent.

"I think, gentlemen, you are looking at it from different points of view," interrupted Mr. Llewellyn John with a tactful smile. "Let us hope that Mr. John Dene will be found. If it can be proved he is dead, then we shall be fully justified in sending to Auchinlech, acquainting his second-in-command with what has happened, and instructing him to assume command of the *Destroyer* in accordance with Mr. Dene's wishes."

The matter was then dropped, although it was clear that the members of the War Cabinet were not at one on the subject either of John Dene or his disappearance.

The Home Secretary promised personally to urge the police to greater efforts.

Slowly and with infinite labour Scotland Yard sifted the enormous volume of evidence that poured in upon it, proving conclusively that John Dene had been seen in every part of the United Kingdom, not to mention a number of places on the Continent. Police officers swore and perspired as they strove to grapple with this enormous problem. Night and day they worked with the frenzy of despair. They cursed the war, they cursed the colonies, they cursed John Dene. Why had he not stayed in Toronto and disappeared there, if he must disappear anywhere. Why had he come to London to drive to desperation an already over-worked department?

One thing that the police found particularly embarrassing was that constables were constantly being called upon, by enthusiastic and excited members of the public, to arrest inoffensive citizens on the suspicion of their being John Dene of Toronto. In some instances the constables would point out that no resemblance existed; but the invariable reply was that the object of suspicion was disguised.

All these false scents were duly reported to headquarters through the local police-stations, with no other result than to increase the sultriness of the atmosphere at Scotland Yard.

An elaborate description of John Dene was sent to every coroner and mortuary-attendant in the country. The river police were advised to keep a sharp look-out for floating bodies. In its heart of hearts Scotland Yard yearned to discover proof of the death of John Dene, whilst all the time it worked steadily through the deluge of correspondence, and listened patiently to the testimonies of the avaricious optimists who were convinced that they, and they alone, could supply the necessary information that would lead to the discovery of the whereabouts of John Dene, and transfer to themselves the not inconsiderable sum of £20,000.

"If ever another blighter comes from Toronto," remarked Detective-Inspector Crabbett, as he mopped his brow, "it would be worth while for the Yard to subscribe £20,000 for him to disappear quietly." Having thus relieved his feelings he plunged once more into the opening of letters, letters that convinced him that the whole population of Great Britain and Ireland had gone suddenly mad.

Articles appeared in many of the German newspapers upon the subject of the mysterious disappearance of John Dene. A great point was made of the fact that he was an inventor, and was known to be in close touch with the British war chiefs. Emphasis was laid upon the extraordinary efforts being made to discover his whereabouts. "It is inconceivable," said the *Koelnische Zeitung*, "that the anxiety of the relatives of the missing man could have prompted them to offer a reward of 400,000 marks for news of his whereabouts, and that *within two days of his disappearance*. Imagine a private citizen in Germany being absent from home for two days, and his friends offering this colossal reward for news of him. What would be said?" The writer went on to point out that behind this almost hysterical anxiety of the English to find John Dene lay a mystery that, whatever its solution might be, *was certainly not detrimental to German interests*.

The *Vorwärts* hinted darkly at something more than John Dene having disappeared, a something that was so embarrassing the British authorities, as to be likely to have a very serious influence upon the conduct of the war.

The *Berliner Tageblatt* openly stated that the British Admiralty was offering the reward, and left its readers to draw their own conclusions. "Victory," it concluded, "is not always won with machine-guns and high-explosive. Fitness to win means something more than well-trained battalions and valiant soldiers; it means a perfect organisation in every department of the great game of war; violence, bluff and intrigue. The country with the best-balanced machinery was the country that would win, because it was *fit* to win."

In Germany, where everybody does everything at the top of his voice, italics are very popular. An excitable people think and live italics, and a daily newspaper either reflects its public or ceases to be.

With great tact the Paris papers limited themselves to the "news" element in John Dene's disappearance, reproducing his portrait, with the details translated from the London dailies.

The neutral press was frankly puzzled. Those favourable to Germany saw in this incident a presage of victory for the Fatherland; whilst the pro-Allies journals hinted at the fact that someone had blundered in giving such publicity to an event that should have been regarded as a subject for the consideration of the War Cabinet rather than for the daily press.

CHAPTER XV.
MR. LLEWELLYN JOHN
BECOMES ALARMED

I

Mr. Llewellyn John was obviously troubled. With the forefinger of his right hand he tapped the table meditatively as he gazed straight in front of him. The disappearance of John Dene was proving an even greater source of embarrassment to the War Cabinet than the internment of aliens. The member of parliament who translated his duty to his constituents into asking as many awkward questions as possible of the Government, found a rich source of inspiration in the affaire John Dene.

Mr. Llewellyn John disliked questions; but never had he shown so whole-hearted an antipathy for interrogation as in the case of John Dene. The fact of the Home Secretary being responsible for the answers constituted an additional embarrassment, as Sir Roger Flynn was frankly critical of his chief in regard to the disappearance of John Dene. He had not been consulted in the matter of offering a reward, as he should have been, and he was piqued.

His answers to the questions that seemed to rain down upon him from all parts of the House were given in anything but a conciliatory tone, and the method he adopted of "dispatching them in batches like rebels," as Mr. Chappeldale put it, still further alienated from the Government the sympathy of the more independent members. In this Mr. Llewellyn John saw a smouldering menace that might at any time burst into flame.

He had come to wish with deep-rooted earnestness that Sir Roger Flynn would take a holiday. He had even gone to the length of suggesting that the Home Secretary was not looking altogether himself; but Sir Roger had not risen to the bait.

"Ah! here you are," cried Mr. Llewellyn John with a smile, that in no way mirrored the state of his feelings, as Sir Roger entered, and with a nod dropped into a chair.

"Eight more questions on the paper," he said grimly. "I suppose you appreciate the seriousness of it all."

"What would you suggest doing?" enquired Mr. Llewellyn John tactfully.

"Get a new lock for the stable door now the horse is gone," was the uncompromising retort.

"I've asked Colonel Walton to step round," said Mr. Llewellyn John, ignoring his colleague's remark.

"It's all that fellow Sage," grumbled Sir Roger. "I went round to see him yesterday, and he was as urbane as a money-lender."

"But surely you wouldn't quarrel— —"

"I always quarrel with a fool who doesn't see the consequences likely to arise out of his folly," said Sir Roger.

"If he would only play golf," murmured Mr. Llewellyn John plaintively.

"He'd resign at the first green because someone had shouted 'fore.' The man's a freak!" Sir Roger was very downright this morning.

"I wish we had a few more of the same sort," was Mr. Llewellyn John's smiling rejoinder.

Sir Roger grumbled something in his throat. Malcolm Sage was too often in antagonism with his Department for the Home Secretary to contemplate with anything but alarm a multiplicity of Sages.

Mr. Llewellyn John, who deeply commiserated with those heads of departments who had suffered from Malcolm Sage's temperament, was always anxious to keep him from coming into direct touch with other Ministers: the invariable result was a protest from the Minister, and resignation from Malcolm Sage.

Once he had been summoned before the War Cabinet to expound and explain a certain rather complicated enquiry in connection with a missing code-book. Before he had been in the room five minutes he had resigned.

At Scotland Yard he was known as "Sage and Onions," the feebleness of the *jeu d'esprit* being to some extent mitigated by the venom with which it was uttered. Nothing short of the anti-criminal traditions of the Yard had saved Malcolm Sage from assassination at the hands of its outraged officials.

His indifference was to them far more galling than contempt. He seemed sublimely unconscious of the fact that he was not popular with the police officials, a circumstance that merely added to the dislike with which he was regarded.

There was much to be said for Scotland Yard, which was called upon to carry out instructions from "a pack of blinking amachoors," as one of Sage's most pronounced antagonists had phrased it. Added to which was the fact that they were dealing with a man who seemed entirely unable to discriminate between courtesy and venomous hatred. Like the German nation, the officials discovered that there was little virtue in a hymn of hate that was not recognised as such.

"It's no good scrapping a man because he doesn't keep to your own time-table," said Mr. Llewellyn John, mentally making a note of the phrase for future use.

Sir Roger had remarked that the Prime Minister lay awake half the night coining phrases which would not win the war.

"This John Dene has caused more trouble at the Home Office than all the rest of the war put together." Sir Roger was obviously in a bad temper.

"We must learn to think Imperially, my dear Flynn."

The Home Secretary made a movement of impatience. "There'll be murder at Scotland Yard one of these days," he announced. "That fellow Sage goads the officials there to madness."

"And yet he's so popular with his own men," said Mr. Llewellyn John. "At Department Z. they would do anything for him."

"Well, I wish they'd do it and keep him there."

Whilst Mr. Llewellyn John and Sir Roger Flynn were discussing Department Z., Colonel Walton was seated at his table drawing diagrams upon the blotting paper, and Malcolm Sage sat opposite, engaged in the never-ending examination of his finger-nails.

"The Skipper's got the wind up, Sage," said Colonel Walton.

"I expected as much."

"I've got to go round there in a quarter of an hour. Sir Roger's trying to force his hand."

"Let him," said Malcolm Sage.

Colonel Walton shook his head with a smile. "That's all very well, Sage; but it isn't the language of diplomacy."

"Ours isn't the department of diplomacy, chief. Why not promise him something dramatic in a few weeks' time? That's bound to appeal to him." For a moment a fugitive smile flittered across Sage's features. "I think," he added, "we shall surprise him."

"In the meantime we must be diplomatic," said Colonel Walton. "That's why I'm not taking you with me this morning."

"You think I'd resign," queried Sage with an odd movement at the corners of his mouth.

"I'm sure of it," was the response, as Colonel Walton rose. "I suppose you know," he continued, "that Scotland Yard is absolutely congested. You can have no idea of what Sir Roger said when I met him in Whitehall yesterday."

"If it's anything at all like what comes through to me——" and Malcolm Sage shrugged his shoulders.

Ten minutes later Colonel Walton was shown into Mr. Llewellyn John's room.

"Ah! here you are," cried Mr. Llewellyn John, as he motioned Colonel Walton to a seat. "Is there any news?"

"None, sir," was the response.

"This is getting very serious, Walton," said Mr. Llewellyn John, "something really must be done."

"Have you tried Scotland Yard, sir?" asked Colonel Walton evenly, looking across at Sir Roger, who made a movement as if to speak, but evidently thought better of it.

"I didn't mean that as a rebuke, Walton," said Mr. Llewellyn John diplomatically. "But this John Dene business is really most awkward. Scotland Yard has apparently been entirely disorganised through your advertisements, and Sir Roger has just been telling me that there are eight more questions down on the paper for to-day. Every day the

Admiralty endeavours to call up Auchinlech by wireless," continued Mr. Llewellyn John, "but they can get no response."

"The thing is, where is John Dene?" demanded Sir Roger, speaking for the first time, and looking at Colonel Walton, as if he suspected him of having the missing man secreted about his person.

"I think the popular conception of the detective is responsible for all the trouble," said Colonel Walton quietly, looking from Sir Roger to the Prime Minister.

"What do you mean?" demanded Sir Roger.

"I think Sage expressed it fairly accurately," continued Colonel Walton, "when he said that if a man disappears, or a criminal is wanted, the detective is always expected to produce him as a conjurer does a guinea-pig out of a top hat."

"It isn't that," said Mr. Llewellyn John irritably. "It's the reward that's causing all the trouble."

"What is the detective for if it's not to solve mysteries?" demanded Sir Roger aggressively.

"I think that is a question for Scotland Yard, sir," said Colonel Walton.

Sir Roger flushed angrily, and was about to speak when Mr. Llewellyn John stepped into the breach.

"You know, Walton, we have to consider the political aspect," he said.

"What is Department Z.'s conception of the detective then?" demanded Sir Roger.

"To watch for the other side's mistakes and take advantage of them," was the reply, "just as in politics," with a smile at Mr. Llewellyn John.

Mr. Llewellyn John nodded agreement.

"You remember the Winthorpe murder case, Sir Roger?"

"I do," said the Home Secretary.

"There Scotland Yard tracked a man who had been three weeks at large. He made the mistake of calling somewhere for his washing, and the police had been watching the place for three weeks."

"That's all very well," said Sir Roger, obviously annoyed. "But you must remember, Colonel Walton, that this John Dene business has a political significance. It's—it's embarrassing the Government."

"But while they are worrying about that," remarked Colonel Walton imperturbably, "they're dropping the 'intern all aliens' cry."

Mr. Llewellyn John smiled.

"I'm convinced," he said, "that there's quite a large section of the public that would like me to intern everybody whose name is not Smith, Brown, Jones or Robinson."

"Or Sage," suggested Colonel Walton slyly.

"Sage!" cried Mr. Llewellyn John, "he ought to be in the Tower. But seriously, Walton. What I want to know is how long this will last?"

"In all probability until the full four months have expired," was the rejoinder.

"Good heavens!" cried Mr. Llewellyn John in consternation.

"I should not be alarmed, sir, if I were you," said Colonel Walton with a smile. "The public will soon get another cry. Sage suggests they may possibly hang an ex-minister."

Mr. Llewellyn John laughed. Colonel Walton's reference was to a previous Prime Minister who on one occasion had enquired of a distinguished general if he had ever contemplated the effect on the public of the possibility of Great Britain losing the war. "They'd hang you, sir," the general had replied, leaning forward and tapping the then Prime Minister on the knee with an impressive forefinger.

For a few moments there was silence, broken at length by Sir Roger.

"But that does not relieve my congested Department," he said complainingly.

"I'm afraid," said Colonel Walton, turning to Mr. Llewellyn John, "that it's impossible for Department Z. to work along any but its own lines. If Sage and I do not possess the confidence of the War Cabinet, may I suggest that we be relieved of our duties."

"Good heavens, Walton!" cried Mr. Llewellyn John. "Surely you're not going to start resigning."

"In the light of Sir Roger's remark, it's the only course open for me," was the dignified retort, as Colonel Walton rose.

"No, no," murmured Mr. Llewellyn John, looking across at the Home Secretary. "You must remember, Walton, that Sir Roger has had a very trying time owing to—to these—advertisements, and—and——"

He paused and again he looked expectantly at Sir Roger, who seemed engrossed in fingering the lower button of his waistcoat.

"Neither Sage nor I have any desire to embarrass you or the Home Secretary," continued Colonel Walton, "but——"

"I'm sure of it, Walton, I'm sure of it, and so is Sir Roger." Again Mr. Llewellyn John looked across at his colleague who, seeming to lose interest in his lower waistcoat button, suddenly looked up.

"The question is, how long is this to continue?" he asked.

For some moments Colonel Walton did not reply. He appeared to be weighing something in his mind.

"We're up against the cleverest organisation in the world," he said at length, "and Sage believes that a single man controls the lot."

"Nonsense!" broke in Sir Roger. "This spy craze is pure imagination."

"In any case it causes the War Cabinet a great amount of concern," said Mr. Llewellyn John drily.

"I think," proceeded Colonel Walton, "that before the expiration of the four months stipulated for by John Dene, Department Z. will have justified itself."

"How?" demanded Sir Roger.

"I can say nothing more," said Colonel Walton, moving towards the door, "at present."

"Well, carry on, Walton," said Mr. Llewellyn John and, with a wave of his hand, "and good luck."

"Those two men have megalomania in its worst possible form," growled Sir Roger, as he too rose to take his departure.

"Well, if they don't make good on this," said Mr. Llewellyn John, "you can decide whether or not their resignations be accepted."

With a nod Sir Roger left the room, conscious that he had to explain to the permanent officials at the Home Office why Department Z. was still in being.

II

During the weeks that followed the disappearance of John Dene, a careful observer of Apthorpe Road could not have failed to observe the trouble that it was apparently giving the local authorities. A fatality seemed to brood over this unfortunate thoroughfare. First of all the telephone mains seemed to go wrong. Workmen came, and later there arrived a huge roll of lead-covered cable. Labour was scarce, and never did labourers work less industriously for their hire.

On the morning after the arrival of the men, Mr. Montagu Naylor paused at the spot where they were working, and for a minute or two stood watching them with interest.

Was there any danger of the telephone system being interrupted?

No, the cable was being laid as a precaution. The existing cable was showing faults.

Mr. Naylor passed on his way, and from time to time would exchange greetings with the men. They were extremely civil fellows, he decided. Mr. Naylor felt very English.

The telephone men had not completed their work when the water-main, as if jealous of the care and attention being lavished upon a rival system, developed some strange and dangerous symptoms, involving the picking up of the road.

Again Mr. Naylor showed interest, and learned that the water pressure was not all that it should be in the neighbourhood, and it was thought that some foreign substance had got into the pipes. Just as the watermen were preparing to pack up and take a leisurely departure, two men, their overalls smeared and spotted with red-lead, arrived at the end of the street with a hand-barrow.

In due course a cutting of some fifteen or twenty feet was made in the roadway, and the reek of stale gas assailed the nostrils of the passer-by.

Obviously some shadow of misfortune brooded over Apthorpe Road, for no sooner were these men beginning to pack up their tools, than the road-men arrived, with a full-blooded steam-roller, bent upon ploughing up and crushing down Apthorpe Road to a new and proper symmetry. In short the thoroughfare in which Mr. Montagu Naylor lived seemed never to be without workmen by day, and by night watchmen to protect municipal property from depredation.

"I'm not so sure," remarked Malcolm Sage to Thompson who had entered his room soon after Colonel Walton had gone to pay his call at 110, Downing Street, "that the ménage Naylor isn't a subject for investigation by the Food Controller."

Thompson grinned.

"Eighty pounds of potatoes seems to be a generous week's supply for three people."

"And other things to match, sir," said Thompson with another grin. "Haricot beans, cabbage, they're nuts on cabbage, salad and all sorts of things that are not rationed. I think it must be diabetes," he added with another grin.

"Possibly, Thompson, possibly," said Malcolm Sage; "but in the meantime we will assume other explanations. Some people eat more than others. For instance, the German is a very big eater."

"And a dirty one, too, sir," added Thompson with disgust. "I've been at hotels with 'em."

"Seven meals a day is one of the articles of faith of the good German, Thompson," continued Malcolm Sage.

"And what's the result, sir?" remarked Thompson.

"I suppose," remarked Sage meditatively, "it's the same as with a bean-fed horse. They go out looking for trouble."

"And they're going to get it," was the grim rejoinder.

"Well, carry on, Thompson," said Sage by way of dismissal. "You'll learn a great deal about the green-grocery trade in the process."

"And waterworks—and gas and things, sir," grinned Thompson.

As Thompson opened the door of Malcolm Sage's room, he stepped aside to allow Colonel Walton to enter, and then quietly closed the door behind him.

"Bad time?" enquired Sage as Colonel Walton dropped into a chair and, taking off his cap, mopped his forehead.

"On this occasion I resigned for both of us."

For once in his life Malcolm Sage was surprised. He looked incredulously across at his chief, who gazed back with a comical expression in his eyes.

"I thought I was left at home for fear I might resign," said Malcolm Sage drily when Colonel Walton had finished telling him of the interview.

But Colonel Walton did not look up from the end of his cigar, which he was examining with great intentness.

"I'm not a sceptic," remarked Malcolm Sage presently, as he gazed at his brilliantly-polished fingernails, "but I would give a great deal for a dumb patriot domiciled in Apthorpe Road."

"Dumb?" queried Colonel Walton.

Malcolm Sage nodded without raising his eyes from his finger-nails.

"I have no doubt that Apthorpe Road is exclusively patriotic; but if we were to ask one of its residents to lend us a front-bedroom and, furthermore, if we spent all our days in the bedroom at the window — —" He shrugged his shoulders.

"There's always the domestic servant," suggested Colonel Walton.

"Not much use in this case, chief," was the reply. "It means that Thompson has had to turn road-mender. Good man, Thompson," he added. "He'd extract facts from a futurist picture."

Colonel Walton nodded.

CHAPTER XVI.
FINLAY'S S.O.S.

I

"Well, I think it's spies," announced Marjorie Rogers, as she sat perched on the corner of John Dene's table, swinging a pretty foot.

Dorothy looked up quickly. "But——" she began, then paused.

"And it's all Mr. Llewellyn John's fault. He ought to intern all aliens. On raid-nights the Tube is simply disgusting."

Dorothy smiled at the wise air of decision with which Marjorie settled political problems. The strain of the past week with its hopes and fears was beginning to tell upon her. There had been interminable interrogations by men in plain clothes, who with large hands and blunt pencils wrote copious notes in fat note-books. The atmosphere with which they surrounded themselves was so vague, so non-committal, that Dorothy began to feel that she was suspected of having stolen John Dene.

"Oh, mother!" she had cried on the evening of the first day of her ordeal at the hands of Scotland Yard, "you should see your poor, defenceless daughter surrounded by men who do nothing but ask questions and look mysterious. They're so different from Mr. Sage," she had added as an afterthought.

"If it isn't the spies," continued Marjorie, "then what is it?"

Dorothy shook her head wearily. She missed John Dene. It was just beginning to dawn upon her how much she missed him. The days seemed interminable. There was nothing to do but answer the door to the repeated knocks, either of detectives or of journalists. It was a relief when Marjorie ran in to pick her up for lunch—Dorothy had felt it only fair to discontinue the elaborate lunches that were sent in—or on her way home in the evening.

"A man doesn't get lost like a pawn-ticket," announced Marjorie.

"What do you know about pawn-tickets, Rojjie?"

"Oh, I often pop things when I'm hard up," she announced nonchalantly.

"You don't!" cried Dorothy incredulously.

"Of course. What should I do when I'm stoney if it wasn't for uncle."

"You outrageous little creature!" cried Dorothy. "I should like to shake you."

"He's quite a nice youth, with black hair greased into what I think he would call a 'quiff.'"

"What on earth are you talking about?"

"Uncle, of course. He always gives me more than anyone else," she announced with the air of one conscious of a triumph.

"Where will you end, Rojjie?" cried Dorothy.

"Suburbs probably," she replied practically. "These old wasters take you out to dinner; but marry you—not much." She shook her wise little head so vigorously that her bobbed hair shook like a fringe. "I wish I had a John Dene," she said after a pause.

"A John Dene!"

"Ummm!" nodded Marjorie.

"Why?"

"Marry him, of course."

"Don't be absurd."

Suddenly Marjorie slipped off the table and, going over to Dorothy, threw her arms round her impulsively.

"I'm so sorry, Dollikins," she cried, snuggling up against her.

"Sorry for what?" asked Dorothy in a weak voice.

"That he got lost. I—I *know*," she added.

"Know what?" asked Dorothy, her voice still weaker.

"That you're keen on him."

"I'm not," Dorothy sniffed. "I'm not, so there." Again she sniffed, and Marjorie with the wisdom of her sex was silent, wondering how long she would be able to stand the tickling of Dorothy's tears as they coursed down her cheeks.

At the end of a fortnight Sir Lyster Grayne decided to close John Dene's offices, and Dorothy returned to the Admiralty, resuming her former position; but, thanks to Sir Bridgman North's intervention, her salary remained the same as before John Dene's disappearance.

All the girls were greatly interested in what they called "John Dene's vanishing trick." Dorothy became weary of answering their questions and parrying their not ill-natured impertinences. Sometimes she felt she must scream.

Everybody she encountered seemed to think it necessary to refer to the very subject she would have wished left unmentioned.

One day she had encountered Sir Bridgman North in one of the corridors. Recognising her, he had stopped to enquire if she were still receiving her full salary. Then with a cheery "I don't want to be gingered-up when the good John Dene returns," he had passed on with a smile and a salute.

At home it was the same. A pall of depression seemed to have descended upon the little flat. Mrs. West tactfully refrained from asking questions; but Dorothy was conscious that John Dene was never very far from her thoughts.

Their week-end excursions had lost their savour, and they both recognised how much John Dene had become part of their lives.

Sometimes when Dorothy was in bed, tears would refuse to be forced back, however hard she strove against them. Then she would become angry with herself, jump out of bed, dab her eyes with a wet towel, and return to bed and start counting sheep, until the very thought of mutton seemed to drive her mad.

Mr. Blair she hated the sight of, he was so obviously satisfied with the course of events. Sometimes she found herself longing for the return of John Dene, merely that he might "ginger-up" Sir Lyster's private secretary.

Week after week passed and no news. The volume of questions in the House died down and finally disappeared altogether. The state of affairs at Scotland Yard returned to the normal. Newspapers ceased to refer either to John Dene, or to his disappearance, and the tide of war flowed on.

Marshal Foch had struck his great blow, and had followed it up with others. The stream of Hun invasion had been stemmed, and slowly France and Belgium were being cleared.

Mr. Montagu Naylor's comings and goings continued to interest Department Z., and Apthorpe Road was still in the grip of the workman.

Day by day Dorothy seemed to grow more listless. It was the heat, she explained to Mrs. West, whilst Marjorie nodded her wise little head, but said nothing. Whenever she saw Dorothy she always "talked John Dene," as she expressed it to herself. She could see that it was a relief.

"You see, Rojjie darling, I should always be a little afraid of him," said Dorothy one day as they sat in John Dene's room. "I suppose that is why I— —" She paused.

Marjorie nodded understandingly, and continued to swing a dainty, grey-stockinged leg.

"You—you see," continued Dorothy a little wistfully, "I've always had to do the taking care of, and he— —" Again she broke off. Then suddenly jumping up she cried, "Let's go to the pictures. Bother John Dene!" and Marjorie smiled a little smile that was really her own.

Finally there came the time when for a fortnight Dorothy would have no one to say to her either "come" or "go," and she and Mrs. West went to Bournemouth, Dorothy inwardly dreading two weeks with nothing to do.

II

Whilst the John Dene sensation was slowly fading from the public mind, Malcolm Sage was continuing with unabated energy the task he had set himself. He was aware that Finlay was being watched even more closely than John Dene had been watched, and Sage realised that it was, in all probability, impossible for him to communicate with headquarters.

By an ingenious device, however, Finlay had at length succeeded in establishing contact with Department Z. It had been reported to Sage that on two occasions Finlay had been seen to leave behind him at restaurants a silver-mounted ebony walking stick. He had, however, always returned for it a few minutes later, as if having discovered his loss.

Learning that the stick was of an ordinary stock pattern, Malcolm Sage gave instructions for one exactly like it to be purchased. An endeavour was then to be made to effect an exchange with that carried by Finlay. It was not until a week later that this was effected, and the stick handed to Thompson.

A careful examination disclosed nothing. The silver nob and ferrule were removed; but without bringing to light anything in the nature of a communication.

"It's a wash-out, sir," said Thompson, as he entered Malcolm Sage's room, the stick in one hand and the knob and ferrule in the other.

Sage glanced up from his desk. Holding out his hand he took the stick and proceeded to examine it with elaborate care. The wood at the top, just beneath the knob, had been hollowed out. Sage glanced up at Thompson interrogatingly.

"Nothing in it, sir," he said, interpreting the question.

"There will be when you next make the exchange," was the dry retort and, with a motion of dismissal, Malcolm Sage returned to the papers before him.

"What's the matter, Tommy?" enquired Gladys Norman a few minutes later, as she came across Thompson gazing at the hollowed-out end of a stick, and murmuring to himself with suppressed passion.

"I'm the biggest fool in London," said Thompson without looking up.

"Only just discovered it?" she asked casually. "Poor old Tommikins," she added, prepared to dodge at the least sign of an offensive movement on the part of her colleague; but Thompson was too engrossed in introspective analysis to be conscious of what was taking place about him.

"We're on the eve of developments," said Malcolm Sage one afternoon some weeks later, as Colonel Walton entered his room, closing the door behind him.

"Anything new?" he enquired, dropping into a chair beside Sage's table.

"I'm afraid there's going to be trouble."

"Not resigning?" there was a twinkle in Colonel Walton's eye. In their infinite variety the resignations of Malcolm Sage would have filled a Blue Book.

"I don't like the look of things," continued Sage, pulling steadily at his pipe and ignoring the remark. "Naylor's playing his own game, I'm sure and," he added, looking up suddenly, "it's an ugly game."

"Bluff, that accusing Finlay of acting on his own about John Dene."

Malcolm Sage nodded his head slowly several times. For some minutes he continued to smoke with a mechanical precision that with him always betokened anxiety.

"It's the dug-out business, I don't like," he said at length.

Colonel Walton nodded. "You think?" he queried.

Sage nodded, his face was unusually grave.

During the previous week it had been discovered that Mr. Naylor was having constructed in his back-garden a dug-out, to which to retire in case of air-raids, and he was himself assisting with the work of excavation.

Finlay had confirmed Malcolm Sage's suggestion that Naylor was suspicious. There had been a quarrel between the two, which had taken place through intermediaries. Naylor had accused Finlay of being responsible for the disappearance of John Dene. Finlay had responded by a like accusation, and the threat of serious consequences to Naylor when the facts were known in a certain quarter.

"We've got to speed up." Malcolm Sage addressed the remark apparently to the thumbnail of his left hand.

Colonel Walton nodded.

"I don't like that dug-out business at all," continued Sage. "The changing of the site too," he added.

"Had they got far with the first one?" enquired Colonel Walton

"About five feet down; but they haven't filled it in yet."

Colonel Walton looked up quickly. His face was grave.

"Naylor says they must get the dug-out finished first in case of a raid. He can fill in the old hole at any time."

"A dug-out after nearly four years of raids?"

"Exactly," said Sage, "that and the unfilled hole and Naylor's own activities— —" He broke off significantly.

"About the reward? It would be awkward if— — Come in."

Colonel Walton broke off at the sound of a knock at the door.

Thompson entered with an ebony walking stick in one hand, a silver knob and a small piece of paper in the other. He held out the paper to Malcolm Sage, who, with a motion of his head, indicated Colonel Walton. He was very punctilious in such matters. Colonel Walton took the slip of paper and read aloud.

"Arrest me late to-night and have me taken to Tower. Slip the dogs to-morrow certain, delay dangerous.

J. F."

For fully a minute the three men were silent. Colonel Walton began to draw diagrams upon his blotting pad Malcolm Sage gazed at his finger-nails, whilst Thompson stood stiffly erect, his face pale and his mouth rigid. Presently Sage looked up.

"I'm afraid there'll be no spring-mattress for you to-night, Thompson," he said. "I'll ring in a few minutes," and Thompson drew a sigh of relief as he turned towards the door, which a moment afterwards closed behind him.

"We can't do it to-night," announced Sage with decision.

Colonel Walton shook his head.

"He must take the risk until the morning," continued Sage. "You'll be here until it's all through?" he interrogated.

Colonel Walton nodded. When thoughtful he was more than usually sparing of words.

"About the reward?" he interrogated, as Sage rose and moved towards the door.

"We'll withdraw it in to-morrow evening's papers," was the response, "if you agree."

Again Colonel Walton nodded, and Malcolm Sage went out, bent on reminding Scotland Yard of his existence.

CHAPTER XVII.
MALCOLM SAGE CASTS HIS NET

I

"I'm afraid there'll be trouble with the people at the Tower," remarked Malcolm Sage, who, with the aid of his briar pipe, was doing his best to reduce the visibility.

"Zero is noon," mused Colonel Walton.

Sage nodded.

"They'll begin to drift in about twelve-thirty," he continued, puffing placidly at his cigar.

"Well, it's been interesting, and it'll give the Skipper a sort of joy day with the War Cabinet," said Sage quietly. "To-morrow ought to be rather a large breakfast-party," he added drily.

"He had the wind up rather badly at one time."

"Celt," was Sage's comment.

Colonel Walton nodded.

For some minutes the two smoked in silence.

"I hope they won't start any of that O.B.E. business," said Sage at length.

"Sure to. It will be a triumph for the Skipper," continued Colonel Walton.

"He deserves it," said Sage ungrudgingly. "He's always believed in us. By the way, I told Hoyle to bring Finlay here after they had got Naylor."

Colonel Walton continued to puff contentedly at his cigar.

Early that morning Malcolm Sage had given final instructions to the various members of his staff. He and Colonel Walton had been working all through the night in perfecting their plans. The demands made upon Scotland Yard for men had at first evoked surprise, which later developed into *sotto voce* ridicule.

"What the devil's up with old Sage and Onions?" Inspector Crabbett had muttered, as he cast his eyes down the list of plain-clothes and uniformed officers required. "Who the devil's going to issue all these warrants?"

Department Z., however, had its own means of obtaining such warrants as were required without questions being asked.

Early that morning Malcolm Sage had got through to Inspector Crabbett.

"That you, Inspector?" he enquired.

"What's left of me," was the surly retort.

"Got that little list of mine?" enquired Sage.

"We're engaging new men as fast as we can so as to have enough," was the grumbling reply. "I've asked the W.O. to demobilise a few divisions to help us," he added with ponderous sarcasm.

"Thank you," said Sage imperturbably, as he replaced the receiver.

Mr. Montagu Naylor had been reserved for Department Z. Sage was determined to get him alive; but his knowledge of the man was sufficient to tell him that Mr. Naylor was equally determined never to be taken alive. He had seen that little corrugated-iron covered building at the Tower that had once been a miniature rifle-range and, involuntarily, he had shuddered.

II

"Was that the telephone?"

Mr. Naylor barked the question down from the first-floor. There was a pad-pad of feet, and Mrs. Naylor appeared from the basement.

"Yes," she replied timidly. "Shall I go?"

"No, I'll go myself;" and Mr. Naylor descended the stairs heavily. Passing into his study, he closed the door behind him and seated himself at the table.

"Hullo!" he called into the mouthpiece, lifting off the receiver.

"Is that twelve Haymarket?" came the reply.

"No," was the suave response. "This is Mr. Montagu Naylor of Apthorpe Road, Streatham. You're on to the wrong number;" and with that he replaced his receiver, pulled out his watch and scowled at the dial. The hands pointed to half-past eleven.

With a muttered exclamation and a murmur about a taxi, Mr. Naylor stamped out of the room, just as Mrs. Naylor was leaving the dining-room. She shrank back as if expecting to be struck.

"Back about two," he grunted. "Keep that damned dog tied up."

"I'll see to it," said Mrs. Naylor in a voice that seemed to come through cotton-wool.

Since post time that morning Mr. Naylor's temper had been bad, even for him. An intimation had come from the local police-station to the effect that several complaints had been made of the savage nature and aggressive disposition of a dog he was alleged to keep on his premises. The officer who had been sent round to call attention to this fact on the previous day, had been prevented from entering the garden by the valiant defence put up by James himself. Mr. Naylor had been out at the time of the call, and Mrs. Naylor had not dared to tell him of the constable's visit and discomfiture. Department Z. was taking no risks where James was concerned.

During the whole of breakfast strange sounds had rumbled in Mr. Naylor's throat, whilst on one occasion, when he happened to catch Mrs. Naylor's eye, he glared so ferociously at her that she let the lid of the teapot fall with a crash into a fast-filling cup. With this the volcano had burst, and the grumbles in Mr. Naylor's larynx matured into deep-throated oaths and execrations.

Three times he had descended to the basement, from whence his voice could be heard in passionate protest against any and every thing he encountered. Mrs. Naylor had gone about the house with the air of one convinced of disaster. Susan, as usual, succeeded in shuffling out of the way just as Mr. Naylor appeared.

As the front door banged behind him, Mr. Naylor's scowl lifted as by magic, giving place to an expression of benignant geniality befitting a prominent and respected citizen.

Mr. Naylor managed the distance to the Haymarket in the time without involving a taxi, thus greatly improving his temper. He was a man who grudged unnecessary expense, and all expense, not directly connected with the delights of the table, was to his way of thinking unnecessary.

That morning, just as Big Ben was booming out the tenth stroke of noon, a commotion was observed to take place outside the Pall Mall Restaurant. Suddenly four men precipitated themselves upon a fifth, who was walking calmly and peaceably towards Coventry Street. In a flash he was handcuffed and thrown, somebody called out "Police"; but before anyone had properly realised what was happening, a motor-car had drawn up and the handcuffed man was bundled into it, struggling vainly against the rope with which his legs had been quickly bound. When a policeman arrived, it was to be told by an excited group of spectators that a man had been assaulted and kidnapped in broad daylight.

Thus was Mr. Montagu Naylor of Streatham secured and conducted to the Tower, there eventually to make acquaintance with the miniature rifle-range.

Whilst Mr. Naylor was rapidly nearing the place of the most remarkable appointment he had ever kept, James was reduced to a state of frenzy by several strange men in the adjoining back-gardens. They were, according to their own account, given to the residents whose houses flanked that of Mr. Naylor, engaged upon survey work. The instruments they had with them seemed to give colour to their words. The apathy of the workmen who for the last few days had surrendered Apthorpe Road to others, different from themselves only in that they belonged to another union and brought with them a steam-roller instead of picks and shovels, seemed suddenly to develop into an unusual activity. Immediately after the departure of Mr. Naylor, the asphalt of the footpath just in front of his gate was picked up with an energy that merited rebuke from any self-respecting father of the chapel. A few minutes later a man knocked at Mr. Naylor's door, and stated that it would be necessary to dig up the path leading to the front door.

At this information a look of fear sprang into Mrs. Naylor's eyes. She was terrified of deciding anything in Mr. Naylor's absence. When the men announced that it would be necessary to descend to the basement, she shook her head violently.

"No, no!" she cried. "Mr. Naylor is away. Come again this afternoon."

It was pointed out to her that the afternoon might be too late, something had gone wrong with the gas, and if they waited until the afternoon anything might happen.

The man was respectful, but insistent. He so played upon Mrs. Naylor's fears by hinting darkly at the possibility of there being nothing for Mr. Naylor to return to by the afternoon, unless the gas meter were immediately seen to, that she consented to allow a man to descend to the basement after being told that it would not be necessary for him to go into any of the rooms.

First, however, she insisted that she must go down and see that everything was tidy. After a lapse of five minutes she returned; but when four men presented themselves prepared to descend the stairs, she resolutely refused.

"Very well, mum," said the foreman, "we'll see what the police can do. Just pop round to the police-station, Bill, and bring a copper," he said to a mate. "Sooner 'ave the 'ole bloomin' street blown up than let us go down and dirty your stairs." There was in his voice all the indignation of the outraged British workman.

Mrs. Naylor wavered. The word "police" had for her a peculiar and terrifying significance.

"You—you only want to go in the passage," she said.

"That'll do us, mum," said the foreman. "You stay up 'ere, Bill," he added, turning to the man he had instructed to go for the police.

Mrs. Naylor led the way to the lower regions, unconscious that not three but seven men were following her, the last four with rubber-soled boots.

She had scarcely taken a step along the passage at the foot of the basement stairs, when her arms were gripped from behind and a pad held over her mouth. She struggled against the sweet-smelling sickly fumes; then the relaxing of her limbs told that she had temporarily left for realms where Mr. Naylor was not.

The basement was composed of a kitchen, immediately on the right of the stairs, and a breakfast-room, the entrance to which lay a few paces along the passage. At the end of the passage was a door leading into the area.

Without a sound the men divided themselves, one went to the area door, two remained by the kitchen door, where Susan could be heard clattering crockery, whilst the other four stood outside the door leading to the breakfast-room. One of them gently turned the handle; it was locked. He made a signal to the two men at the kitchen door. One quietly entered.

A moment later Susan looked up with a start to find herself gazing down the barrel of an automatic pistol, whilst before her eyes was presented a card on which was printed, "Come and make the signal to get the door of the breakfast-room open, otherwise you will be shot."

For a fraction of a second she hesitated, then a strange light flashed into her eyes, suggestive half of cunning, half of relief, and with an understanding nod she walked to the breakfast-room door. One of the men placed her in such a position that she would not be in the way of the entrance of the others when the door was opened.

Very deliberately she knocked and paused — knock — knock — knock, pause, knock — knock.

They waited breathlessly. The sound of a key being cautiously turned was presently heard. A moment after a line of white appeared beside the green paint of the door, as it was slowly and cautiously opened.

Then a score of things seemed to happen at once. The waiting men threw themselves into the room, the man at the end of the passage dashed out into the area, he who had been left at the kitchen-door rushed into the back-yard and whistled.

The breakfast-room was in total darkness; but for the brilliant electric torches carried by the assailants. For a moment there was wild confusion, a shot was fired and then all was quiet.

"Got him, Thompson?" It was Malcolm Sage who spoke; but from a physical substance that was not Malcolm Sage.

"Got them and it, sir," was the response.

"Are you hit?"

"Only in the arm, sir. Nothing to write home about," was the cheery response.

"Here, switch on the light someone," said Malcolm Sage, and a moment after there was a click and a three-lamp electrolier burst into light.

"Get a window open, Thompson; thrust all that greenery stuff out," cried Malcolm Sage.

"Right, sir."

With the aid of the fire-irons, Mr. Montagu Naylor's little greenhouse was soon demobilised and lay a heap of ruins in the area.

"That's better," murmured Malcolm Sage. "What a stink!"

He then turned to an examination of the room. The window had been blocked up with a sort of glass case, on which shelves had been built and flower-pots placed. This had the effect not only of cutting off all communications from outside except from the door; but of preventing anyone from seeing into the room. The atmosphere of the place was heavy and foetid, as the only means of ventilation was the door. There were three pallet-beds, a table and several chairs.

Malcolm Sage shuddered at the thought of living week after week under such conditions. He turned to his prisoners.

On the floor lay two men, handcuffed, each with a member of the staff of Department Z. sitting contentedly on his chest. One was foaming at the mouth with suppressed fury, the other, a heavily-built fellow, lay apathetic. In a corner upon one of the pallet-beds sat a man looking about him in a dazed fashion.

"It's all right, Mr. Dene," said Malcolm Sage. "We'll attend to you in a minute." Then turning to Thompson he said, "Get these fellows up into the car. Keep the two women here under guard. Then we'll see to your arm."

"Right, sir," said Thompson.

The arrival of three closed motor-cars outside "The Cedars" had aroused some interest among the residents of Apthorpe Road. The absence of flowers from the lamps and the buttonholes of the chauffeurs negatived the idea of a wedding, and three cars were scarcely necessary to take Mr. Naylor's small household for a holiday.

A group of neighbours and errand boys gathered outside Mr. Naylor's gate. The windows opposite and on each side were manned in force. Presently the onlookers were astonished to see two handcuffed men half carried, half dragged out of the house and hurried into the first car. They were followed by two more of the men who, a few minutes before, had been engaged in picking up Mr. Naylor's path.

As soon as they were in the car, these men proceeded to fetter their two prisoners.

Apthorpe Road gasped its astonishment.

In the breakfast-room Malcolm Sage drew a chair up to the man seated on the bed, seemingly quite unconscious of what was happening. Leaning forward he lifted one of his eyelids, then turned to the others who stood round.

"Dope," was all he said.

There was an angry murmur from the others. For a moment Malcolm Sage sat looking at the wasted form of what once might have been John Dene of Toronto. Then he turned to Thompson, quite unrecognisable as the foreman gas-mechanic, whose arm was being bandaged with a field-dressing.

"Take him in one of the cars to Sir Bryllith Riley, and explain. He's expecting you. Do exactly as he orders. Take Rogers with you, and then get your wound seen to."

Sir Bryllith Riley was the great specialist in nervous disorders, who had made a special study of the drug habit. Without a word Thompson left the room, followed two of the "workmen," who had raised the patient to his feet. Then half leading, half carrying they took him from the room.

The crowd of spectators, which had been considerably reinforced, received its second thrill that morning at the sight of a short sturdily built man, apparently drunk, being helped into the second car. They noticed that he blinked violently in the sunlight, and those who were near enough saw that his eyes were watering profusely. One or two of the more observant observed that he stumbled as he entered the taxi, and would have fallen but for those supporting him. The second car immediately drove off.

A few minutes later two more men left "The Cedars" and entered the third car, which with the first then drove off, leaving Mr. Naylor's residence in the charge of the "survey" men and two of the "workmen."

In the back-garden James was having a meal—it was to be his last.

"I should like a smoke, chief. I left my pipe behind," said one of the men in the third car, as he took from his pocket a pair of gold-rimmed spectacles and proceeded to put them on.

"Here, try one of these," and a gold-mounted cigar case was passed towards him, a case that seemed strangely out of keeping with the corduroys of the owner.

"Well, it's been a happy day," said Malcolm Sage, as he proceeded to light the cigar Colonel Walton had given him.

"I hope the other fellows have got their lot," said the Chief of Department Z., as the car ran into the High Road.

"Trust them," was the answer. "Finlay wouldn't let Naylor escape him. I should like to know what they're saying at the Tower," he added a moment later.

From half-past twelve until nearly two that day, the officials at the Tower were kept busily occupied in receiving guests. The appetite for lunch of the officer of the guard was entirely spoiled.

"Where the deuce are we going to put them all," he asked of one of his N.C.O.'s.

The man shook his head helplessly.

"It might be a Rowton's lodging-house," grumbled the officer, as he made the twenty-third entry in what he facetiously called the "Goods Received Book." "Damn the war!"

III

"Well, Thompson," remarked Colonel Walton with a smile, "you have earned — —"

"A wound stripe," interrupted Sage.

Thompson grinned, as he looked down at his right arm resting in a sling.

"It was meant for Mr. Dene, sir," he said. "I just got there in time. It was that ferret-eyed little blighter," he added without the slightest suggestion of animosity. Thompson was a sportsman, taking and giving hard knocks with philosophic good-humour.

"Plucky little devil," murmured Malcolm Sage. "He bit and scratched with the utmost impartiality."

Malcolm Sage and Thompson were seated in Colonel Walton's room discussing the events of the morning.

"We were only just in time," said Sage. "Finlay was right."

Colonel Walton nodded.

"It was dope, sir." Thompson looked from Colonel Walton to Malcolm Sage. "Sir Bryllith said he'll be months in a home."

"Yes," said Sage. "He won't be fit to answer questions for a long time. Been doped all the time, nearly three months."

"If there's nothing more——" began Thompson.

"No, Thompson, go and get a sleep," said Colonel Walton. "Look after that arm, and take things easy for a few days."

"Thank you, sir," said Thompson; "but I'm afraid I've forgotten the way," and with a grin he went out.

"You've wirelessed?" asked Colonel Walton.

"The whole story. They're bound to pick it up at Auchinlech."

"And the Skipper?"

"Oh! just what we actually know, I should say," responded Sage, and Colonel Walton nodded his agreement.

"They're puzzled over those announcements withdrawing the reward," said Sage a few minutes later. "We ought to be hearing from the Skipper soon."

"He's already been through while you were changing. I'm going round at five. You're coming too," added Colonel Walton, as he lighted a fresh cigar. "What about Finlay?"

"Gone home to see his wife," said Sage. "He's as domesticated as a Persian kitten," he added with all the superiority of a confirmed bachelor.

In another room Gladys Norman was fussing over a wounded hero.

"Poor 'ickle Tommikins." she crooned, as she sat on the arm of his chair and rumpled the hair of Special Service Officer Thompson. "Did 'ums hurt 'ums poor 'ickle arm. Brave boy!" and then she bent down and kissed him lightly on the cheek, whereat Thompson blushed crimson.

"Department Z. makes its traditions as it goes along," Malcolm Sage had once said. "It's more natural."

CHAPTER XVIII.
THE RETURN OF JOHN DENE

"It's very strange," murmured Sir Lyster Grayne, as he raised his eyes from an official-looking document. "What are the official figures for the last six weeks, Heyworth?" he enquired.

"Seven certainties and two doubtful," was the reply.

"About normal, then?"

Admiral Heyworth nodded.

"Then why the devil should the Hun get the wind up?" demanded Sir Bridgman, a look of puzzlement taking the place of the usual smile in his eyes. "What does the I.D. say?"

"That during the last four weeks thirty-seven U-boats have failed to return to their bases as they should have done," replied Admiral Heyworth, referring to a buff-coloured paper before him.

"That leaves twenty-eight in the air," said Sir Bridgman, more to himself than to the others.

Sir Lyster nodded thoughtfully.

"No wonder they're getting the wind up," mused Sir Bridgman.

"The I.D. says that Kiel and Wilhelmshaven are in a state of panic," said Admiral Heyworth.

"It's damned funny," remarked Sir Bridgman thoughtfully. "Structural defects won't explain it?" He looked interrogatingly across at Admiral Heyworth, who shook his head in negation.

"It might of course be wangle," murmured Sir Bridgman.

Sir Lyster shook his head decidedly.

"The I.D. says no," he remarked. "They're doing everything they can to keep it dark."

"Well, it's damned funny," repeated Sir Bridgman. "What does L. J. say?"

"He's as puzzled as the rest of us," said Sir Lyster in response. "He's making enquiries through Department Z." There was the merest suggestion of patronage in Sir Lyster's voice at the mention of Department Z.

Sir Bridgman lit a cigarette, then after a short silence Sir Lyster said tentatively:

"I suppose it isn't the Americans?"

"Impossible," said Sir Bridgman. "You can't base ships on ether, and we were bound to know, besides frankness is their strong point. They are almost aggressively open," he added.

"I——" began Sir Lyster, then paused.

"It's damned funny," murmured Sir Bridgman for the third time. "Well, I must buzz off," he added, rising. "I shall see you at L.J.'s this afternoon."

"It's a conference, I think," said Sir Lyster. "Walton is to tell us what has been discovered." Again there was the note of patronage in his voice.

"Well," said Sir Bridgman, "I'll try and prevent it spoiling my lunch," and he stretched his big frame lazily. "By the way," he remarked, turning to Sir Lyster, "did you see about that convoy a hundred miles off its course, bleating like a lost goat to know where it was?"

"It might have been very serious," said Sir Lyster gravely.

"Oh! the luck of the navy," laughed Sir Bridgman. "We have to do it all, even teach the other fellows their job. Mark it, Grayne, we shall take over the whole blessed country before we've finished, then perhaps they'll raise our screws," and with that he left the room.

Two minutes later his cheery laugh was heard outside again as he enquired of Mr. Blair if it were true that he was going to double the reward for the discovery of John Dene. A moment later he rejoined Sir Lyster and Admiral Heyworth.

"I forgot about that flying-boat business," he said, and soon the three were engaged in a technical discussion.

For more than three months Mr. Blair had known peace. He had been able to walk leisurely across St. James's Park from his chambers in St. Mary's Mansions, pause for a moment to look at the pelicans, dwell upon the memory of past social engagements and anticipate those to come, receive the salute of the policeman at the door of the Admiralty and the respectful bows of the attendants within and walk up the stairs and along the corridors to his room, conscious that in his heart was an abiding peace.

It was true that a war raged in various parts of the world, and that Mr. Blair's work brought him constantly into close touch with the horrors of that war; but it was all so far away, and his was a nature that permitted the contemplation of such matters with philosophical detachment. A scorched shirt-front, an ill-ironed collar, or an omelette that was not all an omelette should be, bulked vastly more in Mr. Blair's imagination than the fall of Kut, the over-running of Roumania, or the tragedy of Caporetto. National disaster he could bear with a stoical calm befitting in a man of long ancestry; but personal discomfort reduced him to a state of acute nervousness.

The Hun ravaged Belgium, invaded Russia, over-ran Lombardy; Mr. Blair was appropriately shocked and, on occasion, expressed his indignation in a restrained and well-bred manner; but John Dene crashing in upon the atmosphere of intellectual quiet and material content with which Mr. Blair was surrounded, ravaged his nerves and produced in him something of a mental palpitation. Therefore of the two events the irruptions of John Dene were infinitely more disturbing to Mr. Blair than those of the hordes of the modern Attila.

Mr. Blair sat at his table, pen in hand, before him a pad of virgin blotting paper. His thoughts had wandered back to a dinner-party at which he had been present the previous night. His eyes were fixed upon an antique family ring he wore upon the fourth finger of his left-hand. The dinner had been a success, a conspicuous success. He was conscious of having shone by virtue of the tactful way in which he had parried certain direct and rather impertinent questions of a professional nature addressed to him by one of the guests. They related to the disappearance of John Dene. Mr. Blair had experienced an additional gratification from the discovery that he had been able to hear mentioned the name of John Dene without experiencing an inward thrill of misgiving.

As he sat this morning, pen in hand, he pondered over the subject of John Dene in relation to himself, Reginald Blair. Possibly he had been a little weak in not standing more upon his dignity with this rough and uncouth colonial. In such cases a bold and determined front was all that was necessary. Of course there would have been one great contest, and Mr. Blair detested such things; but—yes, he had been weak. In future he— —

"Here, who the hell's shut my offices, and where's Miss West?"

The pen slipped from Mr. Blair's limp hand, and his jaw dropped as he found himself gazing up into the angry eyes of John Dene, who had entered the room like a tornado.

"This ain't a seal tank and it's not feeding time," cried John Dene angrily. "Who's shut my offices?" Then with a sudden look in the direction of the door he called out, "Here, come in, Jasp."

Mr. Blair looked more than ever like a seal as he gazed stupidly at John Dene. His eyes widened at the uncouth appearance of "Spotty" Quinton. Mr. Blair started violently as Spotty, seeing the fireplace, expectorated towards it with astonishing accuracy. Spotty could always be depended upon to observe the rules of good breeding in such matters. When a room possessed a fireplace, the ornaments and carpet were always safe as far as he was concerned.

Mr. Blair gazed stupidly at his visitors.

"I—I— —" he stammered.

Without a word John Dene turned, strode across the room and, opening Sir Lyster's door, disappeared, closing the door behind him with a bang. Sir Lyster was in the act of reaching across the table for a letter that Sir Bridgman was handing him. Both men turned to see the cause of the interruption. Sir Bridgman dropped the letter, and Sir Lyster slowly withdrew his arm as he gazed in a dazed manner at John Dene.

Sir Bridgman was the first to recover from his surprise.

"Why, it's John Dene!" he cried heartily, as he rose and grasped the interrupter's hand. "Where the deuce have you been hiding all this time?"

"What the hell have you done with that girl, and who's closed my offices?" demanded John Dene, looking from Sir Bridgman to the First Lord.

"Girl! what girl?" enquired Sir Lyster.

"Miss West," snapped John Dene.

"Miss West!" repeated Sir Lyster vaguely, then memory suddenly coming to his aid he added weakly, "Yes, I remember. She became your secretary."

John Dene regarded him steadily. Sir Bridgman hid a smile, he always enjoyed a situation that brought Sir Lyster into antagonism with John Dene.

"Yes; but that don't help any," cried John Dene irascibly. "Where is she now?"

"Really, Mr. Dene," began Sir Lyster stiffly, when his gaze suddenly became fixed on the door, which had opened slowly, whilst round the corner appeared the unprepossessing features of Spotty Quinton.

Following the direction of Sir Lyster's eyes, John Dene saw his henchman.

"Come right in, Jasp," he cried, and Spotty sidled round the door cap in hand. Catching sight of the fireplace, he expectorated neatly into it. Sir Lyster stared at him as if he had suddenly appeared from another planet.

"This is Jasp. Quinton, one of my boys," announced John Dene, looking from Sir Lyster to Sir Bridgman with a "take it or leave it" air.

Sir Bridgman advanced a step and held out his hand, which Spotty clasped warmly, first however, wiping his hand on the leg of his trousers with the air of a man unaccustomed to his hands being in a fit condition for the purpose of greeting.

"Pleased to meet you," said Spotty briefly.

"How's the *Destroyer*?" asked Sir Bridgman with some eagerness.

"Ruddy miracle," said Spotty, as he once more got the fireplace dead in the centre.

Sir Lyster seemed temporarily to have lost the power of speech. He gazed at Quinton as if hypnotised by the inequality of his complexion. When he expectorated Sir Lyster's eyes wandered from Spotty to the fireplace, as if to assure himself that a bull had really been registered.

At last by an obvious effort he turned to John Dene.

"I congratulate you upon your escape," he said, "but I thought you were too ill to— —"

"My escape!" replied John Dene.

"Yes, from that place—where was it, North?" He turned to Sir Bridgman.

"Streatham."

"Ah! yes, Streatham."

"I've been up north sending Huns to merry hell, where I'd like to send the whole Admiralty outfit," was the uncompromising retort. "I've come into contact with some fools— —" John Dene broke off.

"Shutting up my offices," he muttered.

"But— —" began Sir Lyster, then paused.

"I've been over to Chiswick and she's not there; flat's shut," continued John Dene.

"Chiswick!" repeated Sir Lyster. "Whose flat?"

"Mrs. West's, and you've shut my offices," he added, with the air of one unwilling to relinquish an obvious grievance.

"But I understood that you had just been released from a house in Streatham," persisted Sir Lyster.

"Well, there's a good many mutts in this place who've been released too soon. You're talking about Jim."

"Jim!" repeated Sir Lyster, "Jim who?"

"My brother. They were all after me good and hard, so Jim came along, and I just slipped up north with your man."

"Then you were the fellow with red hair all over him," laughed Sir Bridgman.

"Sure," was the laconic reply. "They were out for me," he continued a moment later, "and I'd never have got away. Jim didn't mind."

"But where is he now?" asked Sir Lyster.

"He's probably the John Dene that they think was released from that place in Streatham," suggested Sir Bridgman.

"Jim's all right," said John Dene, "but where's Miss West and my keys?"

At that moment the telephone bell rang. Sir Lyster lifted the receiver from the rest and listened.

"Yes, that's all right, thank you, Blair," he said; then turning to John Dene he added, "Mr. Blair has your keys and he also has Miss West's address at Bournemouth."

"Here, come on, Jasp.," cried John Dene, just as Spotty was in the act of letting fly at the fireplace for the sixth time. He turned a reproachful gaze upon his chief.

"But the *Destroyer*?" broke in Admiral Bridgman.

"She has been doing her bit," said John Dene grimly. "She's refitting now. I'm off to Bournemouth, and Spotty's going north to-night with some indents."

"Mr. Dene," began Sir Lyster in his most impressive manner, "your patriotism has — —

"Here, forget it," and with that John Dene was gone, followed by his lieutenant, leaving Sir Lyster, Sir Bridgman and Admiral Heyworth gazing at the door that closed behind him.

As Spotty passed Mr. Blair he turned and, thrusting his face forward, growled, "Ruddy tyke." It was his way of indicating loyalty to his chief; but it spoiled Mr. Blair's lunch.

For some moments after John Dene had gone, Sir Lyster and Sir Bridgman and Admiral Heyworth gazed at each other without speaking.

"Do you think it's drink, Grayne, or only the heat?" Sir Bridgman laughed.

Sir Lyster winced and looked across at him as a man might at a boy who has just blown a trumpet in his ear. Without replying he lifted the telephone receiver from its rest.

"Get me through to the Prime Minister. What's that? Yes, Sir Bridgman's here. Very well, we'll come round at once."

As he replaced the receiver he rose.

"The Prime Minister would like us to step round," he said. "Walton and Sage are there. It's about John Dene."

"Seen John Dene?" asked Sir Bridgman of Mr. Blair, as they passed through the room. "You'd better apply for that twenty thousand pounds, Blair."

Sir Lyster wondered why Sir Bridgman persisted in his jokes, however much they might have become frayed at the edges.

When they entered Mr. Llewellyn John's room it was to find him a veritable aurora borealis of smiles. He was obviously in the best of spirits.

"John Dene has been found," he cried before his callers had taken the chairs to which he waved them.

"We left poor Blair with the same conviction," laughed Sir Bridgman.

"Then you know?"

"I telephoned Sir Lyster," said Colonel Walton.

"Mr. Dene has only just left us," explained Sir Lyster. "He was extremely annoyed at the closing of his office and the disappearance of his secretary."

"But——" Mr. Llewellyn John looked from Colonel Walton to Malcolm Sage, and then on to Sir Lyster in bewilderment.

"Perhaps, Sage——" suggested Colonel Walton.

"You'd better tell the story, Sage, as Colonel Walton suggests," said Mr. Llewellyn John.

"There is an official report in preparation," said Colonel Walton.

Mr. Llewellyn John nodded.

In the course of the next half-hour Malcolm Sage kept his hearers in a state of breathless interest by the story of the coming and going of John Dene, as known to Department Z.

"I gave Mr. Dene the credit of being possessed of more than the ordinary amount of what he calls 'head-filling,'" began Sage, "but I didn't realise at first that he possessed a twin brother; but I'll begin at the beginning."

"When you turned over the matter to Department Z.," continued Malcolm Sage, "we made exhaustive inquiries and discovered that the Huns were determined to prevent the *Destroyer* from putting to sea, and they were prepared at any cost to stop Mr. Dene from going north. In Canada and on the way over they made attempts upon his life; but then, as so frequently happens, they became the victims of divided councils. They wanted the plans. Thanks to, er—certain happenings they learned that the *Destroyer* would not sail without Mr. Dene."

"How?" interpolated Mr. Llewellyn John

"They obtained the guarantee."

"I remember," said Mr. Llewellyn John, "it was stolen."

"Mr. Dene used to leave his safe open with such papers in it as he wanted the enemy to see. That's what he meant when on one occasion he said, 'If you've got a hungry dog feed it.'"

Sir Bridgman North laughed, Sir Lyster turned to him reproachfully.

"Mr. Dene became convinced that an effort would be made to kidnap and hold him to ransom, the price being the plans of the *Destroyer*. Department Z. also became convinced of this, but at a later date. As a precaution John Dene sent to England by another ship his twin brother, known as James Grant. When everything was ready the two changed places; that accounted for the strangeness of manner that Miss West noticed with Mr. Dene a few days before his disappearance."

Malcolm Sage then went on to explain the method by which the false John Dene had been kidnapped, and of Department Z.'s discovery with relation to Mr. Montagu Naylor.

"But all that time what happened to the *Destroyer*?"

"The *Destroyer* was responsible for the extraordinary increase in the mortality among U-boats."

Mr. Llewellyn John jumped from his chair as if he had been thrown up by a hidden spring.

"But—but——" he began.

"Mr. Dene hit upon a clever ruse," continued Sage, "and——"

"But the advertisements! Did you know this at the time?"

"It was known at Department Z., sir, and the advertisements were to convince the Hun of our eagerness to find John Dene so that we might start operations."

"I see, I see," cried Mr. Llewellyn John; "but how on earth did you ferret all this out?"

"We just sat down, sir, and waited for the other side to make mistakes," said Malcolm Sage quietly, "just as the Opposition does in the House of Commons," he added slyly.

And Mr. Llewellyn John smiled.

"It was better to say nothing about the Finlay business," said Malcolm Sage, as he and Colonel Walton walked back to St. James's Square. "It's results they're concerned with."

Colonel Walton nodded. "We must see John Dene, however," he said.

"If only for the good of his own soul," said Sage, as he knocked his pipe against a railing.

CHAPTER XIX.
COMMANDER JOHN DENE
GOES TO BOURNEMOUTH

I

Late one afternoon when Dorothy and Mrs. West were walking along the Christchurch Road on their way back to the boarding-house for dinner, Dorothy suddenly gave vent to an exclamation, and with both hands clutched her mother's arm so fiercely that she winced with the pain.

"Look, mother," she cried, "it's——"

Following the direction of her daughter's eyes Mrs. West saw walking sturdily towards them on the other side of the road, a man in the uniform of a naval commander. In his mouth was a cigar, from which he was puffing volumes of smoke. With a little cry Mrs. West recognised him. It was John Dene of Toronto.

There was no mistaking that truculent, aggressive air of a man who knows his own mind, and is determined that every one else shall know it too.

Suddenly Dorothy released her mother's arm and, running across the road, planted herself directly in John Dene's path.

"Mr. Dene!" she cried, when he was within a yard or two of her.

Several passers-by turned their heads. For a fraction of a moment John Dene gazed at the apparition in front of him, not recognising Dorothy in the white frock and large hat that shaded her eyes. Then with what was to him a super-smile, he held out his hand.

"Say, this is bully," he cried, giving Dorothy a grip that caused her to wince. "I've just been to your apartment-house and found you out." Then catching sight of Mrs. West, "Why, there's your mother," he cried and, gripping Dorothy's arm with an enthusiasm that she was convinced would leave bruises, he guided her across the road. A moment later Mrs. West was having the greatest difficulty in preserving a straight face under John Dene's vigorous greeting.

"I've been chasing all over Robin Hood's barn to find you," he cried, still clasping Mrs. West's hand.

"And according to the papers other people have been doing the same with you," said Dorothy, deciding in her own mind that John Dene ought to spend the rest of his life in uniform. It gave him a distinction that hitherto he had lacked in the ill-cut and ill-made clothes he habitually wore.

"I found these waiting for me at my hotel," he said, looking down at himself, as if divining her thoughts. "I ordered them way back," he added.

"You look very nice, Mr. Dene," said Mrs. West, smiling happily. She had not yet recovered from her surprise.

"All the girls are turning and envying mother and me," said Dorothy mischievously.

"Envying you?" John Dene turned upon her a look of interrogation.

"For being with you," she explained.

For some reason John Dene's face fell. Mrs. West hastened to the rescue.

"We've all been so anxious about you," she smiled. "We—we thought— —"

"And shall I get twenty thousand pounds if I give you up to a policeman?" asked Dorothy. She felt she wanted to cry from sheer happiness.

"Reward's withdrawn. Haven't you seen the papers?" he said practically; "but they nearly did for Jim," he added inconsequently.

"Jim!" repeated Dorothy. "Who is Jim?"

"My brother," was the reply. "He took my place and I went north."

"Ooooooooh!" Gradually light was dawning upon Dorothy. "Then it wasn't you who forgot where the stamps were kept and," she added wickedly, "seemed to disapprove of me so."

"Disapprove of *you*!" John Dene managed to precipitate such a wealth of meaning into the words that Dorothy felt herself blushing furiously. Even Mrs. West appeared a little embarrassed at his directness.

"Here, it's about time we had some food," he said, turning his wrist to see the time.

"We were just going home to dinner," said Mrs. West. "Won't you come with us?"

"I want you to come right along to my hotel. I've booked a table for you."

"That's not very complimentary to our attractiveness, Mr. Dene," said Dorothy.

Again John Dene turned to her with a puzzled look in his eyes.

"You should have assumed that two such desirable people as mother and me were dining out every night, shouldn't he, mother?"

John Dene turned to Mrs. West, his brows meeting in a frown of uncertainty.

"Dorothy will never be serious," she explained with a little sigh. "She's only joking," whereat John Dene's face cleared, and without further ado he hailed a taxi. As Sir Bridgman North had said, John Dene never waited to be contradicted.

That evening many of the diners at the Imperial turned their heads in the direction of a table at which sat a man in the uniform of a naval commander, a fair-haired girl and a little white-haired lady, the happiness of whose face seemed to arouse responsive smiles in those who gazed at her.

Slowly and haltingly John Dene told of what had happened since that Wednesday night some three months before when his brother had taken his place. Although John Dene never hesitated when telling of what he was going to do, he seemed to experience considerable difficulty in narrating what he had actually done.

"And aren't you happy?" enquired Dorothy, her eyes sparkling with excitement at the story of what the *Destroyer*, her *Destroyer*, had done.

"Sure," he replied, looking straight into her eyes, whereat she dropped her gaze to the peach upon her plate.

"I feel very proud that I know you, Mr. Dene," said Mrs. West, her eyes moist with happiness.

"Proud to know me!" he repeated, and then as if Mrs. West's statement held some subtle humour that he alone had seen, he smiled.

"Why do you smile?" asked Dorothy, looking up at him from beneath her lashes.

"Well, it tickled me some."

"What did?" she demanded.

"That anyone should be proud to know me," he said simply.

"Perhaps it's because you've never gingered mother up," said Dorothy pertly.

"Dorothy!" Mrs. West looked anxiously at John Dene, but his eyes were on Dorothy.

"And are you glad to know me?" he demanded

"'Proud' was the word," corrected Dorothy, playing with her fruit knife.

"'Glad' will do," he said, watching her keenly. "Are you glad I'm back."

"'You see I'm your secretary," she said demurely, "and I'm—I'm paid to be glad, aren't I?"

John Dene's face fell.

"When you get to know her better," said Mrs. West, "you will see that she only teases her friends."

"And her poor mother," put in Dorothy. "When do we resume work, Mr. Dene?" she asked, turning to him.

"We'll go back to-morrow a.m.," he said, obviously relieved at the suggestion.

"But our holidays!" cried Dorothy in mock consternation.

"You can have as long a vacation as you like when I'm through," was the answer, and Dorothy drew a sigh of relief. She was longing to get back to work.

That night she and Mrs. West sat up until dawn was fingering the east, talking of the miraculous reappearance of John Dene of Toronto, as they leisurely packed ready for the morrow.

II

For nearly an hour John Dene had sat in his chair listening. From time to time he gave to the unlit half-cigar in his mouth a rapid twirl with his tongue; but beyond that he had manifested no sign of emotion.

Quietly and as succinctly as possible Malcolm Sage had gone over the happenings of the last few months, telling of the discovery of Mr. Montagu Naylor's secret code, how it had enabled Department Z. to enlarge the scope of its operations, how Finlay had hampered Mr. Naylor in his murderous intentions with regard to his prisoner by suggesting the displeasure that would be created in high quarters, if anything happened to John Dene before the plans of the *Destroyer* had been secured.

"I didn't figure on Jim getting corralled," said John Dene at length.

"That was where your reasoning was at fault," was Malcolm Sage's quiet retort.

"I warned him," began John Dene; then a moment later he added, "I'd hate to have anything happen to Jim. He seems all used up."

"He'll be all right in a month or so," said Colonel Walton reassuringly.

"He's always sort of been around when I've wanted things done, has Jim," continued John Dene with a note of real feeling in his voice. "He's a white man, clean to the bone."

Malcolm Sage had already learned all he wanted to know with regard to James Dene. Quiet, taciturn, seldom uttering more than a word or two at a time, and then only when absolutely necessary, he was entirely devoid of the brilliant qualities of his brother, for whom, however, he possessed an almost dog-like affection. All their lives it had been John who had planned things, and James who had stood admiringly by.

"I was tickled to death about those advertisements," said John Dene presently.

"You probably thought we were barking up the wrong tree," suggested Colonel Walton.

"Sure, until you put me wise."

"We were trying to play into your hands and save your brother," said Malcolm Sage, as he knocked the ashes from his pipe against the heel of his boot, and proceeded to stuff tobacco into the bowl.

"If it hadn't been for those advertisements——" began John Dene, then he paused.

"The first hole dug in Mr. Naylor's back-garden would have been filled-in again," said Sage quietly.

"But how did they manage Jim after he'd got into that taxi?"

"The driver released a multiple curtain that fell over his head. As it dropped chloroform was sprayed over it. Quite a simple automatic contrivance."

There was a look in John Dene's eyes that would have been instructive to Mr. Naylor could he have seen it.

"They took him right out into the country," continued Sage, "then brought him to and doped him. He was taken to 'The Cedars' between one and two the next morning. That was where we picked up the scent again," he added.

As Sage ceased speaking, Colonel Walton offered his cigar-case to John Dene, who, taking a cigar proceeded to light it.

"By the way, Mr. Dene," said Sage casually, "do you remember some one treading on your toe at King's Cross the night you were going north. You were quite annoyed about it."

John Dene nodded and looked across at Sage, as if expecting something further.

"That was one of our men."

"But——"

"I told him to tread on your toe," proceeded Malcolm Sage, "so that you might remember that Department Z. was not quite so——"

"Now it gets me," cried John Dene. "It was you who trod on my foot at the theatre."

"At 'Chu Chin Chow,'" said Malcolm Sage, smiling.

"Seems to be a sort of stunt of yours," said John Dene as he rose.

"Going, Mr. Dene?" enquired Colonel Walton.

"Yep!" he said, as he shook hands with each in turn, then with an air of conviction added: "I take it all back. You'd do well in T'ronto:" and with a nod he went out.

"I wonder if that's a testimonial to us, or a reflection upon Toronto," murmured Malcolm Sage, as he polished his nails with a silk handkerchief.

"What I like about colonials," remarked Colonel Walton drily, "is their uncompromising directness."

Whilst John Dene was removing, from the list of things that required gingering-up, Department Z. and its two chiefs, Mr. Llewellyn John was engaged in reading Commander Ryles's report upon the operations of the *Destroyer*. It proved to be one of the most remarkable documents of the war. First it described how the *Destroyer* had hung about the Danish coast, but had been greatly embarrassed by the density of the water, owing to the shallowness of the North Sea. She had carefully to seek out the clear passages where the depth was sufficiently great to prevent the discolouration of water by sand.

After the first few weeks the *Destroyer* had been brought south, there to catch U-boats soon after they submerged. That was where the Germans suffered their greatest losses. Once the *Destroyer* had penetrated right into the Heligoland Bight, her "eyes" enabling her to avoid submerged mines and entanglements.

Commander Ryles had himself witnessed the destruction of thirty-four U-boats. Three times the *Destroyer* had returned to her base to re-victual and recharge her batteries, also to rest her crew. At the termination of the third trip, it had been decided that the boat was badly in need of a thorough overhaul, and in accordance with the instructions received, he had prepared his report and brought it south in order that he might deliver it in person to the First Lord.

When he had finished the lengthy document, Mr. Llewellyn John laid it on the table beside him. For some minutes he sat thinking. Presently he pressed the knob of the bell. As a secretary appeared he said, "Ring through to Sir Roger Flynn, and tell him I shall be delighted if he can breakfast with me to-morrow."

And Mr. Llewellyn John smiled.

CHAPTER XX.
JOHN DENE'S PROPOSAL

Marjorie Rogers had entered the outer office at Waterloo Place expecting to find Dorothy. Instead, John Dene sat half-turned in her direction, with one arm over the back of the chair.

"She's gone home," he said, divining the cause of Marjorie's call.

The girl slipped into the room, softly closing the door behind her, and walked a hesitating step or two in John Dene's direction, a picture of shy maidenhood. Marjorie Rogers was an instinctive actress.

"Gone home!" she repeated as a conversational opening. "Is she ill?" She gave him a look from beneath her lashes, a look she had found equally deadly with subs and captains.

John Dene shook his head, but continued to gaze at her.

He was a very difficult man to talk to, Marjorie decided. She had already come to the conclusion that she had been wrong in her suspicion that he made love to Dorothy.

"You don't like us, do you, Mr. Dene?" She made a half-step in his direction, dropping her eyes and drawing in her under lip in a way that had once nearly caused a rear-admiral to strike his colours.

"Like who?" demanded John Dene, wondering why the girl stayed now that he had told her Dorothy had gone home.

"Us girls." Marjorie flashed at him the sub-captain look. "May I sit down?" she asked softly.

"Sure." John Dene was regarding her much as he might a blue zebra that had strayed into his office.

"Thank you, Mr. Dene." Marjorie sat down, crossing her legs in a way that gave him the full benefit of a dainty foot and ankle. She had on her very best silk stockings, silk all the way up, so that there need be no anxiety as to the exact whereabouts of her skirt.

"I have been wondering about Wessie——"

"Wessie, who's she, a cat?"

Marjorie dimpled, then she laughed outright.

"You are funny, Mr. Dene," and again she drew in her lower lip and raked him with her eyes.

"Who's Wessie, anyhow?" he demanded.

"Wessie's Dorothy," she explained. "You see," she went on, "her name's West and——"

"I get you." John Dene continued to regard her with a look that suggested he was still at a loss to account for her presence.

"As I said," she continued, "I've been wondering about Dorothy."

"Wondering what?"

John Dene was certainly a most difficult man to talk to, she decided.

"She's thinner," announced Marjorie after a slight pause.

"Thinner?"

"Yes, not so fat." How absurd he was with his——

"She never was fat." There was decision in John Dene's tone.

"You know, Mr. Dene, you're very difficult for a girl to talk to," said Marjorie.

"I never had time to learn," he said simply.

"I think it's through you, Mr. Dene." She gave him a little fugitive smile she had learned from an American film, and had practised assiduously at home.

"What's through me?" he demanded, hopelessly at sea as to her drift.

"At first I thought you were working her too hard, Mr. Dene, but," she added hastily, as if in anticipation of protest, "but—but——"

"But what?" John Dene rapped out the words with a peremptoriness that startled Marjorie.

"But when you got lost——" She hesitated.

"Got what?"

"I mean when you disappeared," she added hastily, "then I knew."

"Knew what?"

Marjorie no longer had any doubts about John Dene's interest in Dorothy. He had swung round his chair, and was now seated directly facing her.

"You know she worried," continued Marjorie, "and she got pale and——" Again she paused.

John Dene continued to stare in a way that made her frightened to look up, although she watched him furtively through her lowered lashes.

"Is that what you came here to say?" demanded John Dene.

"I—I came to see Dorothy, and now I must run away," she cried, jumping up. "I've got an appointment. Good-bye, Mr. Dene. Thank you for asking me in;" and she held out her hand, which John Dene took as a man takes a circular thrust upon him.

A moment later Marjorie had fluttered out, closing the door behind her.

"Well, that's given him something to think about," she murmured, as she walked down the stairs. "Wessie must have me down to stay with her. He's sure to get a title;" and she made for the Tube, there to join the westward-rolling tide of patient humanity that cheerfully pays for a seat and hangs on a strap.

For nearly an hour John Dene sat at his table as Marjorie had left him, twirling in his mouth a half-smoked cigar that had not been alight since the early morning. His face was expressionless, but in his eyes there was a strange new light.

The next morning when Dorothy arrived at the office, she found Sir Bridgman North with John Dene, who was angry.

"Just because somebody's lost a spanner, or a screw-driver, they're raising Cain about it. Look at all these," and he waved a bunch of papers in front of Sir Bridgman.

"It's a way they have in the Navy. We never lose sight of anything."

"Except the main issue, winning the war," snapped John Dene.

"Oh, we'll get on with that when we've found the spanner," laughed Sir Bridgman good humouredly.

"I don't want to be worried about a ten cent spanner, and have a couple of letters a day about it," grumbled John Dene, "and I won't have it."

"What I used to do," said Sir Bridgman, "was just to tell them that everything possible should be done. Then they feel happier and don't worry so much. Why I once lost a 12-inch gun, and they were quite nice about it when I told them that somebody must have put it aside for safety, and that it had probably got mislaid in consequence. I never found that gun. You see, Dene," he added a moment later, "we indent everything—except an admiral, and it doesn't matter much if he gets lost."

John Dene grumbled something in his throat. He was still smarting under the demands from the Stores Department to produce forthwith the missing article.

"Now I must be off," said Sir Bridgman, and with a nod to John Dene and a smile to Dorothy he departed.

All the morning John Dene was restless. He seemed unable to concentrate upon anything. Several times he span round in his revolving chair with a "Say, Miss West;" but as soon as Dorothy raised her eyes from her work, he seemed to lose the thread of his ideas and, with a mumbled incoherence, turned to the mechanical sorting of the papers before him.

Dorothy was puzzled to account for his strangeness of manner, and after a time determined that he must be ill.

Presently he jumped up and began restlessly pacing the room. Three times he paused beside Dorothy as she was engaged in checking inventories. Immediately she looked up, he pivoted round on his heel and restarted the pacing, twirling between his lips the cigar that had gone out an hour before.

On the fourth occasion that he stood looking down at her, Dorothy turned.

"If you do that, I shall scream," she cried.

He stepped back a pace, obviously disconcerted by her threat.

"Do what?" he enquired.

"Why, prance up and down like that, and then come and stand over me. It—it makes me nervous," she added lamely, as she returned to her work.

"Sorry," said John Dene, as he threw himself once more into his chair.

Suddenly with an air of decision, Dorothy put down her pencil and turning, faced him.

"Aren't you well, Mr. Dene?" she inquired.

"Well," he repeated with some asperity. "Of course I'm well."

"Oh!" she said, disconcerted by his manner. Then for a moment there was silence.

"Why shouldn't I be well?" he demanded uncompromisingly.

"No reason at all," said Dorothy indifferently, "only——" She paused.

"Only what?" he enquired sharply.

"Only," she continued calmly, "you seem a little—a little—may I say jumpy?" She looked up at him with a smile.

Without replying he sprang from his chair, and once more started pacing the room with short, nervous strides, his head thrust forward, his left hand in his jacket pocket, his right hanging loosely at his side.

"That's it!" he exclaimed at last.

Dorothy continued to regard him in wonder. Something of vital importance must have happened, she decided, to produce this effect on a man of John Dene's character.

"It's—it's not the *Destroyer*" she cried breathlessly at last. "Nothing has happened?"

John Dene shook his head vigorously, and continued his "prancing."

"Then what——" began Dorothy.

"Listen," he said. "I've never had any use for women," he began, then stopped suddenly and stood looking straight at her.

Dorothy groaned inwardly, convinced that she was about to be dismissed. In a flash there surged through her mind all that this would mean. She might be taken on again by the Admiralty; but at less than half her present salary. It was really rather bad luck, she told herself, when the extra money meant so much to her, and she really had tried to be worth it.

"You see, I don't understand them."

The remark broke in upon her thoughts as something almost silly in its irrelevancy. Again she looked up at him as he stood before her rather as if expecting rebuke. Again he span round and continued his pacing of the room.

As he walked he threw staccatoed remarks from him rather than directed them at Dorothy.

"There's nothing wrong with the *Destroyer*. When you're after one thing you don't seem to notice all the other things buzzing around. One day you wake up to find out that you've been missing things. I've been telling myself all the time that some things didn't matter, but they do."

He paused in front of Dorothy, expressing the last three words with almost savage emphasis.

"There's never been anybody except Jim—and the boys," he added, "until your mother was——" He stopped dead, then a moment later continued: "I'd like her to know." To Dorothy his voice seemed a little husky. "May be it'ud please her to think that she had—you see I'm telling you the whole shooting-match," he blurted out as he resumed his restless pacing up and down.

"But that's just what you're not doing," said Dorothy. "I don't in the least understand what you mean, and—— Oh, I wish you could stand still, if only for a minute."

Instantly John Dene stopped in his walk, and stood in the middle of the room looking over Dorothy's head.

"I'm trying to ask you to marry me, only I haven't got the sand to do it," he blurted out almost angrily.

"Oh!" Dorothy's hands slipped into her lap, her eyes widened and her lips parted, as she looked up at him utterly dumbfounded.

"There, I knew what it would mean," he said, as he continued his pacing. "What have I got to offer? Look at me. I'm not good-looking. My clothes are not right. I don't wear them properly. I can't say pretty things. The best I can do is to buy flowers and chocolates and express them. I daren't even hand them to you. Oh, I've thought it all over. What use am I to a woman?" Then as an after-thought he added, "to a girl?" He turned and paced away from Dorothy without looking at her.

"Oh, shucks!"

John Dene swung round on his heel as if he had been struck. His jaw dropped, his cigar fell from his mouth, and he looked at her as if she had said the most surprising thing he had ever heard.

"I said 'shucks'" she repeated. Her eyelids flickered a little and she was unusually pale.

"You mean — —" His voice was far from steady.

"I mean," said Dorothy quietly, "that a man who could invent the *Destroyer* ought to be able to learn how to talk to—to—be nice to a girl." The last five words came tumbling over each other, as if she had found great difficulty in uttering them, and then had thrown them all out at one time.

"Say," he began, hope shining from his eyes. Then he stopped abruptly and walked over to his chair, throwing himself into it with a sigh. "You mean."

"Perhaps," said Dorothy, dropping her eyes and playing about with a fastening on her blouse, "I might be able to help you." Then after a pause she added, "You know you got me a rise."

And then John Dene smiled. "Say, this is great," he cried. "I—I—
—" Then suddenly he jumped up, dashed for his hat and made for the door. As he opened it he threw over his shoulder:

"We'll start right in to-morrow. I'm through with work for to-day. I'll be over to-night."

Then suddenly Dorothy laughed. "Was ever maid so wooed?" she murmured. "But— —" and she left it at that.

As she thrust the pins into her hat, she decided that John Dene had been right. It would have been awkward to—to—well, to do anything but go home.

Just as she was about to lock the outer door of the office, she had an inspiration. Returning to her table she removed her gloves and, after a few minutes' thought and reference to the London Directory, she sat down to her typewriter and for a few minutes her fingers moved busily over the keys.

With a determined air she pulled the sheet from the clips and read:—

"JOHN DENE OF TORONTO. Lesson 1.

Tailors . . . Pond and Co., 130 Sackville Street.

Hosiers . . . Tye Brothers, 320 Jermyn Street.

Bootmakers . Ease & Treadwell, 630 Bond Street.

Hatters . . . Messrs. Bincoln and Lennet, Piccadilly.

When a man knows his job, let him do it and don't butt in."

With a determined little nod of approval, she folded the sheet of paper, inserted it in an envelope, which she addressed to "John Dene, Esq., The Ritzton Hotel, S.W. Immediate," and left the office.

"I wonder what you would think of that, mother mine," she murmured as she left the hotel, after having given strict injunctions that the note be handed to John Dene immediately he returned.

CHAPTER XXI.
MARJORIE ROGERS PAYS A CALL

"Well, mother darling," cried Dorothy, as she jerked the pins into her hat, "you've lost the odd trick."

"The odd trick!" repeated Mrs. West, looking up with a smile into her daughter's flushed and happy face. "What odd trick?"

"John Dene of Toronto. Whoop! I want to jazz. I wonder if he jazzes;" then, with a sudden change of mood she dropped down beside her mother's chair and buried her face in her lap. When she looked up her eyes were wet with tears. "Mother, darling, I'm so happy." She smiled a rainbow smile.

"What did you mean about the odd trick, dear?" enquired Mrs. West greatly puzzled, accustomed as she was to her daughter's rapid change of mood.

"John Dene's the odd trick," she repeated, "and I'm going to marry him." Again she hid her face.

"Dorothy!"

"I am, mother, really and really." She looked up for a moment, then once more she buried her face in her mother's lap.

"Dorothy dear, what do you mean?"

"Oh! he was so funny when he proposed," gurgled Dorothy, "and I just said 'shucks.' That seemed to please him."

"Dorothy dear, are you joking?"

"Not unless John Dene's a joke, mother dear," she replied. "Wouldn't it be funny to call him Jack?" Then she told her mother of the happenings of the afternoon.

"Please say you're glad," she said a little wistfully.

"I'm—I'm so surprised, dear," said Mrs. West, stroking her daughter's head gently; "but I'm glad, very glad."

"I thought you would be, and I shall be Lady Dene. Everybody at the Admiralty says he'll get a title, and you'll have to say to the servants, 'Is her ladyship at home?' You won't forget, mother, will you?" She looked up with mock anxiety into her mother's face.

Mrs. West smiled down at Dorothy; her eyes too were wet.

"But oh! there's such a lot of spade work to be done," continued Dorothy. "I shall begin with his boots."

"His boots!"

"They're so dreadful, mother. They're all built up in front as if they were made to kick with, and when I marry him, if there's any kicking to be done, I'm going to do it."

"Of course you realise, dear, that he's much older than you," said Mrs. West hesitatingly.

"He's a perfect baby-in-arms compared with me," she smiled at her mother, a quaint confident little smile.

"But you're sure that—that——" Mrs. West hesitated.

Dorothy nodded her head violently.

"When——" began Mrs. West.

"It—it was when he disappeared," she said with averted face. "I—I seemed to miss him so much. Oh! but mother," she cried, clasping her mother's knee, "he's so funny, and really he wants someone to look after him. You see," she continued slowly, gazing away from her mother, "it's always difficult to—— What made you love—care for father?" she corrected.

"He was your father, dear."

"Yes; but he wasn't before you married him."

"Dear, you——" began Mrs. West, a flush of embarrassment mounting to her cheeks.

"Own up, mother, that you don't know. You can't say it was the shape of his nose, or the way he ate, or his chest measurement."

"Dorothy! why will you never be serious?" protested Mrs. West.

"I can't, mother," cried Dorothy, jumping up and walking over to the window. "No girl ever really knows why she wants to marry a man," she remarked, gazing out of the window. "It's just a feeling.

I've got a feeling that I want to take care of John Dene, and—and—oh, mother! see to his boots," she finished with a laugh.

"I like Mr. Dene, Dorothy," said Mrs. West with a decisiveness that was with her uncommon.

"I know you do," said Dorothy mischievously. "That's what I'm afraid of."

"Dorothy dear, you mustn't," began Mrs. West.

"And," continued Dorothy relentlessly, "I won't have any poaching. I don't mind his being nice to you," she continued, leaving the window and planting herself in front of her mother, "because you really are rather nice." She tilted her head on one side, a picture of impudence. "Now, Mrs. West," she said, "the sooner we understand each other the better."

Again she was back on the stool at her mother's feet. For some minutes there was silence.

"Mother!" She looked up with grave and serious eyes.

"Yes, dear."

"I always prayed for—for him to come back. I—I—— Oh bother!" as the bell rang.

"I wonder who that is. We won't answer it."

"But we must, dear," expostulated Mrs. West. "It might be a friend."

"Oh, well," cried Dorothy, getting up and going out into the tiny hall. A moment later she re-entered, followed by Marjorie Rogers. "It's Marjorie, mother."

Mrs. West smiled up at her as the girl bent to kiss her.

"I've come to know," began Marjorie, then she hesitated.

"To know what?" asked Dorothy.

"If it's all right."

"If what's all right?"

"J. D."

"What do you mean, Rojjie?" cried Dorothy, blushing.

"Did he propose? You know I ran in this afternoon and gave him a hint."

"You what?" cried Dorothy aghast.

"Oh! I just gave him a sort of hint that he was— —"

"You wretched little creature!" cried Dorothy, seizing Marjorie and shaking her vigorously. There was a look in her eyes that half frightened the girl.

"Help! Oh, Mrs. West!" cried Marjorie, "she's killing me."

"What did you say to him?" demanded Dorothy fiercely.

"I just gave him a hint," repeated Marjorie airily. "I knew he was in love with you."

"What did you say to him?" Again Dorothy shook her.

"Oh, Wessie, if you do that you'll shake all my hair off, not to speak of my teeth. All I said was that you had wasted away when he was lost, and mind, you've got to ask me down to your place, wherever it is, because it's all through me. Oughtn't she, Mrs. West?" she appealed.

Mrs. West smiled a little uncertainly.

"Marjorie, you're a pig," cried Dorothy, "and I don't believe you did go and see him."

"Oh! didn't I, then why do you suppose I've got my new stockings on?" she cried, lifting her skirts.

"Children, children," smiled Mrs. West.

"My chief says he'll be made a baronet, so that'll be all right for the kids," said Marjorie.

"Rojjie!" cried Dorothy in confusion, and a moment later she had rushed from the room.

When Dorothy returned to the little drawing-room a quarter of an hour later, she found that Marjorie had accepted Mrs. West's invitation to stay to dinner.

"Is he going to call this evening?" she asked eagerly.

"Don't be inquisitive," cried Dorothy, conscious that she was blushing.

"You're in love with him, Dorothy, aren't you?" persisted Marjorie.

"Oh, mother, please tread on this horrid little creature," cried Dorothy; but Mrs. West merely smiled.

"You know," continued Marjorie candidly, "he's not much to look at; but he beats all those boys at the Admiralty." She shrugged her shoulders indifferently. "It's nothing but chocolates, lunches and dinners, and take it out in kisses."

"My dear," said Mrs. West with quiet dignity, "you mustn't talk like that."

"I'm so sorry," cried Marjorie contritely; "but you know I get so fed up, Mrs. West. John Dene's so different. If it hadn't have been for Dorothy, I should have tried to get him for myself. I could," she added, looking from one to the other.

"You could probably get anything in the world except what you most wanted, Rojjie," said Dorothy sweetly.

"What I most wanted," repeated the girl.

"Yes, dear, a good spanking."

Marjorie made a face at her. Suddenly she jumped up from the table, and throwing her arms round Dorothy, kissed her impulsively, then a moment later she returned to her seat, a little shamefacedly as Dorothy and Mrs. West smiled across at her.

"I know you think I'm a feather-headed little cat, Mrs. West," said Marjorie wisely. "No, don't deny it," she persisted, as Mrs. West made a movement as if to speak. "But I'm not worldly all through, really, and I do like John Dene, and of course I just love Dollikins," she said with a quaint little smile in Dorothy's direction. "Would you sooner I went?" she asked, looking from one to the other.

"Sooner you went?"

"Yes, after dinner, I know that John Dene's coming to-night, although Dorothy won't own up."

"We shouldn't let you go, should we, mother?"

Mrs. West smiled and shook her head.

"Oh, won't it be lovely," cried Marjorie ecstatically, "when I refer to my friend, Lady Dene. And you will ask me down, Wessie darling, won't you, and get a lot of nice boys."

Dorothy lowered her eyes to her plate and blushed.

Later in the evening when they were all sitting in the drawing-room and a ring at the bell was heard, Marjorie danced about the room with excitement.

"Oh, please let me open the door," she cried. "I promise I won't kiss him."

"No, dear," said Mrs. West. "Dorothy."

With flaming cheeks and reluctant steps Dorothy left the room. It seemed to Marjorie a long time before she returned, followed by John Dene, who, when he had greeted Mrs. West, turned to Marjorie and shook hands.

"His boots, Dorothy," whispered Marjorie a minute later.

Dorothy looked down at John Dene's feet. The ugly American "footwear" had been replaced by a pair of well-fitting brown boots.

"Please, Mr. Dene, may I be a bridesmaid?"

"Marjorie!" cried Dorothy.

"I may, mayn't I?" persisted Marjorie. "I'm sure Dorothy won't ask me unless you insist."

"Sure," replied John Dene genially. He was always a different man when with Mrs. West and Dorothy.

"You hear, Dorothy. If you don't make me chief bridesmaid I shall—I shall create a disturbance and say it's bigamy or something, and that Mr. Dene has already got two wives in Toronto, not to speak of Salt Lake City. And now I must be running away. Oh! Mrs. West, you said you would give me that pattern," she said suddenly.

"That pattern, dear," began Mrs. West, whilst Dorothy felt her cheeks burn.

"Yes, don't you remember?"

"What pattern?" began Mrs. West, then conscious that Marjorie was making hideous grimaces at her, she rose and walked towards the door, leaving John Dene and Dorothy alone.

"No one would ever think you were married, Mrs. West," said Marjorie severely, as they walked into the dining-room. "Don't you know that young people want to be alone when they're only just engaged."

This with such a serious little air of womanly worldliness that Mrs. West's smile almost developed into a laugh.

"Don't you think, Mrs. West, that God must be pleased when two nice people come together?" said Marjorie gravely.

Mrs. West looked at her with slightly widening eyes, then recovering herself, said, "God is always glad because of happiness, dear."

And Marjorie nodded her head as if in entire agreement with the sentiment.

An hour later, when Marjorie had gone, Mrs. West entered the drawing-room, having been sent in by Dorothy to entertain John Dene whilst she wrote a letter.

After a few commonplaces they sat in silence, John Dene smoking lustily, Mrs. West happy in her thoughts. It was the Good Lord, she decided, who had ordained that Dorothy and John Dene should fall in love with each other, and thus crown with happiness the autumn of her days.

"I've been trying to figure out all the afternoon why she said 'shucks,'" John Dene suddenly burst in upon her thoughts in a way that startled her.

"Said 'shucks!'" she repeated. Mrs. West had a habit of repeating a phrase when not quite understanding it, or desirous of gaining time before framing her reply.

"Sure."

"But who said 'shucks'?" she asked, lifting her brows in an endeavour to comprehend, "and—what are 'shucks,' Mr. Dene?"

"Shucks," repeated John Dene in his turn, "shucks are—are——" He paused, then as if determining that this was a side issue he added: "When I told her to-day that I'd never had any use for girls, and—and——" He looked at Mrs. West helplessly.

She smiled.

"She just said 'shucks.'"

"I think she must have meant that you were too modest," said Mrs. West softly.

"Me modest!" John Dene sat up straight in his surprise.

"I think that is what she must have meant."

"I take it that down at the Admiralty they don't figure it out that way," he said grimly. "Me modest," he repeated. "What have I got to give any girl," he continued presently, "and a girl like—Dorothy."

The name seemed to come with difficulty. "I'm all wrong," he added with conviction. "I can't talk — —"

"We love you just for yourself, John," said Mrs. West gently.

For a moment there was a look of surprise in John Dene's eye, then with great deliberation he rose and, walking over to Mrs. West, bent down and kissed her cheek.

"Oh!"

John Dene started up and, turning to the door, saw Dorothy standing on the threshold looking from one to the other, her eyes dancing with mischief. Mrs. West had flushed rosily, and with downcast eyes gave the impression of one who had been caught in some illicit act.

"So this is what you two get up to when I leave the room," said Dorothy severely.

"Sure," said John Dene, "and we'll be getting up to it again, won't we, mother?"

And John Dene smiled.

THE END.